TO MEET AGAIN

Visit us at www.boldstrokesbooks.com

By the Author

The Secrets of Willowra

To Meet Again

To Meet Again

by

Kadyan

2023

TO MEET AGAIN

ISBN 13: 978-1-63679-398-6

This Trade Paperback Original Is Published By
Bold Strokes Books, Inc.
P.O. Box 249
Valley Falls, NY 12185

First Edition: March 2023

Credits
Editor: Shelley Thrasher
Production Design: Susan Ramundo
Cover Design By Tammy Seidick

Acknowledgments

I want to thank the whole BSB team for their dedication and their help.

Thanks again to Shelley for her patience and professionalism.

Thanks to Len for giving me again a wonderful opportunity to tell this story.

A special thanks to Björn Larson for his help on passenger ships before WWII.

To my readers, I hope you will enjoy this book.

Be aware, this book contains racist language common in war slogans and in everyday talks at the time.

Dedication

To my wife, always

In the memory of all the courageous women who were imprisoned during WWII. May we always remember them.

Prologue

London, 2000

Thea looked around and observed the small, still-well-kept garden. Everything was so familiar, but at the same time, nothing was the same. Her heart ached. Every time she came here, she saw new plants in this small patch of land. The owner had loved her garden so much. Today, the beautiful roses were in bloom, and apart from her, no one was here to admire them.

She used her key to open the door. Inside, a musty smell caught her by the throat. No one had been here for three weeks. Not even her mother...her mother. Thea sighed.

What a surprise at the lawyer's office yesterday. Her father, usually so stoic, couldn't help but look at his wife and ask for an explanation too. Her grandmother Dorothy had died, but she wasn't even her grandmother. She was her great-aunt. Why had they done this? Both her mother and her grandmother? Why had they let everyone think they were mother and daughter? It didn't make sense, but her mother refused to talk, to explain.

Thea walked quietly around, looking at the old wallpaper, the pictures, the furniture. Everything was old. Nothing had changed since Thea was born thirty years ago. She remembered her parents' discussions, trying to convince "Granny" that a renovation was necessary because the last time she had done it was "when Thea was born." But "Granny" wouldn't listen. She liked her home just the way it was. It was her home, after all.

Every time she entered it, Thea had the illusion of stepping back in time to the 1930s. Today, however, was very different. Today, she saw things through different eyes. She had loved her grandmother, and she felt betrayed. Why the lies? What did they have to hide? They were both liars.

She had barely opened half the windows to let the fresh air in when the doorbell rang. Smiling widely and her heart beating faster, Thea rushed to the front door.

A tall, slender, blond woman stood there in jeans and a sweatshirt, gazing at her from head to toe with sparkling, happy, blue eyes, which made her shiver with pleasure.

"Pat! Finally." Thea wrapped her arms around her. "Finally. I haven't seen you in ages." They hugged for almost a full minute.

"Oh, Thea, my love. You're right. It has been far too long. We can't keep meeting on the sly."

At the familiar Australian accent she loved, tears filled Thea's eyes.

"That's going to change. I guarantee it. I've got some big news. Come on in. We don't want the neighbours to start gossiping."

Pat burst out laughing. Thea took her hand and led her inside the house.

"Are we alone?" Pat whispered close to her ear as soon as they were out of earshot.

Thea could feel the warm breath on her neck.

"Yes," she replied in a low voice, carefully locking the door.

Pat's lips were immediately on hers as she pressed her against the door. Thea felt elated. It had been so long since they were able to make love. They were definitely not going to miss this opportunity. Kissing, touching…tongue against tongue. She could feel Pat's hands on her hips, and she wanted to tear off their clothes. Thea needed skin on skin now, but she forced herself to stop. Too many quick encounters like this in the last few months had frustrated her. But that was over. Today, Thea would take her time. She needed this.

"Wait. Follow me. We're in no hurry today."

After leading Pat down the corridor, Thea opened the last door on the right, that of her great-aunt's bedroom, and drew her beloved inside. Sensing soft lips on her neck, Thea didn't resist and closed her eyes.

"I won't need time...to come," said Pat, panting. "I'm almost there already, just looking at you in your tight jeans. You are so sexy..."

Thea laughed. Oh, she'd missed this woman so much. "I've been fantasising about you naked on this bed since this morning," she said, slipping her hands under Pat's black shirt.

She didn't care if it was her grandmother's or her great-aunt's bed. She just wanted to make love without anyone disturbing them.

❖

Clothes flew everywhere in a few seconds. Finally, they were naked, alone, and with a big bed. Pat immediately pushed Thea onto the mattress and straddled her. Her blood boiled, her fingertips tingling to touch the soft skin. The trusting grey-green eyes looked at her, waiting, wanting. She almost hesitated...almost. The pleasure of finally being able to caress the soft velvet of that beloved skin sent shivers through her. With a dry mouth, Pat hurried to discover this lovely woman again.

"You're so very beautiful," she whispered. "It's been far too long."

Slowly, Pat plunged her hand into Thea's thick brown hair. An infinite pleasure. Pat couldn't resist any longer.

"We have to stop meeting like this, stealthily. I want more time with you. We have to find a solution," Pat whispered, her cheek on Thea's warm shoulder.

Drawing arabesques, she gently caressed Thea's belly. These brief encounters drove her crazy. Most of the time, they met in a hospital storage room or, when their schedules matched, in each other's rooms, but it was complicated, and she was becoming more and more frustrated.

Fingers grasped Pat's hand, pulling her to the softest lips she had ever tasted. She was so in love with this beautiful woman it hurt. Why was it so hard to live together? They were adults, both had jobs. But London rents were unaffordable, and they had been sharing flats with friends or colleagues when they met a year before.

"I agree," Thea said.

Deep inside herself, Pat felt Thea's kisses on her hand, loved the sensation of Thea's tongue sliding down her arm, the small bites of her soft skin. When Thea's velvet lips touched her own, she almost left her body. "I have the perfect solution," Thea said without pausing.

Pat opened her mouth, welcoming that nimble tongue, deepening the kiss. God. She forgot everything when they were together. Feeling the desire invade her belly again, she closed her eyes and enjoyed the ride. She wanted more, always more. As she began to gently massage Thea's beautiful buttocks, she felt her slide off the bed, away from her.

"Don't you want to know?" Thea asked playfully.

Disappointed that her prey was slipping away, Pat crossed her arms over her chest and, while ogling her girlfriend who was waiting in front of her, played the game.

"Let's hear it. What's your perfect solution?"

Thea smiled and gestured to the walls around them. "This."

Pat frowned. She looked at the old-fashioned wallpaper, the outdated frames, the antique furniture, but she didn't understand. What was the connection between this old place and them?

"My great-aunt left me her house."

"What? Bloody hell…!" Pat couldn't believe it. "Wait a minute. Did you say great-aunt? I thought your grandmother lived here."

"So did I. I got a big shock when the solicitor opened the will and started talking about the niece, the great-niece. Even my father reacted as I did. The only person who didn't flinch, of course, was my mother. She knew perfectly well that Dorothy Baker was not her mother, and now she refuses to tell us why they always lied. To cut a long story short, the house is mine, but I don't have any idea why my great-aunt left it to me. The solicitor didn't know anything more, or else he had been instructed to say nothing."

Pat took in all the information quickly. Indeed, it was a surprise, but after all, it wasn't her family. "I'm surprised your mother didn't inherit the house. If I remember what you told me, I thought they were close."

Looking around, Thea finally shook her head. "I don't think they were. My mother was doing her duty and came by once a month to check on her. But now that I see things in a different light, I don't remember any real affection between them, at least on my mother's part. Now I understand why she never called her Mum. She used 'Granny,' the same word as me. I thought it was for my benefit. I was so wrong."

When Pat embraced Thea from behind, Thea closed her eyes, seeming to let the love between them wash over her. Pat knew she needed their closeness. This revelation had obviously upset her a lot.

"We can live here together, or we can sell the house and buy something else for ourselves, just us. What do you think?" Thea asked.

Surprised, Pat looked around at the old wallpaper, the furniture, the bed—a smile stretched her lips—and the decor. This room was beautiful with its retro charm. "There's no rush to decide. Maybe if your mother won't talk, your great-aunt will."

Disconcerted grey-green eyes stared at Pat. "My great-aunt is dead. How can she speak?" Thea asked.

Pat laughed gently. "All the old people I know have their secret gardens. My grandmother explained that to me when my great-grandmother died, and she told me her story about her life in the bush as a canteen girl. I'm sure there are letters or papers somewhere in this house that explain the story of your great-aunt and mother. We just have to find them."

Thea looked around and checked the cupboard.

"Maybe not here, but in her office, if she had one," Pat conceded, amused at Thea's attitude.

Thea opened the first drawer full of underwear. And closed it. As she opened the second one, a mischievous smile played on her face.

"You're a genius, my love. Look what I've found. Another secret from Auntie Dorothy?" Thea quickly unfolded the red silk dressing gown and pulled it over her shoulders. She twirled around, and Pat admired the beautiful dragon on her back.

"Wow. Definitely not British at all. Your auntie was hiding a lot."

"Here. This one's for you. It'll look good with your eye colour." Thea threw her a pair of light blue, velvety, caress-inducing pyjamas, which Pat immediately put on. Thea suddenly jumped into Pat's silk-covered arms, their lips brushing against each other's, lost in this wonderful kiss—slow, so slow.

Finally, pulling herself together just before they ended up back on the bed, Thea grabbed Pat's hand and led her out of the room. "My great-aunt didn't have a real office, but a nice, cosy little room, her boudoir, as she called it. She spent all her time there."

Hand in hand, they rushed down the corridor, and at the last minute, Thea turned left. Pat almost missed the entrance to the room because she was laughing so hard at the mischievous look in her lover's eyes. She knew Thea enjoyed detective books, so having a mystery in her own family and the chance to discover it was an irresistible temptation.

"Don't get your hopes up. It may take a few days before we find her cache if it's not in this room," Pat said. "The house isn't big, but it must be full of nooks and crannies and secret drawers."

After hearing these words, Thea went straight to the secretary and opened the first drawer. Pens, pencils, scissors...Pat laughed out loud at such enthusiasm.

"Everything has to be in this place. I can feel it. We have to check all the furniture."

The second drawer was full of various pieces of writing paper.

"Maybe you can donate some things to charity?" Pat suggested as she looked at the wall paintings of various landscapes.

There were several styles, but one painting in particular intrigued her. She recognised a view of the old Singapore Harbour from having been there several times before coming to England for her studies.

"Good idea. As soon as we find out all the secrets."

As Thea rummaged through the secretary, Pat was drawn to the old wardrobe. The craftsmanship was a marvel. The old cabinet reminded her of the one in her grandparents' house. As a child, she had loved to dive into it to smell the wax, then rummage through the boxes filled with so many mysterious things. She tried to open this one, but the doors were locked, and no key was visible.

"Do you have the key to the cabinet?"

Thea stopped what she was doing and looked at Pat, rubbing her head.

"It must be somewhere inside one of those drawers, if I remember correctly. I was never allowed to open it myself. Wait a second." Thea pulled out the first drawer, poked around for a moment, and, with a smile of victory, lifted the key into the air. "Ta-da! And there it was! I knew I'd seen it."

❖

Thea handed the key to Pat, and they exchanged a knowing look. Thea was impatient; however, she wanted to include her lover in this search for the truth. Pat's gentle smile of connivance was her reward.

Letting Pat take the lead, Thea, attentive, stayed behind. What was in that cupboard? Why did her grandmother, no, her great-aunt, keep it locked?

With an obvious reverence for the age of the cabinet, Pat inserted the key and opened it. The old doors creaked.

Inside, a treasure was waiting. Thea was sure of it. She could feel it on the tip of her tongue.

"Boxes?" she exclaimed, a little disappointed as she looked around the shelves.

Pat smiled, her eyes sparkling. "You're so impatient! Not just boxes. Your great-aunt's life. Read."

Each box had a label explaining its content.

"Your great-aunt was well organised. Bills, taxes, photos, fabrics, threads, letters…" Pat said.

"Pull the boxes marked letters and photos," said Thea, suddenly very excited.

"Pictures? Letters? From whom? Didn't your great-aunt lead a very solitary life?"

"I never saw her with a friend. She never talked about anyone."

"Do you think she had a mysterious life? A torrid affair?" joked Pat. "That would explain the bathrobe and pyjamas."

"A lover? Are you kidding? I know her husband was killed in France during World War II, and she never remarried."

"So she lost the love of her life during the war. How old was she at the time?"

"She was born in 1920, on the 6th of March, if I remember correctly." Thea thought for a few seconds before adding, "Maybe you're right. She was twenty when our army was trapped at Dunkirk. And twenty-five when my mother was born. She never talked about him or any other man."

After placing the two boxes on the floor, Pat removed the lid and began to rummage through the letters while Thea, a little confused, looked at her. The envelopes were all in chronological order. She grabbed the last one.

"This one is from Singapore, dated six months ago," Pat said.

"Singapore? My great-aunt knew someone who lived in Singapore? Are you kidding?"

Pat pulled the paper out of the envelope. Two blank sheets with very neat handwriting.

"My dear sister…"

"Sister? My great-aunt had a sister? Who lives in Singapore?"

"Maybe this letter is from your real grandmother. It's signed Evelyn."

Still in shock, Thea grabbed the sheets held out in her direction, while, this time, Pat pulled the first envelope from the box.

"This one was posted in Southampton, dated April 24, 1938. From the same person."

"Are they all from Evelyn?" asked Thea as she checked the dates on the stamps.

Quickly, Pat leafed through several letters, taking care not to change their chronological order.

"With the exception of the first one, most of them look like they're from Singapore, in the same handwriting."

Stunned, Thea was caught for a moment in a maelstrom of questions. Could this be her real grandmother? Had they already found the hidden secret? She exclaimed, "We have to read them, all of them."

"You want to do that now? Don't you have band practice tonight?"

Thea shook her head as she looked at the perfectly arranged envelopes. She sighed. "Our contract with the cabaret is over, and the manager didn't want to renew it. He wants to change the style. He said jazz doesn't appeal anymore."

"I'm sorry," Pat murmured, hugging her. "I know how important this one performance a week is for you and your band. Besides, I love your husky voice and your sensual way of wearing dresses from the 50s."

"Thanks. The guys are looking for another contract," Thea said. "In the meantime, we've decided to take a break. So you and I have the weekend to make love and unearth my great-aunt's secret."

After fingering the small box on the side of which was written **Photos**, Thea lifted the lid. Four albums were waiting for her inside. Excitedly, she read the titles aloud: "up to 1920, 1921–1955, 1956–1970, and 1971 to now."

She grabbed the second album, the one to go with the first letter, and opened it. Hindered by its weight, she placed it on the desk, then looked around. For what they wanted to do, they had to be comfortable.

"I suggest we use the dining-room table so we have more room. We'll be able to spread out."

"Good idea. I'll take the letter boxes there."

Before Pat left, Thea stole another quick kiss from her. "To motivate you," she said.

Pat laughed and, with her arms full, left the boudoir.

Once the boxes were on the table, Thea sat next to Pat and hesitated. She was a little anxious about delving into her great-aunt's past. What if she discovered an unpleasant secret? "How do you want to start?"

"From the beginning?"

Pat's playful grin made Thea laugh. She loved this pragmatic woman so much.

"Yes. Of course. Why didn't I think of that? Go ahead, my love. Dig in."

Pat grabbed the first letter as Thea opened the neatly filed photo albums and spotted a black-and-white portrait of a beautiful young blond woman with clear eyes.

Chapter One

London, 22 April 1938

> *My dear sister,*
> *I know this will be very difficult for you to accept, but I am leaving England in a few hours. I am taking a boat to Singapore. Don't worry about me. I have a contract and a husband now. Let me tell you what happened a few weeks ago...*

As I wrote these words, I couldn't forget the last few days. Everything was so vivid and so confusing at the same time, I didn't have time to think too much.

London, 31 March 1938

I was walking down the street looking for the address my music teacher had given me the night before. If only I could get a small contract, I could leave my parents' house. Even though I had been disappointed before, I was hopeful. My teacher was confident. Tonight, I couldn't help but feel that this was my last chance. It had to be. I was so angry at my father. He had pushed me into a corner, and I couldn't do anything but rebel at this injustice. I couldn't obey him and give up my passion. Yet I had accepted everything he had said until now.

Following my family's wishes, I had studied to be a nurse like my mother, like my sister. My father was a doctor and loved medicine, of course. But it was not my vocation. When, two months earlier, I had mentioned that I would like to become a singer, my father had stared at me with a characteristic frown. He wouldn't accept my plan. My mother shook her head but didn't say a word, leaving us alone in his office.

"I hope you aren't serious, my dear daughter."

"Father, as you already know, I've been studying piano and singing for the last few years—"

He interrupted me in his stentorian voice. "For your education. A proper young woman must know music."

"Yes, but what I really love is singing, and I'm good at it. You've heard me many times, and you told me so yourself."

He looked slightly embarrassed by this reminder. "So you'll be singing for your future husband, who will appreciate your talent. I guess you're not busy enough with your studies if you think about such trifles. Maybe it's time we took a serious look at this marriage thing."

My heart sank. I wanted to talk to him about signing a contract to sing in a London cabaret, and my father's answer was a husband. Deep in my soul, I knew we would never agree on the subject. The way he looked at me with his pursed lips, his jaw clenched, I recognised the signs. His anger was growing. I had crossed that line once and would never do it again. After all these years, I could still feel the pain in my back.

"I guess you're right, Father. Maybe I am bored with my studies," I muttered, not really proud of myself.

Tears filled my eyes, but I held them back. I didn't want to cry in front of him. He had just shattered my dreams with one sentence, but he was not to know what he had done—not today, not tomorrow, not ever. My heart hardened suddenly. I almost clenched my fists, but I held back. I didn't want him to know how much his refusal upset me, ever.

"Dinner is ready," my mother said from the dining room.

My father got up and left me alone in his study. I heard the footsteps of my sister, Dorothy, as she came down the stairs, leaving me less than a minute to swallow my emotions. What was I going to do? I almost slapped myself. But instead, I told myself to first go and eat and pretend these last few minutes had never happened, and then think.

The meal was a quiet affair. I listened to the discussions with a distracted ear. Fortunately, Dorothy, two years younger than me, was a chatterbox, and having just started nursing school, she had a lot to ask our father. Her questions kept him busy, and as dinner progressed, he finally relaxed and even allowed himself a smile. My mother, however, was a different story. I could feel her staring at me during every lull in the conversation. She wasn't going to give up easily.

"Evelyn, when are you planning to graduate from nursing school?"

Why was she asking? She knew perfectly well. As an obedient daughter, I answered, "Next May, Mother. In two months."

"All right, then. Perhaps we could organise a party in June with some of your father's colleagues. I'm sure he knows some young, single doctor who would make a good husband for you. You could work at the hospital for a year until you get married next summer. I've always loved summer weddings."

I tried not to react; however, deep inside I was dying a little more. Every sentence was a dagger in my heart.

"You're right, my dear," my father replied cheerfully. "There are two or three promising young doctors I'm thinking of. It would be nice to have a man I could talk to at our family dinner."

Obviously satisfied that all would soon be well, he smiled at my mother.

I couldn't bear it. I wanted to stand up, to scream at them that it was my life they were talking about, not some piece of clothing to buy in a shop. But I held back, looked down, and remained silent. Dorothy's eyes were on me, asking me what I had done now.

At the end of the evening, I could think of only one way out of this trap: to leave. How would I do that? I had no idea. I certainly didn't want to get married, and I didn't want to become a nurse. I wanted to sing. I was good at it. I'd even come close to getting a contract the previous month at a good West End cabaret. When the owner found out I was only twenty and single, he withdrew the offer. I would have needed parental consent, and he didn't want to bother with that. Knowing I wouldn't get it, miserable, I left without arguing.

I skipped the afternoon classes at the hospital to look for the address I had written on a piece of paper. At the door, I frowned. What was this place? Certainly not a cabaret. If someone other than Marian, my music teacher, had given me this address, I wouldn't have ventured into this part of London. It was daylight, yet I felt myself under the microscope of watchful eyes. Without waiting, I knocked on the door, which, to my astonishment, opened very quickly.

"Are you Evelyn?"

"Yes...yes."

The man was tall and looked quite serious. He glanced left and right before finally letting me in. What had I gotten myself into?

"Come on in. I'm James Deacon, by the way. The piano is over there. We've got less than an hour to give it a try before the place opens. I called in a big favour so we could do this audition. I hope you're good."

Cabaret? It didn't look like a cabaret. Not understanding everything James was saying, I followed him down the corridor, ignoring the various doors we passed. A man carrying crates of bottles jostled me without even looking at us. What was this place? When he stopped by the piano in a large, dimly lit room, I knew.

"Is this really a cabaret?"

"Yes. Of course, it is. Do you think I can keep a piano in the little room I rent?"

James seemed as bewildered as I was. "What did Marian tell you?"

"Just that you were looking for a singer and that it was urgent. Are we going to perform here?"

I wasn't very happy. If I had to go against my parents' wishes, I couldn't stay in London. I had been very clear with my music teacher. Why had she sent me to this address?

"No. It's only for your audition." He hesitated before settling down behind the piano. "What song do you know?"

"What style do you play?"

"Anything to make the customers happy. Why not start with something easy?"

He played the first few notes, and I smiled. I knew the song "Minnie the Moocher" well. As I started to sing, I took off my hat and coat. James looked at me intently with his blue eyes. All of a sudden, he changed the music, and I followed him effortlessly. After almost ten songs, he stopped and, with a small smile on his lips, looked at me without saying anything. He was a handsome chap, full of youthful charm. All the women must have been after him.

"You're good," he said, seeming a little surprised. "I like your contralto voice with its light, dusky timbre."

Suddenly I heard applause from the shadowy part of the room and tried to see who it was. A tall man leaning on a cane approached slowly, but never stumbled despite having his eyes on me.

"If you don't want to go with that good-for-nothing, I'll give you a job, girl. You'll attract customers for sure, pretty as you are."

Under his slightly too-strong gaze, I tensed up. I had the feeling this guy wasn't who he seemed to be. I would never have worked for him.

"Leave her alone, Mac. She's with me." Standing up, James took his coat and hat and prepared to leave. "Are you coming?"

Grabbing my things, I followed him to the opposite side of the room we had entered. All the while Mac's eyes never left me. When we reached a larger door, James held it open to let me through. Outside, the rain had started again. Grey clouds darkened the sky. This street, which I didn't recognise, was bigger than the one I had come down, and I realised I had entered this place through the back door.

"I live nearby. Come and have tea at my place, and we'll talk."

At his place? Alone? I paused for a moment. James laughed.

"Only to chat about our project. I promise you that. Even though you're a pretty thing, you don't have what I like."

What was he talking about? Incomprehension filled me. Even though I wasn't interested in marriage, I knew I was pretty, with a nicely curved body. My breasts were neither small nor large. Men generally found me attractive, if the inappropriate comments I received at the hospital were anything to go by.

After a few hundred yards, James turned left into a narrow street and opened the first door on the right of a not-so-old, but shady house. After a few steps up the stairs, he stepped aside to let me into a very small room. I knew it wasn't right for me to be alone with a man here, but at this point I didn't care. I was here against my father's wishes, ready to break all taboos and look to my future without his approval.

James lit the small burner under the kettle.

"I have a contract…no, I have two contracts, to be exact. One in Singapore with the Goodwood Park Hotel and another on the London-Singapore ship to pay for the cabin and passage. My singer ditched me last week to get married." He grinned. "To a man she'd just met. I guess she wasn't ready for the adventure. Are you?"

A boat? Singapore? Asia? My God! So far? Could I go that distance? Could I really leave everything behind? I wanted to run away, to take control of my future, but was I ready to go to the other side of the world? I was stunned and just stood there, arms flailing, not moving or speaking.

"If you're not interested, tell me now, but don't waste my time." Jaw clenched, James looked desperate.

Coming to my senses, I held up a finger to interrupt his diatribe. "Give me a minute. My teacher never mentioned going abroad."

"She didn't say anything? I did tell her whom I was looking for and why."

He looked really distraught and started walking up and down talking to himself. In this small room, I was becoming more and more claustrophobic. "Stop moving, and let me think for a moment!"

James froze. The kettle sang.

"I have a few questions to ask you before I make my decision. In the meantime, give us some tea. I'm thirsty after all that singing." Could I do that? Leave everything behind and go with him? A stranger? Jump into the unknown?

He looked at me, and I looked back at him. *No, my dear. I am not just a pretty thing. I'm a woman who doesn't let herself be pushed around.* I was proud of myself for standing my ground for once. He was not my father and had no authority over me. Even in the silence of the room, I could tell he was getting the message, because he slowly poured the hot water into the teapot and sat down without a word.

I perched on the one chair and raised the cup to my lips. "Tell me more about the contracts," I asked after the first sip.

"The ship leaves Southampton on the 23rd of April. It's a P&O passenger ship."

James handed me brochure number 346 with a ship drawn on the first page as he continued his explanations. I flicked through it, looking at the timetable and the prices. Fifty-eight pounds for one-way in second-class? I nearly choked.

"In the evening we will entertain the passengers. The contract calls for a small cabin for the two of us. I've also negotiated a two-year contract in Singapore at the Goodwood Park Hotel. It's not the Raffles Hotel, but it's a good one. If we're lucky, maybe we can get a contract with the Raffles later. A lot of people with money—bankers, planters—go to these places, so we can expect tips on top of our salary. They provide accommodations and a return ticket at the end of the contract."

"They don't provide the outward ticket?"

"Yes, of course, but we will earn extra money to perform on the boat. It will keep us busy, and it will give us time to rehearse. It takes four weeks to reach Singapore, you know. We'll arrive on the 20th of May. Our contract at Goodwood Park starts on the 22nd of that month, so we'll just have time to settle in a bit."

I was just getting into the heart of things. "How much? And don't try to be dishonest. I want to know everything."

James stroked his chin and remained silent for a few seconds. He stared at me, stood up, and opened a small cupboard. Without hesitation, he handed me some papers.

At first, I saw only a jumble of legal terms with a logo and names on a letterhead. I closed my eyes. It couldn't be any harder than reading medical terms. I just had to concentrate. Gradually, everything became clearer. The salary wasn't bad, but I was a bit annoyed that only James's name was mentioned on the contracts. "And the singer's name?"

"Read carefully. The contracts are in the names of Mr. and Mrs. Deacon. We'll have to get married before we leave." His voice faded at the end of the sentence. He looked away.

"I'm sorry?" I was shocked. I couldn't believe what I was hearing. I felt as if my jaw was locked open, my eyes probably so round that I could never close them again.

"It doesn't matter…"

"What? I don't know you. I should marry you and…"

My cheeks were heating and certainly getting redder and redder. Just imagining him touching me…Suddenly he started laughing. His shoulders were shaking so much I thought he would collapse in front of me. "Sorry, sorry…" Still laughing, he wiped his eyes.

"Except for a piece of paper, this union will be a marriage in name only. I will not touch you. You have my word. I had the same agreement with the last singer before she left me," he said bitterly. "I had to lie at the time of the contract because the management didn't want to provide two cabins on the boat and two rooms in the hotel. Otherwise, they would have deducted it from our salary. Don't worry. I'm not interested in your feminine attributes."

From the way he stared at me, I knew I was missing something important. I stared back.

"So, do you agree?"

At that moment, the smile that lit up his face really made him look like an angel with his blond hair and blue eyes. I felt that I should have fallen in love with him. However, in my heart I knew I would never be attracted to a man, no matter how handsome he was. I couldn't get engaged or married like my parents wanted. Not if I wanted to be myself. That didn't leave me much choice.

"Yes. I agree. There's just one little problem. I'm twenty years old, so I need parental consent to marry you. And believe me, I'll never get it from my father."

Appearing surprised, he looked at me for a moment before bursting out laughing and allaying my fears.

"No problem. In this part of London, I'll get you a parental-consent slip without any trouble. We just need to discuss a few practical details before we go to the other side of the world. Some more tea?"

Tell our parents I'm sorry. I have to live my life.
Love,
Evelyn

Chapter Two

Colombo, 14 May 1938

My dear sister,
When I arrived in Southampton on the 23rd of April with my new
husband, I was terrified. In front of me was this huge, black-painted
ship with two smoking chimneys and two masts: the SS Rajputana.
Could I leave? Should I leave?

The activity on the jetty and the noise were comparable to Victoria
Central Station at peak times. I couldn't believe it. Everywhere I
looked, I saw movement: a man, a car, a cart with luggage. Men in
uniform were striding around with purpose; others, dressed normally
like us, were passengers. James was walking beside me, but although
I didn't really know him, I could tell he was as nervous as I was.
Leaving everything behind was never easy.

"You stay here with the luggage. I'll find out where we have to
go."

He pointed to the one and only gangway onto the ship. Leaving
me there with two large suitcases, he started to walk away. I was not
happy to be left behind, so, ignoring our belongings, I followed him.
He stopped.

"I asked you to wait for me there."

"Why? There's only one gangway. It's the only way to get into
this...monster. So why should I wait for you on the platform in the
middle of all this chaos?"

Smiling my sweetest smile, the one I reserved for annoying men, I took his arm.

"Let's go together. It'll save time. And who knows? If I charm the crew, maybe I can help us get a better cabin."

He didn't really seem convinced by my arguments, but he went back to get our luggage, and together we climbed the gangway. On the deck of the ship, a very nice gentleman in uniform checked our tickets.

"Are you part of the entertainment? Glad to have you on board. Passengers who spend four weeks at sea with only a few ports of call are bored."

He smiled at me and ignored James completely before pointing to another uniformed man beside him. "Max will help you find your cabin. You just have to go with him."

He handed the man our tickets and whispered something to him.

As we followed Max, I was in awe. The wood of the bridge was perfectly polished. Everywhere I looked, everything seemed to be clean and well maintained. James was chatting casually with Max, and I gleaned some information about the ship: "passenger and ocean liner," "built in Scotland in 1925," "good and sturdy ship," "interior design by Lady Elsie Mackay," and so on.

"A woman designed this ship," I exclaimed, slowing mid-deck. Surprised that a woman could do this, I almost screamed, and everyone present looked at me. A little embarrassed, I blushed.

Max promptly corrected me. "Not the ship, madam. Just the interior of the ship."

His attitude expressed his disapproval. I could almost read his mind. A woman could never design such a perfect piece of engineering. James grabbed my hand before I made a fool of myself by expressing my opinion. "My wife is a bit tired after the train. Perhaps a little rest and refreshment will do her good before tonight."

I pressed my lips together so as not to make a scene. How dare he? We would have a discussion later, alone. James had to feel my nails digging into his hand and winced a little. That was good. Next time he wouldn't speak for me.

"Anyway, Lady Mackay died in 1928 trying to fly across the Atlantic Ocean with another pilot," Max said before opening a door and entering the place that would be our home for the next four weeks.

The small cabin was beautiful, with polished wood everywhere, two bunk beds, and some custom-made furniture. The small, round window let us see the sky and a bit of the sea, but that was all. I wouldn't spend much time here. Too cramped.

"Thanks, Max. Could you tell us where we should perform? And please call me James."

Max sat back and smiled. James really had a way with people.

"You'll have to entertain the first-class passengers in the music room on A deck from four to six p.m. and eight to nine p.m. every day. Usually, it's just the piano. This time it will be a nice change to have a singer too."

He looked at me sharply, as if he doubted my abilities. "Madam, if—"

Suave, I interrupted him with a smile. "Evelyn. Please, call me Evelyn, Max."

"Yes, thank you, Evelyn. A word of advice. It would be better if you didn't walk around alone."

When I winced, he added quickly, "We are almost at full capacity with 553 passengers, and 482 of them are men. A beautiful woman like you…we wouldn't want you to get into trouble."

I could understand his concern, but the glance he gave James annoyed me. That knowing look between two men when they talked about women reminded me of my father and his friends. When they wanted to have a serious discussion, the weaker sex had to leave the room. For them, our brains could not grasp the subtlety of the political game or anything else. Women could slave away—in hospital, at home, in the fields—see an accident or death and deal with it, but men thought the world was theirs to do with as they pleased.

"I'll discuss this issue with my wife. Thank you, Max."

As soon as he closed the door, hands on hips, I stood in front of James. I had to set things straight immediately. "Never answer for me. Do you understand?"

"What are you talking about? I didn't—"

"What about right now? I'm your wife on paper only. We have a partnership. That's all. I'm capable of thinking for myself. Do you think I ran away from my parents to let you treat me the same way they did?"

James opened his mouth and closed it again. He raised his hands in peace.

"Please keep your voice down. I'm sure the wall is very thin. You don't want anyone to know about our business. Do you?"

I looked at him with disdain, very angry, but I lowered my voice.

"No. I don't want anyone to get involved in our business and stick their nose where it doesn't belong. I need this contract as much as you do." To hide the trembling of my lips, I turned around, took off my hat, and opened my suitcase. I hated it when my body betrayed my feelings. "I'll sleep in the bottom bunk," I added without looking at him.

For a little while James kept silent. He was watching me, evidently sizing me up. Apart from the few rehearsals we'd had, he didn't know me. For the past month, we had spent our time together on music and singing. We had to choose about forty songs to start with. Some of them we hadn't had a chance to rehearse. We hoped to do that on this trip.

"I'm going to look at the piano in the music room. Join me when you're done here…if you want."

❖

After unpacking my clothes, I freshened up a bit using the water from the jug. The whole ship was vibrating under my feet. Were we about to leave? I rushed out and walked as fast as I could without running to the upper deck. Many people were there, some waving to friends or family who had stayed on land, and others, like me, just watching the commotion. A deep sorrow filled my heart. I was leaving behind my dear sister, my best friend, and she didn't know it yet. In a few days, she would receive the letter I had posted on the pier. By then she and my parents would be worried. I should have thought of that and told them a lie…another one.

A blast from a foghorn startled me. Kids were running along the jetty, waving with both arms. Were they the children of some of the men on board or just kids playing? One yard…two yards. The land where I was born was moving away. Fear gripped me. What was I doing? Going to the other side of the world with a man I barely knew. Was I insane? I forced myself to breathe slowly, deeply, like I did during my breath training before singing. Yes. To calm my fear, I needed to sing. Singing would be my escape. The music room was on A deck.

I tried to orient myself. I assumed I was on B deck. I had noticed that our cabin was on C deck, in the forward part...the bow of the boat...of the ship. I had never been to sea before, and these marine terms, which I had learned at school, were buried deep in my memory. When I finally spotted the stairs going up, I noticed that everyone was starting to leave the railing, most of them going down, supposedly to their cabins on C and D decks.

The weather was quite fine for England. The hazy sun was giving a little warmth on A deck as I tried to find the music room.

"Ma'am?" asked someone behind me.

With a smile, I turned toward a man in a white uniform. He was so tall I almost had to take a step back to avoid a stiff neck.

"Hello, sir. I'm looking for the music room."

"It's not open yet, ma'am," he replied politely.

"I am Evelyn B...Deacon, the singer for this trip. My...husband went in earlier to check the piano." The words had barely left my lips when I heard music and recognised one of our songs. "I guess if I follow the music, I'll find the piano, won't I?"

The man in uniform smiled, his dark eyes sparkling with humour. "Yes, ma'am. I'm John Carter, the ship's third officer. Pleased to meet you. Let me show you the way."

"Thank you, Mr. Carter. I hope I'll be able to find my own way around the ship in the next few days."

He pointed the way with his arm and walked beside me.

"It's easy to navigate around a ship. This one is not that big. Most of A deck is reserved for first-class passengers: lounge, music room, smoking room. The lounge and smoking room on B deck are for second-class passengers. The two dining rooms for first and second class are on C deck. In general, the aft part of the ship is reserved for second-class passengers. I recommend that you do not venture there alone." Mr. Carter stopped in front of a glass door.

With all the windows surrounding the room, I could see James playing, lost in his music. For at least a minute, with the third officer beside me, I watched him string together chords. He was excellent, and I was lucky that we were well matched. A slight cough reminded me that I was not alone.

"Thank you, Mr. Carter."

"Have a good trip, Mrs. Deacon. I think we'll have the opportunity to meet again."

Leaving the friendly officer, I entered the music room. The decor was very elegant, with lots of dark, polished wood reflecting the light, comfortable armchairs, and small tables. The chandeliers hung from the beams. Did they move with the roll of the ship? The music stopped.

"Ah, it's you. Are you feeling better?" Obviously realising the awkwardness of his words, James raised his hand. "Sorry. Wrong thing to say. Look. I can see you have quite a temper, and I don't want to argue with you. Let's make a deal. I'll try to stay out of your way as much as possible, and you do the same. Like you said, between you and me, there's just a piece of paper. We have a professional agreement. That's all."

Did he mean it? I stared at him. He was so handsome with his candid blue eyes. Why didn't I feel anything for him? Not even the slightest spark? Nothing. What was wrong with me?

"I agree. Anyway, we have a lot of rehearsing to do if we want to be ready when we arrive in Singapore."

James began the first note of "Stormy Weather." I laughed. "I hope this isn't a premonitory song for the trip…or our relationship."

Fingers running over the piano keys, James smiled faintly.

As usual, every afternoon, after almost two weeks of navigation, I was sitting quietly in the music room. Our cabin was so small I felt claustrophobic if I stayed there too long. The music room was bright and almost empty most of the day. The view from here was fantastic. From time to time, women or men would come here to read in peace. For my taste, the lounge, even the one on A deck, was too noisy, with many gentlemen talking about their new jobs somewhere in India or Malaysia. Some were returning home with their new wives after a holiday in England. When I learned that these poor men couldn't marry for the first five years of their overseas contract, I was surprised. From time to time, I would see James talking or laughing with a group of men. He kept his end of the bargain and left me alone.

So much to see, so much to write about in my diary or to Dorothy. We had crossed the Suez Canal the day before, which was an incredible experience. The shore was so close I could almost touch the desert sand with my bare hand. I never imagined that it could be like this. With the sky so blue, the air so dry and warm, it was nothing like England here. It was hard to write down a feeling, a sentiment. I looked at my blank page and saw only mental images: Port Said, the children laughing and jumping in the water, the desert…

When I heard the piano, I looked up and winced. A man, his friends encouraging him, was trying to play. When the woman beside him began to sing, I knew I couldn't linger here. It was impossible for me to remain stoic when I heard someone sing out of tune. Annoyed and not knowing where to go, I put all my things into my bag and left the music room.

With the temperature high and the sun shining, the shaded part of the deck was full of people, and the other part of it was too hot to stay there. Resigned, I went down two levels and entered my cabin. The sight that met my eyes left me speechless. Two men, half-naked, with their trousers down to their ankles, were embracing on my bed. MY bed! I immediately recognised James and John Carter, the third officer. As a nurse, I had seen a few penises during my training, but never two of them rigid at the same time. When my gaze met James's and then John Carter's, my facial temperature soared. I wasn't a shy person by any means, but this was still a bit too much for me. Still shocked, I hurriedly left the cabin. Taking a deep breath, I climbed up to the B deck and walked to the railing. The open sea with the mountains on the horizon calmed me slightly. The ship was moving at a good pace. What I had seen…James with another man…How could this be? Passengers were strolling behind me, chatting. I was shaking inside. Fortunately, no one came to check on me. Was this why James had told me not to worry about our fake marriage?

"Evelyn…" James's voice. "Could we…could we talk?"

Was it fear that made him hesitate?

"Please…let me explain."

I turned and stared at him. He looked down. Anger rose instantly. My voice swelled with barely contained rage. "What do you want to explain? On my bed? You did it on my bed?"

"Keep your voice down, please." James looked around furtively, and before I could react, he grabbed my arm and dragged me with him toward our cabin. I tried to resist. "He's gone. Please come. We need to talk. Don't make a scene. If the captain finds out about this, he'll put us ashore in Aden, the next port."

I didn't really understand what he was talking about, but if the captain wanted to get rid of James and Carter, so be it. "That's your problem, not mine," I said when we were in our cabin.

"Don't you see? The contract is in our names. If I can't stay, you can't stay. Think about it, Evelyn. Don't you see why my promise not to touch you after we were married was so easy for me to keep? Maybe I should have been more honest with you, but I couldn't. I was…"

"Scared?"

He lowered his head in defeat. "Yes," he admitted, tears in his eyes. "It's happened before, and I barely escaped. I know you must be disgusted, but I…"

Disgusted? No. I was angry. I should have been repulsed, but a voice inside me told me I wasn't pure as the driven snow in all this. I had never been with a man, never wanted to be with a man for some reason I didn't really understand. However, I couldn't analyse what I was feeling at the moment.

"As I told you, you can do what you like with your free time, but not in my cabin."

"We can't go anywhere else, Evelyn. Passengers are not allowed in the crew's quarters. Could we say that the place is mine from two to four p.m.?"

His expression grew pleading. He insisted, despite my pout of disgust at finding them on my bunk. Yet I could understand the logic of his request.

"My bed is off-limits."

"You could take the top bunk. You know…two people upstairs… it's a bit…like…dangerous."

Imagining the two men on the upper bed falling down during the heat of passion, I couldn't resist and burst out laughing. James, obviously bewildered, stared at me. "Sorry. Just a vivid imagination. I'll take the top bunk."

"Thank you," He seemed so grateful I couldn't stay mad at him.

"Don't ever put me in that awkward position again. Do you understand me?"

"I understand you. I promise."

He walked away, leaving me alone with my thoughts. I looked at my cabin with the hastily made beds, and the anger started to rise again until I remembered that we had a contract, nothing more. Ginger Rogers's voice teased me with her song "We're in The Money." She was right about that. James was my meal ticket. Without him I had nothing.

Chapter Three

Singapore, 15 December 1938

My dear sister,
I'm sorry I've been so busy these past few months. You can't imagine this city. It's so full of life everywhere, all the time, day and night. We arrived in Singapore on the 22nd of April. Let me tell you about it.

Even before the ship docked in Singapore, from the deck I saw that it wasn't at all like home. Bare-chested people were everywhere, others in uniforms, shouting in strange languages, pulling a handcart, using a donkey cart, carrying trunks, luggage, waiting for passengers... From time to time I could recognise Indians, but most of the workers in the port were Chinese.

I was a bit suffocated by the smells, and, beside me, James evidently was too. With the heat, I was sweating a lot. All the dresses I owned were made of wool, and since the Red Sea I had suffered every time we stopped somewhere. Changing the items in my wardrobe to lighter fabrics would be my priority. I had never imagined such heat and humidity. John Carter—we'd become friends since I'd walked in on them in my cabin—had warned us about the climate the day before we arrived in Singapore when he said good-bye to James.

"Shall we?" James pointed to his arm with his chin. I grabbed it like a lifeline. "Don't worry. Someone should be waiting for us on the dock...at least I hope so."

I forced a hesitant smile onto my lips. James sounded as intimidated as I was. In a way, this speculation reassured me, and I relaxed a little. "I guess the big adventure is just beginning now, for both of us."

James stopped in front of our cabin so we could get our bags. "I want to thank you for…you know…John…"

I knew what he meant. Over the past month, I had learned who my husband really was: an excellent pianist with a big heart and a taste for men. I could live with that.

"I don't mind. You know that. When we got married, I didn't expect you to be…my husband. In a way, it's better like this. It made things clearer."

James stared at me for a long time. Finally, seeming convinced that I was telling the truth, he nodded. A knowing smile twinkled in his eyes. "I understand. You're right. She was beautiful."

"What are you talking about?"

"Mrs. Tradewick was very beautiful."

At the mention of her name, I felt a twinge of sadness. What did he mean? Jane was nice, and we had a lot of laughs. "What? What are you implying?"

"Just that she was beautiful, with her long red hair. Nothing else."

He was lying openly. I could easily perceive his innuendo. Recalling certain memories—her hand touching my arm, her lips close to my ear—I felt my cheeks grow warm. "It wasn't like that!"

"I saw the way you looked at her. Believe me, it *was* like that. It was like that for her too. Why do you think her husband forbade her to come to the music room the last few days before they disembarked in Penang?"

Speechless, I shook my head. No. It wasn't like that. James was distorting everything with his dirty mind, wasn't he? "Don't compare your actions to mine, James. We have nothing in common. Now let's hurry before the person waiting for us loses patience and leaves without us."

As we made our way along the platform, my head was spinning in all directions. So many people were passing each other that we had to pay attention to everything. The coolies, in their baggy trousers, carrying heavy crates on their bare shoulders, moved on without paying attention to the others. The handcarts, loaded more than necessary, gave me the creeps when they passed a little too close to us. James's voice rang out as a man in a pointy hat carrying a hoist with buckets on each end nearly knocked him over.

"This way, Evelyn. There are fewer people." He pointed with a suitcase to a less crowded area.

I followed him. Indeed, most travellers seemed to be using this area, where street vendors of all kinds were lined up, shouting unknown words: *otak*, *kaya*, *popiah*, *satay*, and *mee goreng*. I suddenly recognised the words coffee and tea and chicken rice. Some of the passengers, accustomed to life here, were laughing as they rushed to purchase their favourite dishes, trying to encourage the newcomers.

"Ah. Here's our car, I think."

The relief in James's voice was obvious. I read the sign with our name on it before I saw who was holding it. Amazed, I slowed my steps. My mouth dropped open for a moment before I realised the rudeness of my reaction. A huge man, made even taller by his light-grey turban and his salt-and-pepper beard reaching halfway down his chest, stood waiting for us, stoic in the midst of the tumult. His long jacket and trousers matched to his headdress, perfectly ironed, gave him a natural dignity.

"Mr. and Mrs. Deacon, I presume," he said in his deep voice in excellent English. "I am Dalbir Singh, one of the drivers of the Goodwood Park Hotel. The car is just over there."

He pointed to a well-polished black car parked a few yards away. As he grabbed one of the two suitcases, I studied him from the corner of my eye, but not discreetly enough. His dark eyes met mine.

"I am a Sikh, madam. My parents came from Punjab in 1885, but I was born here."

I smiled at his explanation and nodded. Looking around, I saw a group of men, bare-chested with just a long piece of cloth wrapped around their loins. Some were crouching, smoking a cigarette, while others were standing, talking. Their dark skin glistened with perspiration.

"What are these men doing?" I asked our driver.

"They are waiting for work. When the passengers have left, they will unload your ship. Please," he said, opening the back door of the car.

I sat down in the immaculate interior.

Dalbir Singh didn't mind the traffic. He cut through the lines of handcarts, forcing them to stop abruptly, passing trolleys and bicycles. More than once I clenched my jaws, sensing the impact, but each time, everything went smoothly. After a while I realised that he kept driving almost at the same speed and that the others did the same, anticipating possible crossings.

"You will certainly have to use the rickshaws," said Dalbir Singh, pointing to a handcart with a small roof that spilled out at least four children and one adult. "It's cheap and very comfortable to get from one point to another in Singapore."

Hardly imagining myself being pulled in this cart, I kept silent, busy admiring the white houses with their large archways cluttered with objects or the people wearing both western costume or dresses and the more oriental outfits of the other inhabitants.

A woman in a sari, followed by a maid carrying packages, walked past our car without looking. Our driver avoided them brilliantly.

Gradually, as we drove out of the city centre, the houses became fewer and farther between, giving way to parks surrounded by palms and other trees I didn't know. The bushes were bursting with flowers in every shade of red and purple. As the car slowed, I had my first glimpse of the hotel where we would be working for the next two years.

The Goodwood Park Hotel was massive with its tower and pointed roof. The entrance, framed by two huge white porticoes, was impressive. As our car pulled up, I could hardly shake off the tremor inside my chest. Everything was so much grander than I had expected. When James had told me that he had a contract with a hotel in Singapore, I thought it would be a small place in the centre of the city. I didn't expect this huge hotel surrounded by lawns and all these tropical trees. I saw hardly any buildings nearby.

We got out as a porter rushed up to unload our luggage.

"Enjoy your stay in Singapore, Mr. and Mrs. Deacon. I suppose we'll see each other again."

As Dalbir Singh was about to get back into his vehicle, I asked him, "What are those beautiful fan-shaped trees?"

Following the direction I pointed, he smiled. "They are called the traveller's palm trees, madam. I think of them as the emblem of Singapore because so many of them grow here. But I personally prefer banyan trees."

He pointed to a huge tree a little farther on. I had seen several of them and was impressed by their size.

"If you're interested in the flora of Singapore, I suggest visiting the botanic gardens, madam."

"Evelyn! We are expected," James suddenly reminded me.

I waved to our driver and hurried after my husband.

A smiling man greeted us immediately upon entering. The ceiling of the hall was so high it made me dizzy.

"I am Walter Siemens, the assistant manager. Welcome to our hotel. We have been waiting for you. Our guests will be happy to have a new entertainment."

"James Deacon."

"Evelyn Ba...Deacon," I replied, still looking around and very intimidated. "It's a..."

I couldn't find my voice, but Mr. Siemens finished for me. "An impressive room? Yes. It is. The owner renovated the old Teuton club and turned it into a hotel only nine years ago. We are a direct competitor to the Raffles. The Prince of Wales even stayed here in '36. You'll see that we attract quite a crowd in the evening with our orchestra. I'm sorry to rush you, but as it's already Friday, you'll have to start tomorrow afternoon. Weekends are the busiest days for us, and we have already announced new entertainment for Saturday teatime. On Saturday and Sunday, you will start at three p.m. On the other days, it will be at four p.m. As stipulated in your contract, you are free every Monday. Joseph is our concierge. He will show you to your room. If you have any questions, ask him. He has been here for twenty years."

Mr. Siemens pointed to an old man with white hair and a bright smile. His deep-blue eyes sparkled with mischief as soon as the assistant manager walked away. He adjusted his uniform before addressing us.

"Come with me. The porter will take care of your suitcases. I suppose more luggage will arrive later?"

"Yes. We have two trunks too," confirmed James.

"Don't worry. The baggage handlers will take care of it. Before I show you the staff quarters, we'll take a quick detour to the lounge.

This will be the place where you perform every day. Food and non-alcoholic drinks are free for the entertainment staff. A word of advice, sir. If you drink too much in your spare time, never go where customers can watch you."

"I don't get drunk," James replied promptly.

"And never be late."

Grimacing, I stared at James. Being on time would be a real challenge for him. Our exchange didn't fool Joseph. "I see."

The piano on a platform took up the entire back of a huge room.

"On weekends this room is often full at teatime. It is usually packed after dinner when the band is on and the guests start dancing. Singapore is rich, and people want to have fun."

Still following Joseph, we walked through long corridors in the service area of the hotel. Joseph explained where each one led—kitchen, laundry, delivery—until we reached a lift.

"This is the staff lift. There's a shortcut from the lobby, of course. Your room is on the second floor."

As the doors opened, Joseph walked to the left and pointed to a door in the middle of the corridor.

"The last two rooms are the suites of the director, deputy director, and their families."

As Joseph inserted the key, the last door opened, and a very well-dressed woman came out into the corridor. She slowly walked toward us. I could see that she was beautiful, with her light-red hair and porcelain skin with just a touch of makeup. She stopped a few feet away before examining us from head to toe. Sweating in my travel outfit, I felt uncomfortable.

Quickly, Joseph took off his uniform headgear. James also took off his hat. As a proper lady, I kept mine on.

"Good morning, Mrs. Wilford. Our afternoon entertainment couple has arrived. Mr. and Mrs. Deacon. Mrs. Wilford," Joseph added reverently.

My husband straightened up and gave her a winning smile as he took her hand between his own.

"Pleased to meet you, Mrs. Wilford. I hope you will do us the honour of coming to our first performance tomorrow."

Following Joseph and James's lead, I smiled and gently squeezed her hand. "Nice to meet you, Mrs. Wilford."

Again, she looked at me coldly from head to toe, and a warning crept up my spine.

"I expect you will find the room to your liking. And, of course, I'll be there for the show, but I suppose I'll also check the rehearsal to make sure you're as good as you say you are on paper."

Her charming smile belied the menace in her tone. Immediately I was on my guard.

"Excuse me, but I have important business to attend to."

Waiting for her to disappear into the lift, Joseph let out a deep, relieved breath before opening the door to our room.

"Be careful with her. She's a bitch," he muttered. "If she can stab you in the back, she will."

"Who is she?" I was very curious, because I seldom felt so much dislike for someone I had just met.

"The director's wife, Clara. He is a fair man, but her? She thinks she owns the place and the staff. If convention and fear of criticism didn't hold her back, she would treat us like her slaves."

Joseph entered the room. "This is your home for the next two years. Enjoy it. If you need anything, just ask me."

"Thank you, Joseph. We won't hesitate," said James, shaking his hand as I finally took off my hat.

The room was well decorated and well kept. It wasn't very big, but, at first glance, it had everything we would need. I was relieved to see two beds and a large fan.

"I don't think you'll be able to meet your conquests here."

"You're quite right there, my dear. Not with the boss's accommodation so close to ours," James replied, clearly annoyed. "I would have preferred a little more privacy."

Opening the suitcase and pulling on my robe, I began to sing "Isn't It Romantic?" to cheer him up. By the time I finished the song, imitating a French accent like in the movie *Love Me Tonight*, James had collapsed on the bed, laughing his head off.

CHAPTER FOUR

Singapore, 8 January 1940

I felt satisfied today when I got back to the hotel. I loved Mondays. They were our day off, and I used them to stroll around and see the beautiful city of Singapore. I loved the vegetation, the climate, the people. Walking around Little India with all the women wearing saris made me imagine what India was like. I had the same feeling in Chinatown, with all the traditional junks in the harbour. Other places were very British with their cricket pitches, but I also saw Australians, Malaysians, Japanese, and many other nationalities. The place was a wonderful melting pot that I couldn't get enough of. The food, whether from small restaurants or street vendors, enchanted me. I could never decide between masala dosa, murtabak, Hainan chicken rice, or a simple laksa, not to mention the succulent pepper crab or all the conceivable varieties of noodles.

I couldn't imagine ever going back to England, especially now when war had been declared in Europe. Everyone was following the news very closely. It was a strange feeling, as if people here were waiting for something serious to happen, though Germany had not yet sent its troops west. They appeared content with Poland and the surrounding countries. The French spoke proudly of their Maginot Line, which frightened the Germans, while the British merely mentioned the strength of their navy. Some well-informed journalists, more concerned with Asia, wrote long articles about the conflict between Japan and China. The war had been raging there long before

I arrived in Singapore. To tell the truth, from here, I was more afraid of the Japanese than the Germans. I wrote to my sister once a month, and to my delight, she wrote back. Of course, my parents were furious, but they had begun to calm down. Dorothy had been angry at my departure and wrote me that she had cried a lot because she was left alone. But she understood why I did it. Her acceptance relieved me of some guilt. We exchanged our different points of view on everyday life and about these wars.

But the conflicts were all far away, and most of us in this paradise were living a good life. I had a roof over my head, food, a little money, and a job I liked. James was James. We were friends; however, apart from our performances, I rarely saw him. This suited me, as I was discovering feelings for a very beautiful young Indian woman, Nisha, whom I met by chance at our tailor's shop. She was extremely sweet, and we laughed a lot together. During the past three months, Monday afternoons were ours. I knew she wasn't in love with me, because Nisha often talked about her fiancé waiting for her in India, which broke my heart, but I couldn't stop seeing her. She was the light, and I was the moth. James had been right all along.

At first, I had fought this inclination, but I soon had to admit that I was attracted to women. What would my father have said? A singer and a lesbian at that. Yet I was not mistaken about myself. During the past year and a half, I had quietly read everything I could on the subject, from Radclyffe Hall's poems and novel, *The Well of Loneliness*, to Richard Freiherr von Krafft-Ebing's *Psychopathia Sexualis*, and so many others. All these descriptions fit me perfectly. Of course, I was not what the experts called a "garçonne," although I sometimes wore trousers when I went into the jungle with young men and women I had met. I was twenty-two, and life was beautiful and carefree. Our contract with the hotel was up in five months, so we still had time to find another one. I had to talk to James to find out what he wanted to do next. Maybe try the Raffles?

I had barely made it through the hotel entrance when Joseph rushed up to me and grabbed my arm to lead me into the concierge room.

"What have you done?"

Distraught, I stared at him. He looked terribly worried.

"What do you mean, Joseph? I haven't done anything. Why are we here, in this sordid room?"

"Mr. Wilford has been looking for you all morning, and let me tell you, he doesn't seem happy." Joseph was a kind man, who had befriended me from the beginning of my stay. He had given me a lot of good advice.

"Did he ask only about me or James too?"

Frowning, Joseph hesitated while rubbing his chin. "No, just you. Why only you, if you didn't do anything?"

A shiver ran down my spine. I shook my head. "I don't know. It's my day off. I haven't even been here."

"You'd better go see him right away. You know him." Joseph seemed still doubtful. He gently took my hand in his and looked me in the eyes. "I am your friend. Don't forget that."

Swallowing hard, I forced a smile. What did he know that I didn't? "Thank you."

As I reached the front of the management office, I took a deep breath before knocking on the door.

"Come in."

Mrs. Trudy, the manager's secretary, was sitting at her desk. She was always here. Sometimes, I wondered if she slept here. She was like a guard dog with a bone—never smiling, never a kind word. She smiled only at her boss. The way she glared at me made me shiver. If a look could kill, I'd be dead on the spot. But what could I have done?

"Mr. Wilford has been searching for you all day." She pursed her lips as if she were chewing on something bitter, ready to spit it out.

I refused to apologise for my absence. I held her gaze. "It's my day off. I just got back."

Mrs. Trudy picked up the phone. "Evelyn Deacon is here…Yes, sir."

She stared at me for a few more seconds before showing me the manager's door. I knocked and entered. "You wanted to see me, sir?"

Mr. Wilford stood up and, with a serious expression, pointed to a chair. "Do you know where your husband is?"

He was neither friendly nor angry. Just annoyed, perhaps. I shrugged, not comprehending his question. "No. He had some business to attend to. I went to lunch with a friend."

As he remained silent, I became worried. "What's going on?"

"He's been arrested."

I jumped to my feet. "But why?"

Mr. Wilford grimaced with what looked like embarrassment. Deep down, I knew. A small voice began to chant, *No, no, no. not that. He promised.*

"He...he was caught with...a man..." Visibly upset or embarrassed, Mr. Wilford could not hold my gaze. "In an unseemly position...in bed."

I opened my mouth to speak but immediately closed it again. What could I say? The idiot had been caught. I had to react like a real wife. I couldn't let on that I knew about his escapades. I sank into the seat and put my hand on my chest, acting out the role of my life as my mind raced. What was going to happen now? Would they release him? Convict him? Send him back to England?

Mr. Wilford pushed a piece of paper across his desk. A handwritten name and phone number.

"The name of the policeman who called me this morning to warn me, and his number."

"Is he going to jail?"

"I'm afraid so."

"What will happen to me? What about the contract? Will you have time to find another pianist for tomorrow?"

The director shook his head. "I'm afraid that's not possible. The contract has both your names on it. It says that your conduct must be exemplary to work here."

I felt frantic. I couldn't lose this job. "But I'm not responsible. I haven't done anything wrong."

"I'm sorry, but your husband's behaviour reflects on you, on us. I don't want a scandal to taint my hotel. I'm not a bad man, you know. You have until tomorrow to vacate the premises. And as the contract has been breached, you have no return ticket to England. You'll have to pay for it yourself."

Stunned, I stared at him blankly. He couldn't hold my gaze but finally said, "That's all, Mrs. Deacon."

What could I do but leave? I couldn't yell at him. He had a right to save the good name of his hotel. I was furious with James. I could have killed him. He had promised! Quickly I left the office, ignoring Mrs. Trudy's murderous stare. A last shred of decency prevented me from running to my room.

When I closed the door, I felt drained. Only an hour earlier I had been so happy, and now I was in a maelstrom. I looked around but saw nothing. In shock, I collapsed heavily on my bed and stared at myself in the wall mirror without moving.

How long did I remain prostrate? Three knocks on the door brought me out of the nothingness I was in. I took a deep breath and opened it. Joseph was standing there. The sadness in his eyes told me that he knew. Keeping a secret in this place was almost impossible. It was a miracle that James had kept his for so long.

"May I come in?"

I stepped aside and pointed to the room. My lips trembled. I struggled to hold back the tears. "You've heard," I said in disappointment.

"Yes, I have. I'm sorry." Joseph shook his head, his expression sad. "It's not the end of the world, you know, Evelyn."

Forgetting my status as a distinguished woman, I sniffed. "Is that true? To me, it looks like it. What will I do now? I have to leave here tomorrow. I'm stuck in Singapore, with no job and no roof over my head, with just a little bit of savings."

I was whining and hating myself for it. It wasn't like me to cry about my fate, but a wave of self-pity had hit me.

"Let me know when you're done complaining so we can really talk about your situation." Leaning against the cupboard, Joseph crossed his arms and stared at me. "At least you're not crying too much…I hate it when women cry and moan."

Sniffling, I fought back my tears and clenched my fists. "No. I'm not crying. I don't feel sad. I feel angry…" A mirthless chuckle passed my lips as I stood up and walked to the window. I turned around. "I swear I'm not unhappy for James. I'm furious at him. That dirty son of a bitch! I could kill him! He promised!"

Joseph's lips stretched into a small smile. "This attitude suits you much better. Why did you marry him? You don't love him."

I lowered my eyes without answering. Was it that obvious?

"I see. The contract to come here," Joseph said.

Suddenly I felt ashamed. Joseph was my friend, but he must have hated me for lying all these months.

"You're not the first, you know."

What? What was he talking about?

"Getting married on a contract...to a man...like that."

I frowned.

"I knew from the beginning who he was and what his tendency was," Joseph added. "We have a lot of them around here. Some get caught, and others are smart enough to remain anonymous. At first, I just wondered why you agreed to this marriage. I think I know now. No law against you women, but be careful."

What was he talking about? Me and the law? Suddenly understanding, I blushed. "I—"

Joseph raised his hand and smiled. "You're my friend, Evelyn. You don't need to explain yourself. Here. I've written down some addresses for you." He pulled a folded sheet of paper from his pocket. "The first is a boarding house. It's cheap and clean. I know the landlady, Mrs. Yeo, a trusted widow. She's not the friendly type, but she won't interfere in your affairs. I've contacted her. She has one room left, and she'll keep it for you until tomorrow."

He handed me another paper. "On this one I wrote the name of a place where they could use a good singer. The Blue Tiger is a reputable cabaret. Don't go singing in seedy places. And the last one..."

He gave me another paper. "This is the name and address of a good divorce lawyer. I thought you might want your freedom now."

Stunned, I took the papers and looked at him. Lost in my emotions, I couldn't speak. He had thought of everything. Grateful, I rushed into his arms. "Thank you, Joseph. You are a very good friend."

"I just hope you don't forget good old Joseph when you're famous," he teased me. "If you could pack up James's things, I'll put them in the storage room tomorrow."

Unable to make a sound, I nodded.

"Well, I've got to go. If the boss catches me with you, I'll hear about it for a month. You're an outcast now, my dear. Good-bye."

Alone, I sat down on my bed again, though I was no longer deep in despair. Little pieces of paper with addresses and a few words of support from a friend could change everything.

Almost two years before, I had turned my life upside down by making personal choices to be happy. I was going to do it again, out of obligation. I needed to pack, but instead I picked up a sheet of paper and began to write to Dorothy. Writing to my sister was like confiding in a diary. Deep in my soul I could hear the song "I Ain't Got No Home."

CHAPTER FIVE

Singapore, September 1940

As I was putting the finishing touches on my makeup, I heard someone call, "Evelyn, you're on."

"I'm coming!" I hurried across the small corridor, where Andy, the Chinese owner, was waiting for me as usual. A thin man in his fifties, he spoke good English despite a strong Chinese accent. In the months I'd been working here, I'd always seen him dressed the same: a dark western suit with a red tie.

"Full house tonight," he said, peering discreetly through the curtain. "A few new people are in the right-hand corner."

I glanced around quickly before entering the stage. Yes, I could see them. Men and a handful of women. They occupied two large tables.

"They work at the hospital," Andy explained. "I've been trying to get these doctors here for some time. They'll be good for the Blue Tiger's reputation. I need you to be excellent tonight."

That man infuriated me every time he talked to me, sounding like he thought I wasn't doing my job properly. I was a professional performer, for God's sake, not a teenager learning to sing. Since I'd started working here eight months ago, the audience had grown a lot. But Andy was never happy and refused to admit that customers came to hear me. He wouldn't give me a raise or more hours and was always criticising my dresses, my hair, my voice, and even the songs I didn't choose myself. If only I could have gone somewhere else, but the competition was fierce and the good opportunities rare. Andy wouldn't give me six nights a week, only three, and on that salary, I didn't have enough money for a better room or a ticket back to England. He was well aware of this fact. Moreover, the commitment that bound us prevented me from working in another cabaret in my spare time. Each time, he reminded me that he was the one who had given me a chance when I was in trouble. I'd had no choice but to sign an exclusive one-year contract with the bastard. When I heard the first note of "Let Yourself Go," I knew the stage was waiting for me.

Every night when I started to sing, the crowd would chatter, but gradually they would quieten as the music for the first song came on. I had only three musicians with me: the pianist, the bass player, and the drummer. We played mostly jazz, but not always. Usually, at the end of the show, we allowed some private requests. Sometimes, people would take advantage of the music to dance on the open space in front of me.

As usual, I sang and enjoyed myself, taking care to draw as much attention as possible from the doctors' table in order to please Andy without neglecting the other customers. One of the women at this table was different. Not only did she barely speak to her colleagues and drank little, but she wore trousers and a jacket, a rarity in Singapore. Mostly ignoring her fellow diners, she quietly watched my every move. Sometimes our eyes would meet, and each time a chill ran up my spine. She was beautiful, with short, barely wavy, blond hair. Few women dared to cut their hair that short in those days. Most of us wore it shoulder-length or longer, in a bun. As a blonde who admired her films, I adopted the Ginger Rogers style as soon as I left the Goodwood Park Hotel. Curling my hair every day to get the same look was time consuming, but the compliments I received were worth the trouble. Some men had even told me that I was as beautiful as Ginger Rogers herself.

That night, forgetting all my immediate problems, I sang my favourite love song from the bottom of my heart as I fantasised about the beautiful stranger sitting quietly there.

❖

The next Saturday when I arrived at the club, I was still thinking about that woman. Doctor or nurse? I had to admit that I had been disappointed not to see her on the other two nights of the week when I was singing. Perhaps she was busy, or, worse, she wasn't as interested in me as I was in her. Taking a deep breath, I changed my clothes and put on my makeup while chatting with the other performers who came before me. I was the main attraction of the evening, but Andy had other dancers and singers in the afternoon, and some were still there when I arrived.

I talked for a moment with Mei Ling, who had just finished her number before returning to serve in the room. She slipped sensually into her red cheongsam, a beautiful Chinese-style dress covered with small golden dragons and open to the top of her right thigh. I admired her beauty and her long, black hair before she pulled it up on the back of her neck in a bun.

"Evelyn? It's time!"

As I walked down the hallway, I didn't want to think about my beautiful stranger. Would she be there? Andy was waiting in the same place, half watching the customers and half watching the artists.

"They're back," he said with a smile. "You did a good job last time. Do it again."

At first, I didn't understand what he was talking about until I realised with a pang that the doctors were there again tonight. I opened the curtain a little to confirm what he'd said. Yes, they were sitting at the same table, but the beautiful stranger wasn't among them. Was she late? Was she in the bathroom? Would she come? I was so disappointed that Andy had to grab my arm to remind me that I had a job to perform.

"What's going on with you? They're waiting. Can't you hear the music? The musicians have played the introduction three times now."

I looked at Andy as if I had never seen him before. Lost in my world of hurt feelings, I had forgotten the notion of time. Gradually the music and the voices of the customers reached my ears. I straightened my posture and stepped onto the stage. Moving sensually in my shiny blue silk dress, I drew all eyes to me. I strode to the microphone, smiling, while the musicians played "How Deep Is the Ocean." With a slow shake of my head, I observed the crowd. Most of them were young gentlemen of all nationalities, and some had come with the woman they apparently wished to court. Others were planters, businessmen, or tourists. All clearly wanted to have fun. The people at the Chinese tables drank a lot and laughed loudly, while those at the Western tables seemed more subdued.

For most of the song, to avoid disappointment, I averted my eyes from the doctors' table, but if I ignored them completely, Andy would threaten to fire me. I finally glanced over. There she was, looking at me. My heart beat a little faster.

Just like last time, she was wearing white trousers and a white shirt. My voice caught in my throat for a fraction of a second, and I noticed the pianist's glare. Discreetly I shook my head and smiled wider.

When the first note of "My Funny Valentine" began, I couldn't resist approaching the stranger. However, not wanting to embarrass her too much, I moved toward the man sitting next to her before returning to the stage and finishing my song by looking into her eyes. I had never been so attracted to anyone.

We continued this little game for several weeks. Every Saturday night she was there, and my heart was racing. Her eyes on me were like a velvet caress, sensual and exquisite.

One weeknight at the end of October, I was late coming into the club. I sang there on Wednesdays too, but we had fewer customers than on Fridays or Saturdays. I liked the change of pace, the more intimate atmosphere with the customers. On this occasion, the musicians and I would try out the new songs that we often rehearsed in the morning. I was in the middle of my performance when I noticed her sitting at a small table at the back, all alone. What was she doing here on a Wednesday? Fortunately, I knew the lyrics so well that my wandering mind didn't miss a word. After the performance ended, still reeling from the emotion, I had quickly exited the stage, ready to change, when Andy stopped me.

"A customer asked to have a drink with you."

Although this was part of the game, I winced. "I'm tired, Andy, and you know I don't like to do that."

"It's part of your contract." Clearly annoyed at my resistance, he stared at me, hard. "She's waiting," he added, pointing to the room. She is? Was it…? Could it be…? I followed Andy's gaze to the small table at the back. Yes, it was her. I took a deep breath to calm my racing heart. "I'll do it, but let me change first."

Andy couldn't understand why I didn't want to meet her in my stage clothes. I sighed. "It's a woman thing."

Incredulous at my answer, he nevertheless released my arm. I hurried off to the dressing room to remove my dress and stage makeup.

Ten minutes later, or maybe a little longer, I stopped at her table. She looked up and smiled shyly. For the first time, I could see that she had deep-green eyes and a smile to die for. Add to that a dimple on one cheek, and I was swooning.

"Please, sit down." Her voice was deep, a little husky. She seemed nervous. I'd never seen a nervous nurse before. "What are you drinking?"

"What are you having?"

"White wine."

"Then the same."

She gestured to the waiter, pointing to her glass. We watched each other and waited in silence. As soon as my wine arrived, I took a sip, hoping the alcohol would calm my nerves. I should have ordered a whiskey for that to be the case.

"Joan Cliver."

"Evelyn Baker."

"I know. I asked the bartender," she admitted with a slight smile. "I love to hear you sing. You have a beautiful voice."

I could tell from her accent that she was Australian. "Thank you," I replied, embarrassed. I didn't understand why, but she made me feel shy.

"I—"

"Are you—?"

The surprise of speaking at the same time made us laugh and lightened the mood. I apologised. "I'm sorry."

"No. Go ahead."

"Are you a nurse?"

"A doctor…specialising in tropical diseases."

To my surprise, she gave me a big, mischievous smile. My heart missed a beat. She was...beautiful, but more than that. I couldn't find the perfect word to describe her. Not knowing why, I stammered, "My father is a doctor. I studied to be a nurse before I changed careers."

Why had I told her that? Joan raised her eyebrows at my admission. "Quite a move. I take it your father wasn't very happy."

"Not really. I acted without his permission." To stop telling her my life story, I asked, "Why did you want to have a drink with me?"

Joan blushed and looked down. In the blink of an eye, she could go from calm to nervous. I raised the glass to my lips.

"I...I wanted to ask you if you gave...singing lessons."

Luckily, I hadn't had time to take a sip; otherwise, my surprise would have made me splash everything around me. I put the glass back down. "Do you want to learn to sing? Any reason?"

"They say it's a tradition to sing a song for the children in the hospital at Christmas. That's what they told me when I arrived in August." Joan hesitated before adding, "I don't know how to sing, so maybe you could help me with something simple."

"A Christmas song? A song you like?"

"Anything, as long as I don't sound ridiculous."

Joan was sweating, staring at me with her green eyes, begging me to agree. For the first time since I left England, I felt weak, without willpower. She hypnotised me, fascinated me. I couldn't say no to her, but on top of that, I also needed money. Who said never to mix business with pleasure?

"I can do that. I've already given lessons to a few socialites, so I have experience. When are you free?"

The tip of her tongue moistened her lips nervously. I stared at her without moving and resisted the flash of desire that exploded in my stomach. I tried to take a long, quiet breath to calm myself.

"Sundays every fortnight or Mondays when I work on Sundays. Is that okay with you?"

"I'm free. Another singer is here for those days," I explained with a touch of bitterness.

Seeming relieved, she smiled. "I know. I asked around. I guess there's a story there."

I frowned. It was none of her business. Joan held up her hand to stop my answer. "Maybe if we become friends, you'll tell me one day."

Friends? So I wasn't the only one who felt the attraction between us. "Do you want to start tomorrow?"

"I'd love to, yes. Where would you like to practice?"

"I can't do it in my room. The landlady would kick me out."

Joan grimaced as she shook her head negatively. "I live in a guesthouse near the hospital. I haven't had time to look for something more permanent since I arrived."

Sadness filled her eyes as she must have realised that our lessons might not be possible. I couldn't let that happen. Every fibre in my body told me that she was the one I had been waiting for.

"The botanic gardens? Nine o'clock tomorrow morning?"

Surprised, she gave me an anxious look. "In public?"

The fear in her eyes disturbed me. I tried to reassure her. "Believe me. Not many people are in the botanic gardens in the early morning, and there is less chance of rain then than later in the day. I know a secluded spot."

She didn't look convinced.

"Trust me. It's one of my favourite places in Singapore."

"If you're sure."

"I am. Meet me at the entrance tomorrow at nine."

I stood up and held out my hand to not only seal our agreement, but to touch her. I will never forget that first time we touched. A spark, a softness, overwhelming feelings rushed through me. When I let go of her hand, I was surprised that I was still in the cabaret with music playing.

"See you tomorrow."

With wobbly legs, I walked out into the street. What had just happened? The song "I've Got You Under My Skin" was playing in my head, and I couldn't stop it.

Chapter Six

Have you chosen a song?" I asked as we walked side by side to an area of the garden I knew well.

Seeming embarrassed, Joan sighed. "Not really."

When I'd seen her arrive in a light green floral dress and matching wide hat, I'd been surprised. Even with her short hair, she looked very feminine, a far cry from the woman I met at the cabaret. I couldn't help glancing at her dress again.

"What are you looking at?"

"Your dress. No, you in a dress. It suits you. It's different."

She blushed.

I smiled, then blushed back. I couldn't believe I had dared to compliment her. I felt so comfortable with her.

"I like your dress too," she whispered shyly. "The blue matches your eyes perfectly."

A little embarrassed, I bit my lower lip.

Sensing that after this personal exchange, we needed time to recuperate, I pointed to some large tropical trees or flowers, such as hibiscus and bougainvillea, whose names I had learned on arrival. I loved this park. It was so green, so lush. The sun was already high, but my large straw hat was doing its job well.

"Not too hot for you?"

Joan burst out laughing. Not a little girlish laugh, but a laugh from deep inside. Lovely.

"I'm from Australia, south of Darwin. My parents have a farm there. If you want warm and wet, you'll have to visit them during the rainy season. The weather here is wonderful, always the same all year-round. Showers almost every day, usually in the late afternoon, and that's it. Paradise."

"Wait until you get a real storm, and you might change your mind," I told her, teasing. "It's scary."

Still laughing, Joan teased me back. "For a Brit perhaps, but for us, thunder and lightning are as common as kangaroos."

A shiver of delight ran down my spine under her mischievous gaze.

"This is it." I pointed to a bench under a large, magnificent tree surrounded by bushes. The place was hidden from view, and no one would disturb our peace unless they took the little path we were on. "You see, it is very secluded, as I promised. We won't attract many people. I don't think we'll even see anyone during our session."

Joan looked around. The light in her eyes as she smiled at me made me blush. "It's lovely," she murmured.

Every time her sight grazed me, a warmth spread from my belly to my spine. It was wonderful yet so scary. From the beginning, the effect this woman had on me was breathtaking. Swallowing hard, I forced the words out of my mouth.

"If your song is mainly for children, how about *My Darling Clementine*? It's well known and very easy to sing." Without waiting for an answer, I stood in front of her and began on the first verse.

Sitting down, Joan listened to me. Her eyes were on my mouth, my face, and I was trying not to become too distracted. Mission almost impossible. However, she was a client, and I had to remain professional. I forced myself to remember that I also needed money.

"Good idea about the song," she said, sighing. "The kids will love it, and I already know most of the words."

I could barely hear the end of her sentence. She had lowered her head and, avoiding my gaze, was staring at the ground between her feet. I didn't understand her attitude. One minute she was very sure of herself, yet the next she appeared shy and introverted.

"Would you like to try it so I can assess the work we'll have to do?"

Suddenly, Joan raised her head. Her look of fear and misery melted my heart. She was no longer the confident doctor or the subtle seductress. The transformation was incredible.

"I can't do it. That's the problem," she admitted in a breath.

Surprised, waiting for her to elaborate a little, I stared at her. Did she sing out of tune? Along her clenched jaw, the muscles moved slowly. She was gritting her teeth.

Gently, I sat down beside her and took her hand. Without really being aware of what I was doing, I stroked the soft, warm skin with my thumb. I could have gone on like this for the rest of the day, but she turned her hand and took mine. I was momentarily breathless.

"Tell me," I whispered. "I am your friend. You can trust me."

On the verge of tears, Joan swallowed. She hesitated for a long moment before taking a deep breath.

"I…I used to sing as a child. I loved it, actually. I sang to the cows, the chickens, when I was alone with them."

I smiled. I could totally picture Joan as a youngster singing to the animals. She must have been so cute.

"One day…I was eight years old…I had this song in my head that I couldn't sing perfectly. So I kept trying. My mother had asked me to look after my little sister, who was two years old and still a bit wobbly on her feet. It annoyed me. She was so demanding and kept interrupting me. I couldn't concentrate, so I climbed onto the platform of the windmill, leaving her down below, and practised my song. I was so focused that I didn't realise she would try to follow me…"

Sensing what was coming, I tightened my fingers around her hand. Joan added a little pressure.

"She fell, and I didn't even notice. I continued to sing the damn song atop my windmill as my little sister lay on the ground a few feet below me."

Looking straight ahead, Joan wiped her tears with her free hand.

"She died two days later without regaining consciousness, and I never sang again. It was my fault. My parents didn't really blame me. They said it was an accident, but I knew. I never told them what I had done. I was so afraid they would reject me."

A whirlwind of emotions came over me. I soon understood the full implications. "And you became a doctor to save lives."

Joan turned her head sharply and stared at me. "How did you know?"

Gently, I drew her hand into my lap so I could hold it between my fingers.

"This is the kind of thing that changes the course of a life. But now it's time for you to forgive yourself and let your little sister's soul go in peace. In return for one life, you have saved many as a doctor, and you know it. If you trust me, I will help you sing again."

"To free me from my memories?" she asked bitterly.

"To find yourself again. To find the happy child who loved to sing for the animals. Your memories are yours. Good or bad, they are precious. They are what make us who we are."

"A singer and a philosopher?" She was teasing me.

Shaking my head, I laughed, happy to see the joy back in her eyes.

"Far from it. Maybe a singer who hasn't always made the right decisions in her life." Joan opened her mouth, probably to ask a question, but I stopped her. "That's for another conversation."

"I agree. Will you be able to help me? Do you want to?"

Her hopeful gaze didn't leave mine. I nodded. Just to put the joy back in her face, I would go to hell. "Let's simply start. Can you hum after me?"

"Hum? I think so. Maybe...I've never tried."

That day we just hummed the notes of the scale, sitting on a bench, tucked away in this park. I hadn't had such a good day since James was arrested. As we parted, we were both smiling, and I was hoping for our next lesson to be even better than this one.

Sitting on the park bench, I was waiting for Joan. In two months, she had made enormous progress. I was so happy for her. She still couldn't sing using her full voice, but we were close. My stomach clenched in anticipation, and my fingers tingled. I was in love. For the first time in my life, I was truly in love. She was so beautiful inside and out, so sweet. When she talked about her patients, I could see in her eyes the hope of saving them.

Today was going to be a beautiful day. The sky was very blue, blue like at home in winter. It was so rare to see this kind of colour here. The birds seemed as happy as I was, and they kept singing. One of them was squawking loudly, and I hoped it would go away before our class started.

Joan hadn't come to the cabaret last night. With her work at the hospital, this had happened before, but she never missed our lesson. Our meetings had become the highlight of my week. As the lessons progressed, we extended our time to a full day together. Lunch was the first stop after the singing lesson. Then we strolled down the street to digest our food, followed by a cup of tea to cool down. We talked a lot and smiled like two great friends discovering each other, but what I felt in my heart...what I could read in Joan's green eyes...

She simply appeared on the path after going around the bushes. I smiled and so did she, but I could see that something was wrong. Her face was a little too white, her eyes too dull. Tiredness exuded from every pore of her skin. She wasn't wearing a dress as she usually did on her day off. Her trousers and shirt looked as if she had slept in them. I stood up.

"Good day, Evelyn. Sorry I'm late."

Worried, I immediately grabbed her hands. "What's the matter? You look terrible."

Avoiding my gaze, she looked down and shook her head. I tightened my fingers around hers.

"Tell me," I asked gently.

She raised her head. Her lips trembled. Tears slowly rolled down her cheeks. "He died last night."

Joan fell into my arms, squeezing me so hard I could barely breathe, but I didn't care. Joan was in my arms, and she was crying. She needed me. Without letting go, I guided us to the bench so we could sit down. Her head was on my shoulder, her tears sliding down my neck. She was sobbing now. I tightened my grip on her back and began to caress her, murmuring comforting words. I didn't know who had died, but my beloved was in distress, and nothing else mattered. Gently, I laid my cheek against her soft hair, smelled its sweet, flowery scent, and couldn't resist placing a kiss on it.

Gradually the tears dried up, but Joan, huddled against me, didn't move. Despite the heat and the perspiration, I savoured every second of our contact. I cursed the Singapore climate for a moment.

Between the temperature and the humidity, I would have needed to shower every hour to stay cool.

"I'm sorry. I didn't mean to..." She sniffed again before sitting up.

She looked at me with such pain in her beautiful eyes that I couldn't resist the urge to relieve her. My feelings for her silenced my conscience, and I kissed her slowly on the cheek. "You're safe with me," I whispered between small kisses along her jawline to her mouth.

Her lips were so delectable, I couldn't stop. I intensified my kiss, tasted her mouth, her tongue. My heart was dancing, my senses racing. I felt out of control. With my palms, I held her head in place, devouring her beautiful lips. She moaned. Or was it me? The lack of air in my lungs made me pull back a little so I could take a deep breath. My head was spinning. I felt like I had run a marathon...and won. Joan looked as out of breath as I was. I saw apprehension in her eyes. Suddenly I realised what I had done. For the first time in my life, I had truly kissed a woman. And it was divine.

Shocked by my own behaviour, I felt a wave of guilt sweep over me. What would she think of me? Abruptly, I released her head and tried to stand up, but she grabbed my shoulders and, before I could do anything, kissed me back. Not just a little peck on the lips, but a passionate, fiery kiss, like the one we had just exchanged. The fire exploded inside me. When one of her hands slowly slid down me and came to rest on my chest, I thought I would faint with happiness. My hand imitated hers. My heart beat like crazy as soon as my fingers touched her soft nipple. She moaned, I moaned. We were kissing on a bench in the Singapore botanic gardens, where everyone could see us.

"We have to stop," she said breathlessly, her lips against my cheek.

I didn't want to. Just the thought of kissing her more made me swoon. Without waiting, I initiated another, even more passionate kiss that lasted several minutes.

"You're right," I finally replied, staring at her, panting.

She smiled and kissed me again.

In her arms, I lost track of time. Her kisses, so powerful yet so delicate, intoxicated me with desire. I could have enjoyed just a little touch between my legs. "Touch me...now," I ordered her.

I grabbed her hand and guided it to the right spot under my dress. Immediately a storm exploded inside me. I was flying outside my body. I no longer saw a blue sky, only stars. No more birds were singing; I heard only the blood pumping through my veins. Huddled in Joan's arms, I gasped. She kissed my forehead, my hair, caressed my cheek, whispered soft words. I stepped back to get a better look at her and smiled slowly.

"I..."

I touched her soft lips with my index finger, silencing her. No words were necessary. We stayed like that, looking into each other's eyes, for a long time. The distress in her gaze had disappeared. Only hope and desire remained. I could understand it. I felt so elated.

"I guess our lesson today is over. I like this new song," I told her, teasing.

"I love it too, more than anything you can imagine."

Joan's husky voice caressed my senses. She was so seductive that my desire returned in full force. I stood up abruptly and pulled her with me.

"If we stay here, I'll make love to you on this bench, and someone might catch us. We have to move."

"You're right. I shouldn't have—"

"I kissed you, and I don't regret it."

She seemed surprised by the certainty of my admission.

"If it's okay with you, I'd even like to continue," I added, certain of her response.

Joan moistened her lips with the tip of her tongue, and I almost fell over. My heart rate was rising again. "I'd like that too, but where?"

It was a big question that had been swirling around in my head for several minutes. We needed privacy. My room was out of the question, and from what I understood, so was hers.

Joan gently took my hand in hers and pulled me along. "Shall we get a bite to eat first?"

"You're right. It will clear our heads. Hainan-style chicken rice?"

She nodded.

"You still have to tell me what made you cry," I said as we walked.

With a suddenly sad face, she froze on the path. Her fingers tightened on my hand. "I lost a patient last night. He was nine years old. His parents brought him to the hospital too late. There was nothing I could do."

She was silent for a long time after her revelation. I wanted to hug her and never let go, but we were in plain sight, and the garden at that hour was full of mothers with their children. Taking her arm, I encouraged her to walk beside me as I sang "Smoke Gets in Your Eyes" in a low voice, a song I knew she loved in this new version.

Chapter Seven

Joan's kiss was taking me to unknown shores. I couldn't get enough of her lips, her tongue. Every encounter brought its share of frustrations. Every separation became a drama. As soon as we met again, my hands flew all over her. My mind was focused on one thing only: her. My eyes were closed, and I could hear her moaning, or was it me? Suddenly, another unusual sound in the park reached my ears. Not a moan, but a scratching sound. Somebody! In a hurry, I separated from her, grabbed her hand, and started humming the song as we had done at first.

"Can you feel it? The breath should not come from here, but from there."

I placed Joan's palm on my stomach. She looked at me as if I had suddenly gone mad. Unperturbed, I continued to hum and move her hand in an attempt to show her the difference. Two running children were on us in an instant. Obviously surprised to see someone in this remote part of the park, they stopped dead in their tracks. I let my voice grow louder while keeping her hand moving between my chest and abdomen. Understanding lit up Joan's eyes. Shaking her head, she smiled. A few seconds later, the parents appeared, clearly surprised by our presence as well.

Annoyed, tightening my lips, I stared at them. "Sorry. Private singing lesson."

The mother opened her mouth in an O-shape, while the father urged his boys on. They had quickly realised they were in the way.

"Sorry. Go ahead, children. Come on, dear. We'll find another place."

As they left, we remained silent. A sigh of relief passed through my lips.

"That was close. Well done," Joan whispered. "I didn't hear anything. I was busy…"

She stared at me with her sparkling, mischievous eyes, that little smile I liked so much digging into her dimple. My urge to jump on her came back…again. I sighed in frustration. With my arms around my chest, I stood up suddenly. "This has to stop. I can't stand meeting like this anymore."

Panic flashed across Joan's face. She stood up in turn and grabbed my hands. "What do you mean?" Alarm filled her voice.

Before I could explain that I just wanted more, she pulled me against her.

"I love you, Evy. I don't want to let you go or stop seeing you. You are my air when I need to breathe, my food when I am hungry, my water when I am thirsty. Don't…"

I put my finger gently on her lips. "I don't want to stop seeing you, my impetuous one. I love you too. That's not what I meant."

She took a deep breath and rested her forehead on my shoulder. "Don't ever scare me like that again. You hear me?"

"I hear you, my darling Joan."

I kissed her tenderly on the lips, fast enough that she couldn't capture my mouth again and send me to heaven…again.

"So what did you want to say?"

"This park doesn't give us enough privacy for what I want to do to you. I dream about it at night…awake or asleep." I blushed at my bluntness, but I continued, raising my arms to the sky. "We need a place where no one can catch us. It's so frustrating!"

Joan laughed at my outburst. She kissed the back of my hand and led me down the path. "I couldn't agree more. Come with me. I want to show you something. A surprise."

Curious, I followed her toward the exit of the botanic gardens. For the past four months, since I had started teaching her, we had eaten at Wang's, a small Chinese restaurant not far from the park that made delicious noodles, but today Joan dashed in the opposite direction and hailed a rickshaw.

"We're not going to Wang's?"

"No. We're not."

"Where are we going then?"

"You'll see."

Although she seemed a little nervous, Joan wouldn't reveal anything. I continued to pester her throughout our journey, but she stood firm. I felt like an annoying brat, yet she kept smiling at all my attempts.

I recognised the block where she asked the rickshaw to stop. We weren't far from the hospital, and it was on my way to the Blue Tiger. This street, in Chinatown, was very busy. Porters, handcarts, and rickshaws competed for space with cars and trucks. With one hand against my back, Joan led me through the arcades of Chinese furniture and tableware shops. She pushed open a heavy wooden door before entering a narrow alley. Curious, I followed her through the maze to a red door with a colourful demon poster stuck on it. She entered it, smiling. A beautiful, lush garden was hidden between four walls. Singapore would never stop surprising me.

"What is this place?" I asked, turning my head to either side of the cobbled path as I followed Joan.

"We're behind the shops. The owner still lives on the ground floor, but now that his wife has died and his children have families of their own, he rents out the first floor. A colleague of mine used to live here, but he gave notice last week. Come on. I'll show you."

As we climbed the stairs, Joan became visibly more excited, and, in turn, trepidation consumed me. Had I understood correctly? A flat to rent? A flat where we could be together without being watched? When I reached the big wooden door, I was out of breath. Was it the excitement?

I thought Joan would knock or ring a bell, but instead she reached into her bag. My heart beat even faster. Could it be? When I saw the key, I put my fingers to my throat. She inserted it into the lock and turned. I fought dizziness. Slowly, with hope in her eyes, she gently took my hand and helped me across the threshold. The smell of fresh paint invaded my nostrils. Apart from a table and chairs, the flat was empty.

"Are you renting it?" I croaked.

"I wanted to surprise you. But like you said, I've had enough of being constantly on the lookout. The work isn't finished yet. The workmen have to bring in the furniture, and we have to decorate…"

I jumped into her arms. I wanted to melt into her. She withstood the onslaught of my lips, my kisses, and asked for more. "It's perfect," I murmured. "Maybe I could help you arrange it."

My tone was hesitant, uncertain. I didn't want to impose. Seeming embarrassed, she cleared her throat. "I...I guess...I was kind of hoping...that you'd want to...live with me here..."

Speechless, I stared at her.

"There are two bedrooms if you don't want to...you know..." she added immediately, blushing. "I don't want to assume that we..."

Overwhelmed with tears, I hugged her. "Yes, my love, a hundred times, yes."

Immediately, she squeezed me to her chest and lifted me into the air, spinning around. My feet suspended above the ground, I laughed out loud. For the first time since James had been arrested and sent back to prison in England for a five-year sentence, I felt safe and wildly happy.

"And I don't want to sleep in any other room than yours."

She put me down slowly, letting me slide down her. I wanted her so much I was dizzy. My smile was so huge that my cheeks hurt. The happiness in my heart threatened to burst it. I wanted to rip off our clothes and make love on the floor.

A few sharp knocks against the door stopped us. Taking a deep breath, Joan released me to open it while I fixed my hair and checked my outfit.

"Mr. Chee. What a nice surprise! Please come in."

"I'm sorry to disturb you, Miss Cliver, but I heard you were here, and I wanted to check some things with you."

A short, kind-faced man in traditional Chinese clothing entered the flat. He was elderly but looked fit. His intelligent dark eyes roamed the room before landing discreetly on me. He bowed slightly.

"Let me introduce my friend Evelyn Baker. She is going to share this wonderful place with me. I wanted to show it to her so she could organise the room where she will be giving her singing lessons."

Singing lessons? Here? I tried to keep a straight face and continued to smile at Mr. Chee. "I'll be discreet. Don't worry. I don't have many customers."

"Oh, I'm not worried, Miss Baker. It will be very nice to have some life in the house. Anyway, I'm often in my shop watching my employees. If you are free, we could have a Chinese tea sometime. I have some very good products that I import myself for the rich Chinese businessmen in Singapore. They like the taste of home."

I smiled sweetly at him. "It will be a pleasure, Mr. Chee."

He turned to Joan. "The furniture will be back tomorrow. After that you can move in whenever you like, Miss Cliver."

"Thank you, Mr. Chee. I was just talking to Evelyn about this point. As I'm at the hospital all day, she'll be the one to check that everything is in order. If you agree, I'll let her do the decorating."

Joan gave me a mischievous look, daring me to object. Did she think I was a fragile little thing who couldn't measure up to the challenge? I was in love with her, and she was in love with me, but apart from singing and kissing, we hadn't done much together and didn't know each other very well. That was about to change.

"What time are you having the furniture moved in, Mr. Chee?"

"First thing in the morning."

"I'll be here."

Joan and Mr. Chee looked at me with wide eyes, clearly surprised that I wanted to be here at dawn. I deliberately batted my eyelashes in their direction.

"With Joan away, I can't very well let men do as they please with a female interior, can I?"

"You've done wonders, again," Joan whispered in my ear as I showed her the Ming-style wardrobe that adorned our living room. "The original furniture was really ugly, but I didn't dare tell Mr. Chee that."

I laughed and placed a kiss on Joan's cheek. "Let's just say that Mr. Chee is more sensitive to my charm than to yours...or to that of your male colleague."

To tell the truth, I was quite proud of myself. In just over two weeks, I had managed to make this flat to our liking, well, just about. I had actually had a choice of Chinese and other furniture, but some of it was more Chinese than others. I didn't like the style—too over-ornate or too dark—so when Mr. Chee had agreed to let me rummage around in his storerooms, I made some major changes.

"You've put a spell on the old brigand." Joan laughed, looking around. "I can't believe you got him to replace all the furniture we didn't like or that was too uncomfortable."

I leaned against my latest acquisition and crossed my arms over my chest. "If you want, I can ask him to put the old chairs back," I said seriously.

Joan gave me an alarmed look. "Those instruments of torture? Certainly not! I didn't think it was possible to make such uncomfortable things." ˙

As she had soon found out, I loved to provoke her. "They were beautiful with their delicate sculptures."

"They should be banned by the medical academy as objects that can cause deformities. Can you imagine a child growing up with that?"

Outraged, Joan had once again run headlong into my trap. When she saw my smirk, she interrupted her tirade. "You got me again."

The speed at which she came toward me gave me no time to react. She put her hands on either side of my face and pressed her body against mine. "Your little provocative side is showing more and more."

Immediately my heart raced as I felt her hot breath on my cheek, but I looked as contrite and innocent as possible. "Don't you like it?"

Joan laughed. "On the contrary, I love it," she replied before melting on my lips.

Her fingers unclasped the muslin blouse I was wearing over my negligee before sliding down my hips, slowly pulling up the light fabric, and gently working their way to my private parts. God, I loved this woman! In a few seconds, she was able to make me forget my name and all the melodies I had ever learned. In my head, so glorious was the moment, Beethoven's *Ode to Joy* and a song I was practising and loved, "Dream a Little Dream of Me," were fighting.

CHAPTER EIGHT

Singapore, 6 December 1941

Time passed too quickly, and I was swimming in total happiness. The war in Europe seemed so far away. Dorothy's letters arrived only sporadically and told of night bombings, the terror of sirens, shelters, and aerial combat. But she also told me about this man she had met in the hospital. My sister was in love, and I was so happy for her. He seemed a nice, sweet man. They were speaking about marriage, and Dorothy wanted me to come home. But I couldn't. It was too far and too dangerous to travel by sea because of the German U-boats.

When a letter in August 1941 told me that our father had died of a heart attack, I was saddened not to have seen him again, not to have told him about my new life, though it certainly would not have changed his outlook. That I was living with a doctor would have met with his approval. But that it was outside the laws of marriage and, God forgive me, that it was a woman? What a sin!

Despite the horrible news from Europe and the pessimistic news from China with the Japanese advancing from massacre to massacre, I couldn't see life in anything but rosy hues. Joan was everything I could have imagined in a Prince Charming: beautiful, intelligent, serious, but with a discreet sense of humour, calm in stressful situations, yet passionate, yes, very passionate. I glanced around at our neatly furnished and decorated flat. Was there anywhere we hadn't made love? Against the front door, on the table, on the floor by the Chinese cabinet, between the chairs…Each place had its memorable souvenir.

Once a week, I drank tea with Mr. Chee, and each time, he made me taste a different one: green, black, oolong, pu-erh…It seemed that he wanted to educate me in this field: our "horrible" English tea should be reserved only for the poor without taste buds. I must admit that as weeks went by, I understood more and more what he meant. Within a few months, he had managed to convert me to drinking it without sugar or milk. It was all the easier because every week, after our meeting, he gave me a small box of the one tea we had tasted that day.

Had he guessed my relationship with Joan? He certainly had, but it didn't seem to bother him. Nor did my singing career in the club run by Andy, a business associate of his. I didn't dare plunge too deep into those waters. Anyone who took too close an interest in my boss's business tended to end up in the bay among the Chinese junks. The word opium was often whispered very quietly among the staff, and some had assured me that there was a smokehouse just a stone's throw from the cabaret. I refused to let all these rumours sully my cloud of happiness. Perhaps it was unconsciousness, perhaps obstinacy.

The two light knocks on the door and the sound of the key turning in the lock brought a smile to my lips. Like every time Joan came home from the hospital, my heart beat a little faster. I got up from the sofa. She immediately placed her bag on the pedestal table before I leapt into her arms and we touched, joined in the now-familiar dance. I didn't give her time to put down her jacket, held with her fingertips over her shoulder.

"Good evening. Did you have a good day?" I asked her, running my fingers through her hair, which was a little shorter than it had been this morning. "Did you manage to get your hair done? It must have been a quiet day then."

"Yes. A day to my liking. Not too many patients, no last-minute emergencies. I'd love more of that." Joan sighed, kissing the tips of each of my fingers.

"I love your short hair so much." I gently brushed both of my index fingers against her earlobes.

Joan closed her eyes in obvious pleasure. "I know."

"I can't get enough of it."

Her ash-blond hair slipped through my fingers like silk.

"I know."

Her breath quickened, and her voice became hoarse. I knew how this conversation would end and looked forward to it.

Leaving my left hand in her hair, I fumbled between us to undo the buttons on her shirt one by one. As soon as the opening was big enough, I found a breast and grabbed it. I heard the sound of the jacket landing on the floor, Joan moaning. Oh, that sweet music in my ears. It had been my favourite song for several months. I tickled the nipple mercilessly before moving on to the other. I was so blinded by my desire that it took me a few seconds to realise that Joan had unbelted my housedress, and it was now lying at my feet. I found myself naked and offered to her sight and, above all, to her skilful fingers. Occupied with her soft breasts, I had no time to stop her hand as it moved down my torso to slip between my legs. Desire exploded in my belly. Unable to resist, I collapsed against her, clinging to her shoulders as she began a back-and-forth movement. The coolness of the door against my back did not calm my inner fire, nor did Joan's lips on my mouth. She held me tightly between her and the door. I moaned continuously. As the sound seemed to accelerate the movement of her hand, the noises in my throat increased. I wanted to scream but knew, for our safety, that I should not. I bit Joan's shoulder and put one of my legs around her waist.

"More, my love," I found the strength to whisper.

The two fingers that suddenly penetrated me made me see thousands of stars. Gasping, I let her continue for several seconds, savouring every vibration, every tremor.

Catching her hand, I stopped her and slowly slid against the door, taking her with me. Her quick breath against my ear instantly rekindled my desire. But this time I would be the one to make her see the light even in the darkness of our home. Not surprisingly, it didn't take long. No sooner had I placed my lips between her legs than she reared back and exploded.

"I love my homecomings," Joan joked, "especially with this kind of welcome."

"Short hair looks wonderful on you. When you're dressed in trousers, I can't resist you."

It was so true. I loved her boyish chic. Every time I saw her in the street or at home, her look so feminine in her walk and so masculine in her gestures, the way she acted, the way she spoke, a little shiver of excitement ran up my spine.

"You could also cut yours short like Louise Brooks does. You'd look so sexy in the twenties fashion."

Stunned, I put enough space between us to stare at her and sighed.

"I'd be out of the cabaret in a heartbeat. You know Andy. The men who come to listen to me want glamour—finger waves or pin curls. I'm successful because my hair looks a bit like Ginger Rogers's does. Clients love it when I sing her songs."

"I know," Joan replied, gently stroking my face. "I was fascinated by the resemblance from the start. I'm not surprised the men are too. My colleagues remarked to me about it the other day after seeing *Kitty Foyle*."

"I love that film."

"I realised that. We were at the movies together, you know." Joan laughed. "If you haven't told me a hundred times, you've never said it once."

I couldn't help but pinch her cheek hard, causing her to twitch and moan, before placing my lips gently on the sore spot. Her protest vanished as if by magic.

"Food's ready. Come and eat," I said, standing up.

Joan sighed, then grabbed my outstretched hand and stood up as well. Immediately her arm went around my still-naked waist. Night had fallen. In the darkness of our flat, I knew that no one could see us. I took the opportunity to kiss her languidly once more.

After several seconds, she left my lips to catch her breath. "If we continue like this, we won't be eating any time soon."

"Are you that hungry?" I asked, capturing her beautiful mouth once again.

In answer, she led me into the bedroom, to our bed, and laid me down slowly. Then, very gently, she undid the mosquito net, taking care to protect us from those indelicate aggressors who had already taken advantage of us while we were making love in the hallway.

That night, when I fell asleep in Joan's arms, the only song that came to mind was "Me and My Girl." Perfect for us.

Chapter Nine

W hat's going on? What's all the fuss?"
Joan's voice woke me from the deep sleep I was in.
What an evening! We had eaten very late and fallen asleep even later,
driven by a primal urge to keep touching each other until the end
of the night. When I listened, I could hear the street criers. Usually
they stayed in the main street to sell their wares—tea, coffee, food or
newspapers—to the workers who started early. What were they doing
in the alley?

"What time is it?" I asked with a yawn, my voice still hoarse
from sleep.

"Nearly five o'clock. I'll go have a look. This commotion isn't
normal."

Joan, accustomed to sudden awakenings from her shifts at the
hospital, looked fresh as a daisy. She got up, dressed quickly, and
went out.

The night was over. I dragged myself out of bed to wash with
plenty of water in the room reserved for that purpose. The pan of
cold water I threw over my shoulders made me shiver but also
immediately cleared my head and washed away the night's sweat.
Dressed in a large, light tunic, I was heating water for breakfast
when Joan, out of breath, returned to our house holding a crumpled
newspaper. The look she gave me stopped all my movements. At once
I imagined a catastrophe. Had England surrendered to the Germans?
Had submarines sunk another passenger ship?

"The Japanese attacked Pearl Harbour this morning at 7:49 a.m. local time, 1:49 a.m. for us. The newspaper says that the American fleet has been wiped out. The United States is in the war."

Like a carp out of water, I opened my mouth, then closed it again. What was going to happen now? I had never heard anyone mention this possibility. Of course, everyone was talking about the distant war in Europe, about the young British plantation workers who had wanted to enlist but had been sent back to Malaysia to continue the rubber production needed for the war effort. I often heard Chinese people at cabaret rehearsals talking about the Japanese invasion of their country and the imperial army's desire to conquer Asia. But attacking the United States?

"What does that mean for us?"

I felt selfish for thinking of myself first. Joan ran a hand through her messy hair, then sighed.

"I have no idea. For now, not much, I suppose. We'll have to wait and see. Pearl Harbour's a long way from here."

I nodded. She was right. Time would tell.

"Go wash up. The water for the coffee is almost hot. Would you like some porridge, eggs, and bacon, or do you want me to go and buy some Chinese buns?"

Joan hesitated for a second. "It's still early. Why not make time for a traditional breakfast?" She walked away to the room we used as a washroom before stopping and turning back to me. "Just cook the bacon. I'll do the rest. It's my turn to make breakfast."

She disappeared with a smile as I grabbed the pan. Inwardly, I was shaking. Since the signing of the agreement on 27 September 1940, making Japan a member of the Tripartite Pact with Germany and Italy, everyone had been silently following Japan's progress in Southeast Asia. An attack on the US would change the balance, but how?

The British and other foreigners in Singapore were reassured that the British navy and air force were among the best in the area. According to the newspapers, although the Japanese had invaded Indochina over a year before, they were still a long way off. But could they be trusted? If things went wrong, Australia or South Africa would remain our last resort.

"The bacon will burn if you don't turn it over, sweetheart."

I was startled by Joan's voice so close to my ear. Indeed, lost in my thoughts, I had forgotten an important part of breakfast, the sacrosanct bacon that had to be crisp but not burnt. With a fork, I flipped the sizzling slices while Joan tended to the toast. She took over the stove while I served the hot drinks.

"Do you think they'll make it here? For months, I've heard rumours at the club about anti-colonial agitations fomented by Japan, and some have even started talking about leaving Singapore."

Joan continued to bustle about in silence. I liked her calmness, the efficiency of her movements. Watching her made me feel better. She placed the bacon on our plates, along with an egg with a perfectly centred yolk.

"This morning the war became global with the attack on the Americans. At least Roosevelt will no longer have to hide to help the British in their war against the Germans. As for leaving Singapore, let's wait a while before we rush out on the boats. My patients need me. But if you want to be safe…"

Joan sat down opposite me and reached for her cup. Silent for a moment, she took a sip before adding, "I'm not suggesting you go back to England. You'd be trading one peril for another, but my parents will gladly host you in Australia, if you like."

I almost choked on my piece of toast at this wild suggestion. Trying to keep my composure, I gently placed my fork on the edge of the plate and took several deep breaths.

"Listen to me, Joan, for I will not repeat myself. Where you are, I am. Where you go, I go."

Without adding anything else to my rather biblical phrasing, I picked up my fork and started eating again. Joan had not taken her eyes off me, and when I looked back at her, she was still watching me. I waited for her words, but they didn't come. She merely nodded. We understood each other.

For more than a year since we had dared to declare our love, it had only grown, but without ever becoming invasive. She was my soul mate, and I was hers. We communicated as much through our silences as through our words.

That evening, on a Sunday, my boss, in a panic, told me that his favourite singer had boarded the first ship to South Africa that day and that I should replace him immediately. The renegotiation of my contract took only ten minutes. Andy had said yes to all my conditions.

As I began my singing tour, the song "It's a Long Way to Tipperary" took on a different meaning than usual.

Chapter Ten

Singapore, 12 February 1942

"You have to go," Joan said. "You can't wait any longer. The Japs will be here in a few hours."

"I can't leave you."

We stood in the middle of the barracks. Holding back my despair, I whispered even though the nurses around were busy with the twenty patients lying on the beds and didn't care about us.

"I can't leave the love of my life," I argued, tears in my eyes.

Joan bluntly grabbed my arm and pulled me with her into a small storage room.

"Listen to me carefully. Wounded soldiers who were fighting around the Pierce Reservoir and the Holland Road arrived here this morning. Do you understand what that means?"

I couldn't believe my ears. I swallowed. "From the reservoir? Oh, my God. The Japanese are that close?"

I could feel the panic rising. But to leave my beloved behind? To go alone? Without her?

"You have to come with me. Your place is reserved on the boat that leaves this morning."

"You know I can't leave my nurses and the wounded. I took an oath as a doctor."

In her beautiful green eyes, I could see her determination. I loved that quality about her, but at that moment I hated it. Tears rolled down my cheeks. With her fingertips, she swept them away tenderly.

"You'll take the boat with the other women and children and go to Australia as planned," she whispered. "You have my parents' address. I'll meet you there as soon as I can. A colonel told me that all the medical staff and wounded will be evacuated in the next few days, so I'll be following you closely, maybe even tomorrow. Trust me. We'll be together soon."

Desperate, I held her close. I wanted to believe her. To think otherwise was impossible. I sniffed. "You are the love of my life. You know that, don't you?"

Caressing my cheek, she smiled that bright smile I loved so much. "I know. And you are mine. We belong together. Don't worry. Wherever you are, I will find you. I promise you that."

Slowly, her lips took possession of mine in one last desperate kiss. As usual, I felt like I was melting.

"You have to go now. As we said, take only the essential clothes. The money, the jewellery, hide them on your body and wear one of my pairs of trousers. It will be easier for the journey. This is not a fashion show. It's going to be crazy on those boats with all the families. Don't take any chances. Promise me that."

If she hadn't been so serious, I would have laughed at her. She was staying in Singapore with the Japanese army on our doorstep, and I was the one who had to be careful? In the distance, explosions rang out. I could clearly make out machine-gun fire.

"I'll do everything to be safe. But you have to promise the same thing, Joan."

"I love you. And I promise. Sing to me every night before you go to sleep, and I'll listen. Now go!"

She opened the door, leaving me no choice but to get out.

"Doctor! We need you here!" called a nurse as soon as she saw Joan.

My love smiled at me one last time before turning away and rushing to her patients. My feet seemed riveted to the floor. Each step away from her seemed more difficult than the last. In the corridor, on the stairs, chaos reigned. Bloody streaks on the tiles showed the horror of the situation. Stretcher-bearers were trying to make their way through the wounded, sitting or lying where there was room. Everything appeared to me like in a fog, as if my heart and soul had been left behind. The sense of loss was unbearable. But I had made a vow, and I would keep it. For Joan.

Outside the hospital, trucks and cars stopped, pouring out streams of bloodied soldiers and civilians. I could smell smoke in the atmosphere and hear explosions and gunfire in the background. Despite the reassuring rhetoric, Singapore was lost. Unlike all the locals—Chinese, Indians, Malays—I was lucky. As a Brit, I could leave and save my life. To reassure Joan, two days before, I had put us on the departure lists, but I never thought I would use my passage…alone. Joan must have known that she wouldn't come with me, but she hadn't said anything. With a heart full of shame at my escape, I flagged down a rickshaw to go to our flat. Despite all that was happening, he was calmly waiting for customers. I looked at my watch: ten o'clock. I had to hurry if I wanted to get to the pier on time. The boat wouldn't wait.

Madness—no other word could describe the quay. Women and children were everywhere, some of them crying or shouting, a few men in uniform trying to organise as best they could, non-Westerners trying to get through by waving wads of cash…chaos. Even though we had been instructed to bring only one suitcase per person when checking in, most of us had ignored the order. The soldiers were adamant, and abandoned luggage was piling up on the platform, to the delight of the city's poor. There was simply not enough room on board. The *Giang Bee* was a passenger steamer, and seeing all these people boarding continuously, I was afraid that we were already far too many. The crew tried to help everyone settle in, but it was a struggle. I tried to find a place in a cabin downstairs, but four occupants were already in each two-person cabin. The beds were given mainly to families with small children.

"Evelyn?"

Stunned to hear my name, I turned around in the narrow passage.

"I thought it was you." Clara Wilford smiled, clearly not in the least embarrassed to approach me. "Although I was surprised that you hadn't left Singapore since…the case."

Why was she so happy to see me? She had never said good-bye or anything to me when her husband had expelled me from the Goodwood Park Hotel after my ex-husband's indiscretion.

"Mrs. Wilford, Clara. I'd say it's a pleasure to see you again, but the circumstances are not what I'd call a pleasure."

She twitched at the use of her first name. I congratulated myself inwardly. If she thought I was going to be her maid, she would be disappointed. This old boat had seen better days and was certainly not capable of carrying so many passengers. I pointed to our surroundings and said, "All the cabins are full. If I can find a blanket, I'm going to sit on the deck."

"On deck for the whole trip? But it will be very uncomfortable."

Horror flashed across her face. She was still carrying her suitcase, so she didn't have a cabin either. I stopped a passing crew member. "Where could we find a blanket to stay on deck? All the cabins are full."

He grinned. "Sorry about that, ma'am. You'll have to talk to the chief about accommodations."

"Is there no other cabin?" asked Clara. "You can't expect us to sleep on the floor outside."

The crewman looked around, and seeing no one within earshot, he leaned over to us and said softly, "Better the deck, ladies. If we are attacked, you can easily reach the lifeboat. That's my advice to you, but feel free to look for a cabin."

He touched his head in a little bow and left.

"An attack?" Clara was disconcerted. She swallowed several times before finding her voice again. "No one told us about an attack. We're going to Australia to be safe. We are civilians. The war is not about us."

She had been so mean to me that I couldn't resist returning the favour.

"The Japanese have a navy, don't they? And submarines too. And planes. Have you seen any of our planes protecting us? The Japanese have been bombing Singapore for several days now, and no one is standing in their way. Let's face it, Clara. The city is finished, and we're lucky to be on board at all. Imagine the Chinese and Indians who have no choice but to stay."

I felt like a bitch, but my attitude helped me think less about Joan. If Clara had been a friend, I would have confided that I hadn't considered the possibility of sinking until that nice crew member told us. Now I was thinking of nothing else.

"I'm going to sit by the lifeboat. Do what you like." I tightened my grip on the handle of my suitcase and headed for the nearest staircase.

"I'll go with you," Clara said in a resigned tone before following me.

Her concern was palpable. Like all of us, she was plunging into the unknown. The bridge was crowded. Other people had had the same idea as I had. A little farther on, I heard a crew member raising his voice at some women, trying to send them back downstairs, while another handed out blankets. I grabbed one and looked around for some space.

"You can't stay here," insisted the man who appeared to be in charge. "It's not safe. You have to go downstairs."

In another way, he was as annoying as Clara, who hadn't stopped complaining for a minute while we were sneaking in.

Upset, I projected my voice as I used to at the cabaret to drown out the din of the customers.

"It's full downstairs. Shall we sit in the corridors or, better still, in the captain's cabin?"

The sailor glared at me. "I'll find you a spot."

"And the others?" I pointed to the people around us. I persevered. "What if we are attacked? Will you help me climb the stairs over everyone else to a lifeboat?"

Even in the dim light I could easily see his face turn white, his lips pursed. He glowered at me, clenched his fists, and left.

"Well done," said a woman sitting on the floor to my right. "You've shut him up. Good for us. He had been pestering us for at least fifteen minutes. Why didn't he try to convince the gentlemen?"

With her hand holding a cigarette, she pointed to several men and couples farther down the deck.

"I'm Frances McBride. Come join us."

Pushing herself over a little, she pointed to a spot beside her. Some of the women also shifted, giving Clara and me enough room.

"Evelyn Baker. Nice to meet you."

Frances laughed heartily as she shook the hand I held out to her. "*Nice*. You have to say that very quickly, given the circumstances."

Clara held out her hand hesitantly. "Clara Wilford. My husband is the manager of the Goodwood Park Hotel."

"Good for you," replied one of the women sitting next to Frances, wryly. "Welcome to our beautiful suite. Tonight is a special service. A little decadent. You'll appreciate it, since you're used to posh hotels."

The shadow of a smile passed over everyone's lips. Clara tensed.

"Ah, Ruth, leave her alone." Frances laughed. "I'm sorry, Clara, but I guess no one cares what your husband does these days. By mutual agreement, our little group has decided to forget about propriety. Hey, listen up!"

I didn't hear anything. I was about to ask Frances for clarification when she added, "Vibrations. Can't you hear vibrations? The engines. We're leaving."

As usual in the tropics, the night was falling fast, and, with the attacks, the streetlights weren't working. A few lights coming from the harbour made it possible to see the houses in the background. Indeed, we were moving…at last.

"Good-bye, Singapore," said Ruth. "I'll be back."

Some women joined her, and others, like me, remained silent. Joan was on my mind. When would she be on a boat? Tomorrow? Tears came to my eyes. A gentle hand rested on my shoulder.

"We all leave someone or something behind. My husband is fighting with his men right now. He knows we have lost, but he wants to give us time to escape. My children are in England, safe and sound. At least I hope so."

Frances's gentle voice put a smile on my face. Joan was not in combat units. The Japanese would respect the medical staff.

"Most of us here have husbands in the war. What about you?"

I hesitated for a second too long. Clara stifled a little sniffle, and I knew in a flash that she would betray me.

"I'm divorced. No husband in combat."

"Good for you," Ruth remarked. "I don't have a husband either. I was headmistress of St. Hilda's School. My staff left a few days ago. I'm the last one. What do you do for a living?"

"I'm a professional singer."

"That's why you look familiar," said a woman sitting a little farther away. "I heard you a few years ago. In '39, if I remember correctly. You were singing at the Goodwood Park Hotel, weren't you? You have a beautiful voice."

"Thank you. Yes, that was me. After my divorce, I changed venues. A cabaret in Chinatown, the Blue Tiger, gave me a chance."

Clara giggled but didn't comment. Why did I have to run into her here?

"Could you sing something for us?" asked a voice in the darkness. "Anything at all?"

The voice was pleading, and I didn't know whom the request came from. In the dark night, I could hardly even make out the people sitting next to me.

"Please, to take our minds off things" came from many voices somewhere. For two seconds I wracked my brain for the perfect song. Then, thinking of Joan, in a low voice, I started "You Are My Sunshine." It suited my mood. I wanted hope in my life. Soon the women and men present were singing along.

The horrible night was ending. I had never slept so badly, lying on the deck on my very thin blanket. We were stuck together for lack of space, and every time someone moved, she woke her neighbours. Fortunately, in the tropics, at this latitude, it was never very cold. And we were lucky enough not to have any rain.

In the early morning, a crew member handed out a few cups with some hot tea.

"We have to share a cup? How awful! Never in a million years," Clara said in protest.

She wasn't the only one to react like that. All these housewives were used to a gentle life, surrounded by servants. The sailor looked at them without saying anything. He just shrugged and continued to pass the drinks.

"For God's sake, this isn't a holiday cruise! You'll have to adjust." Ruth lectured them, drinking from the same cup as me. "We don't have a contagious disease. But if you don't want tea, that's fine. There will be more for the others."

Even louder, she addressed the sailor. "Thank you, sir. Tea is welcome."

He nodded and smiled.

I was praying that the ship would move faster. The sooner I got to Australia, the sooner I could start looking for Joan. Every time I thought back to our last conversation, my heart sank, and I was afraid. Yet I was sure we would find each other.

"What's that?" shouted someone farther up the deck, pointing to the sky.

Everyone turned their head in the indicated direction. In the cloudy blue sky, I could barely make out a few black dots. Planes?

"Are they ours?" asked another hopeful voice.

The high-pitched wail of the warning siren provided the answer. Fear swept over me.

"They're not going to shoot at civilians, are they?" shouted a woman not far from me.

Silence answered. All our attention was riveted on the growing black spots.

"Get down! Protect yourself!" someone shouted.

With what? Our blankets? Someone huddled against me, then someone else.

The planes were getting closer and closer. Terrified, I closed my eyes. My thoughts went to Joan. Lying on the deck with my back to the wall, humming to myself, I remembered my first encounter with this wonderful woman.

A gentle hand grasped mine. I squeezed it tightly. Bullet sounds, an explosion. The ship rocked. We were shaken in all directions. Screams, cries for help. Lost in my own terror, I couldn't move. I should have. I had trained as a nurse long ago, but I remained there clutching the hand, fearing for my life.

"They've gone," Frances murmured, a tremor in her voice. "They've gone. It's over."

I finally opened my eyes. With a sad expression, she offered me a weak smile before letting go of my hand. Grateful for this small comfort during this moment of terror, I nodded. Now that the threat had passed, some people began to call for help.

"They've got wounded and dead on the other side," said Ruth, stopping beside us breathlessly.

"Did you go there already?" Frances asked, apparently surprised.

"Yes, I did. According to my students, I'm a nosy parker. I like to know what's going on around me."

She winked at me. Raising her voice, she said, "We need a doctor. Anybody?"

No one answered.

"I'm a trained nurse," I heard myself say. "A long time ago."

"It's better than nothing. Let's go, my multi-talented friend."

For several hours, helping the wounded took my mind off the fear of another Japanese attack. We had grouped them in a corner of the deck, and I went from one person to another, giving priority to the most seriously injured. Women, including Ruth and Frances, were changing bandages, handing out water to the lighter casualties.

A young man, terror in his eyes, stopped me by clutching at the bottom of my trousers. "Madam, am I going to be all right?"

I knelt beside him. A glance at his wounds confirmed my first diagnosis. Trying to hide my tears, I took his hand. Without a hospital, he would not survive, and he certainly knew that.

"I don't want to die alone, ma'am," he said, his breath weak, then added, "Don't cry, ma'am. It's not so bad. I don't feel anything at all."

Such a brave young man. He was breathing more and more heavily, and his skin was so white. The makeshift bandage couldn't absorb his blood as it flowed onto the deck.

"My dream...was to...enlist, to fight for my country..."

With a bandage in her hand, Ruth approached us, a question in her eyes. I shook my head. She nodded and walked away to another wounded man.

"What...what's your name?"

"Matt...Matthew Sterling... I heard you last night. Would you...? Would you sing for me?"

I wanted to sob, to howl at all the gods of the earth. It wasn't fair to that kid. I lacked courage, but I had no right to break down.

He needed a song to help him go in peace. So, rejecting the horror of the situation, I took a deep breath and sang "There'll Always Be an England." Matthew smiled and closed his eyes. All around us, many men and women, wounded and unwounded, joined their voices to mine.

Chapter Eleven

As daylight faded, with a heavy heart for Matthew's death, I returned to my side of the deck. Ruth forced some hard biscuits into my hands and ordered me to eat them. As I nibbled silently, I brooded. At that moment, I understood why I could never be a nurse: losing a patient was too painful. When I sang to my clients, they were happy. I couldn't stand death.

"Look! Boats!"

All faces turned in the direction the young man pointed. The siren pierced our eardrums once again. The Japanese! Again! Two sinister shapes were rapidly growing on the horizon. Lights flashed on the warships, and it seemed that our ship was responding.

I leapt to my feet, frightened, ready for anything. A scramble began on deck. People were shouting, asking what was going on.

"Is everyone okay?" asked Frances, next to me. "We have to stay calm and together. They haven't shot at us."

"Not yet," quipped a voice in the growing darkness.

Frances sighed. A man shouted the word torpedo. A wave of fear pierced my heart. Were we going to sink? Yet nothing happened. No explosion, only those flashes of light that were exchanged from one ship to another.

The crew members were running around on the deck, and we were trying to stay out of their way. Soon sailors lowered two lifeboats. At the same time, an officer shouted, "We must evacuate. The Japanese will sink the ship." When some people approached the railing with their luggage, he added in a loud voice, "No luggage."

Suddenly I was glad to have all my valuables in a small pouch tied around my waist. However, I didn't want to leave all my stuff behind. Quickly I opened my suitcase, spread my shawl on the floor, and threw in all my essentials before tying the four corners.

"You're a smart girl," said Frances, next to me, imitating me.

Around us, others did the same. With my little bundle clutched to me, I made my way as best I could to the railing. Panic broke out between those trying to get on the lifeboats first, people in the cabins wanting to get to the deck, and those waiting their turn. A crewman started to lower the first small boat filled with women and children. Unfortunately, it had taken bullets during the air attack and sank as soon as it hit the water. Helplessly, we could see and hear women screaming their children's names before they drowned. I couldn't believe we could do nothing. Horrified, I saw a little boy move his arms and then gradually disappear.

"Let us do our job!" shouted one of the crew. "The other lifeboat can help them."

No sooner had he said this than one of the descent ropes of the second boat broke, spilling its passengers into the sea. People screamed as they fell. Cries for help echoed from the deep, dark water. Even in the dim light of the dying day, I saw at least three people go under. Tears streamed down my cheeks. I could do nothing for them. The frantic crowd was tossing me about, was dragging me along. Couples, families were trying to stay together, while people downstairs were shouting and screaming, pushing their way out. The panic was growing fast, and no one stopped me as I rushed to one of the two remaining lifeboats. I was almost on board when I stumbled forward. Unable to hold on, I saw the railing coming fast. I was already imagining the plunge into the deadly waters when Frances grabbed my arm to steady me.

A little surprised to still be on the deck, I let myself be guided, and together we climbed aboard. The little boat was already crowded, and people were still boarding even as the crewmen began to lower it. I could swim, but I could easily visualise the sharks circling, waiting for us in the tropical sea.

When the lifeboat hit the water, a sigh of relief escaped from every mouth. Some of the men immediately grabbed the oars, while others helped the survivors climb aboard. The other boat that launched just after us did the same. Many people were still on board the ship, but without a lifeboat, I couldn't imagine how they could get off. Before anyone could do anything, the Japanese started shelling the *Giang Bee*. The ship quickly keeled over and began to sink. From the deck, people jumped into the sea and swam toward us or any other floating object. As the flames escaped from the ship, its bow slowly rose into the air. The angle became steeper and steeper. Women were rushing off the deck with their children in their arms. Despite the lack of space, we wanted to save as many as possible. When our boat began to move away, I stood there watching them drown, speechless with horror.

"We can't abandon them," protested one of the men.

"We have to leave if we don't want to be caught in the wake of the ship as it sinks," replied the sailor at the helm in a tense voice.

One by one, the cries for help died out as we moved away, leaving the people to drown. My heart and soul shattered, I began to cry, and I wasn't alone. Those still in the hold of the *Giang Bee* disappeared with her. The Japanese ships departed without offering any assistance, leaving us to take care of ourselves in the middle of the ocean.

"Where are we?" a woman asked as we finally touched the beach.

"Somewhere south of Singapore, in the Banka Strait, I think," said the man in charge of the lifeboat, the only crew member on board with us.

A few metres farther on, the other lifeboat also ran aground. Despite the night and the waves, we had managed to stay together.

The sun was already high in the sky, and those of us who didn't have hats had made one from a shirt or some other piece of cloth. I had used a shawl folded into a turban to protect my head but was glad we could finally settle down in the shade of a tree.

The men were talking. Sitting in the sand, I felt helpless. Why hadn't they included us in their conversation? Following my gaze, Ruth giggled. "Typical male behaviour, isn't it? They're so predictable, don't you think?"

Not understanding, some of our companions frowned. Pointing at the men, she explained. "They don't invite us to take part in their discussions, even though we're concerned and in the majority."

"They just want to save us," said one of the women, whom I had never met before.

"And what will they decide?" Ruth said, sounding angry. "There are fifteen of them and at least sixty of us, with nine children. We need water, food, and shelter. But I'm pretty sure they're talking about walking."

Frances tried to calm her. "Come on, Ruth. Give them the benefit of the doubt."

But Ruth, despite being overweight, jumped to her feet and walked toward them. Curious, I followed her. For the past four years, I had been making decisions for myself and by myself. I had no desire today to leave my fate in the hands of a few men. I wanted Joan to be proud of me when we met again.

"We can't stay here. We have to look for a village." said one of the men.

"We're somewhere in the Riau Islands. If the Japanese aren't already there, we could find some Dutch settlers to help us," answered another, who seemed to know the area.

All the men agreed among themselves. I then took the opportunity to participate. "We need water, food, and shelter."

"We know that, ma'am. What do you think we're doing?"

Before I could add anything sarcastic, Ruth intervened. "If you had included us in your discussion, we might be more supportive. As a teacher, I know children. They are my life. Without water and hats, the younger ones will be dead by the end of the day."

All the men stared at us as if we didn't know what we were talking about.

"Listen, miss," said the tallest man.

"No, she's right," interrupted the coxswain of our lifeboat. "My sister lost a child to heatstroke after he just played outside for a day. Nobody noticed until it was too late. We have to keep the younger ones out of the heat."

The two crewmen in the other lifeboat didn't intervene. Perhaps our coxswain was their superior. I didn't know the navy's insignia. In any case, soon after, everyone moved into the forest to escape the sun. The lack of a trail and the density of the jungle didn't make it easy for our group to move forward.

"We can't continue in this terrain," Clara complained after a while.

Most of the women agreed, especially those with young children.

"We don't know where we're going. It may be hours before we find a path. We need water," said another.

Soon, supported by many voices, they went to argue with those who had taken the lead in our group. I looked at my fellow survivors. The bottoms of their dresses, covered of mud, were in tatters, and their shoes wouldn't withstand this treatment for long either. All of them, men and women, looked exhausted, sweat dripping down their faces and bodies. The mosquitoes, buzzing in our ears, attacked without respite. Walking in this heat without water would kill us faster than the Japanese would.

"Okay, guys," said our coxswain. "Let's go in pairs in different directions. In half an hour, if you don't find anything, you come back here."

Before everyone wandered off in all directions, one of the men, who was bald, suggested, while dabbing his face, "Perhaps the older men can stay with the women to protect them from the wild animals."

I nodded. Well done. This guy was smart. He had spared the pride of those who were as tired as the children and some of the women, though no one was fooled.

I was twenty-three, young and fit, but the fatigue was already creeping into my muscles. I could imagine how the older men must feel. Let the men be useful for once, I thought. Save your strength. A selfish thought, but what more could I do? Yesterday I had rescued some of the wounded on board the ship. None of them were with us, and I feared they had all drowned.

I pushed back the sweet torpor I was sinking into to go help the survivors. Moving from one seated person to another, I worried about minor injuries and suggested ways to keep clean any scratches that might become infected. Soon Frances and Ruth joined me. Ruth gave advice on how to combat dehydration, while Frances asked for people's names, date of birth, and where they were from so that she could record the information in her notebook.

"What are you doing?"

"I'm making a list with the name of the boat and the survivors. Even if we die, maybe someone will find it. At least our families will know what happened to us."

Before I could react, the woman in front of us commented sarcastically, "How lovely. But you know, I'd rather tell them myself. I'm Margery Barnes. Pleased to meet you."

She smiled, acting as if we were at a country club having tea. Despite her snobbish tone and staid gestures, the people around her pulled themselves together and started talking to each other. I was glad to see them come out of their apathy. Even Clara started a conversation with her neighbour.

Reaching the trail was not the worst part of the day, nor was guessing which way to go, but arriving at a planter's house and finding it empty devastated us. Most of the women were crying, and some of the men were grimacing and biting their lips to keep them from shaking. Keeping a stiff lip was very British and often so annoying.

"There must be a well or a river somewhere," Frances said encouragingly, standing in front of the deserted plantation. "A dwelling can't do without water. We have to find it." She walked around the building, and I followed her lead.

"Also a banana or papaya tree. I've never seen a house without fruit in the tropics," said one of the men.

A good number of us, ignoring our fatigue, wandered around. Five minutes later, on my right, I heard, "Water!" followed almost immediately by "Papaya!" Hope returned to my heart a little.

As I hurried in the direction of the voices, I tripped over a root. Ruth, who was walking not far from me, came to the rescue. Since I was unharmed, she just held out a hand to help me up.

"You're a lifesaver," she said with a smile. "Look around you."

Stunned, I stared at her. What was she talking about? This field was full of weeds. I couldn't recognise a single edible vegetable.

"You, my dear, have spent too much time in the city without visiting the wonderful countryside. In front of you lies a local vegetable garden with sweet potatoes, taro, and yams. We'll have a full belly tonight if we can find some way to cook them. Let's ask for help. We need to dig up enough tubers for everyone."

Later, satiated, I looked around at all the people lying in the main room, most of whom were women and children. The couples used a different room, and the single men another one. We had water, food, and shelter, our basic needs were met, and I was alive. What more could I ask for after last night?

All day long, whenever despair came over me, I thought of those who had drowned. I was lucky to be near a lifeboat and able to get into it. Very lucky.

My sweet Joan. I closed my eyes for a moment, praying that she was safe and on her way to Australia. It was dark, and I had made a promise. Gradually I projected my voice into the darkness to sing "Rock-a-Bye Baby." This time no one sang with me. The mothers lay on the dusty floor and hugged their children just a little tighter.

Chapter Twelve

The sky was clearing. Dawn was approaching. I was so exhausted from the previous day's walk that I had slept relatively well, even on the hard, dirty floor. If only I could let Joan know I was alive. She would be worried sick if I wasn't at her parents' house when she arrived.

Trying not to disturb anyone around me, I got up and walked outside. I needed some peace to calm my troubled mind. Perhaps watching nature slowly awaken would do the trick. In the distance I heard what sounded like dogs barking. I went down the few steps and sat on the last one. Hot tea would have been nice…with a muffin.

"Are you thinking about breakfast like I am?" asked a voice I recognised immediately.

"Busted, I guess," I said with a smile.

Ruth was coming in from the garden with sweet potatoes in a bucket.

"Not quite what I had in mind," I admitted, pointing to the vegetables.

She laughed quietly. "Neither did I. A nice hot tea, honey, and toast with butter and jam."

"You shouldn't hurt yourself with these sweet thoughts, ladies," joked a male voice from nearby.

Our sailor was standing on the terrace trying to smooth his wrinkled shirt. "Sorry about my outfit."

Laughing, we replied in unison. "Your apology is accepted, sir."

Pointing to her own clothes, Ruth added, "We aren't in a fashion show, unless it is called disorderly fashion."

I laughed. I really liked Ruth's dry sense of humour. It reminded me of Joan's. The sailor smiled too.

"You ladies are great for morale. It's going to be very important in the days ahead. What have you got there?" He pointed to the bucket with the vegetables.

"Sweet potatoes. If we're going to walk, it's best to do it on a full stomach, don't you think? I'm Ruth Carter, by the way."

"Petty Officer Albert Johnson, at your service. And you're right about the walking and the full belly, ma'am." He stared at me blankly, his eyebrows raised in question.

"Evelyn Baker. Glad to have you on board, Mr. Johnson. Without you, we'd still be out on the water going in circles."

I was sincere. This man seemed to know his stuff, and I was glad he was with us.

"I'm going to try to get some bananas for the children. It'll cheer them up. Don't leave without me." He grinned.

We watched in amazement as he disappeared into the jungle. Where would he find bananas? We had looked everywhere yesterday, and they were all too green to eat. Maybe he would have better luck, or maybe he just wanted some time alone to think. As the higher officer, the weight of responsibility must have crushed him.

"Let's get these sweet potatoes cooked before everyone wakes up. Do you know how to start a fire?"

Incredulous, I looked at Ruth with wide eyes. A fire? Was she joking?

Ruth grinned. "We're going to need a man, poor fire-making women that we are."

To our delight, one of the men on the other side of the house had already anticipated this need, and the flames were crackling happily. All we had to do was clean the sweet potatoes and put them in the water to cook.

Four of us sat and chatted as I heard the others waking up in the house. I was thinking of finding a place to clean up a bit when the guy talking in front of me froze in mid-sentence, his mouth open.

Frowning, I stared at him. He was looking at something behind me. The fright on his face was enough to alarm me. I turned my head slightly and came face-to-face with a rifle barrel and bayonet. In an instant my mouth went dry, and fear gripped me. Japanese soldiers. I couldn't breathe. I shook all over.

"Oh my God," Ruth whispered, slowly raising her hands in surrender.

Around us, many soldiers approached silently, weapons at the ready. They entered the house. Immediately I heard screaming, shouting, and even gunfire. I was petrified. We had hoped to escape. It was wishful thinking, I realised now. The Japanese were all over Asia. No one could send enough troops to stop them, not with the war raging in Europe. What would become of us?

Within five minutes we were all gathered in front of the house—the men on one side, and the women and children on the other. I noticed more guns pointed at the men than at us. An officer, I suppose, was barking at us and at his ten fighters. How many were dead in the house? My brain refused to count. Albert wasn't there. He hadn't returned from his search. I was worried the Japanese would shoot without question when he joined us. Glancing cautiously at Ruth, I said "Albert" without making a sound. She shook her head gently and whispered, "He's safe as long as no one says anything."

Everyone else among us was too frightened to notice that the sailor was missing. The only thing on my mind was survival. The Japanese officer shouted again, and one of the soldiers brutally separated the two remaining crewmen from our group. With their uniforms it was easy to recognise them. Before anyone could realise what was going to happen, the Japanese executed them. Some of our group moved a step, but the guns pointed at them dissuaded them from protesting further.

"They can't..." breathed a woman behind me.

I heard someone crying, children questioning their mother. The officer barked an order, and the soldiers began to push us down the dirt road.

"Please let us have food and water," Frances said. "For the children..."

She walked toward the officer, but a rifle butt from the nearest soldier stopped her. She collapsed like a stone. Ruth and another woman rushed to help her.

Where did I get the courage to address the officer, pointing to the bucket on the fire and the children?

"Food for the children."

I imitated eating with my hands. I begged the enemy and hated myself for it, yet it was our only chance to survive.

A soldier went to see what was in the pot and reported to the officer. Barking again, he pointed at me and the food. I took this as an agreement and rushed to the canteen. Ruth and two other women followed me.

"Keep the water," I ordered them. "It is boiled. We must save it."

Ruth stared at me darkly, appearing determined. Clearly fighting back her fear, she turned and hurried toward the house. No one stood in her way. I was terrified for her, but triumphantly she returned with several empty bottles. I hastily filled them with the cooking water. Ruth went back inside again with one of the two women, whose name I didn't know yet. When she stopped on my level, she handed me several bundles, including mine. Under the threat of Japanese rifles, I opened them very slowly and placed a bottle and some potatoes inside each one. They were quickly distributed to the strongest among us. As I passed, Frances waved at me while holding a dusty, bloody handkerchief to the side of her face.

No one spoke of Albert, and no one saw him. As we walked along the dirt road, pushed by the soldiers, I hoped he would stay safe and thought of Joan.

❖

Of course, we had to wait again. What was I thinking? When I looked around, all I saw was despair. I suddenly felt so self-centred.

The last few years I had been totally selfish. Me, only me. James's indiscretion, whining about a subsistence job at the Blue Tiger, ignoring the war in Europe, in China. I hadn't even had the curiosity to learn about the culture of that part of the world—me, a poor colonialist Brit, lost in my own glittery world. Last year, I was so enthralled in my love for Joan that nothing else mattered. Just me and her. I knew nothing about the geography or history of the area.

According to Ruth and Frances, these islands, Dutch colonies, south of Singapore, were tiny, and using a boat was the only way to leave them. We had been at this pier for several hours, huddled with prisoners arriving in small groups. Some were like us, castaways from a shipwreck, with nothing but the clothes on their backs when they were lucky. I had seen a nun give her white dress to a British woman who arrived here in her underwear. There were also Dutch-speaking planter families with some luggage, even trunks. A barely organised chaos.

"Where do you think we're going?" asked a woman from a different group.

The soldiers separated all newly arrived men from the women and children.

"A bigger place. A prison, I suppose," Ruth answered honestly and matter-of-factly.

I heard gagging behind us. Clara's whining voice cut through the murmurs. "A prison? Why? We are not criminals."

Even after those two days of nightmare, Clara hadn't understood that nothing would ever be the same again. She still clung to her world of wealth and glamour. Since our initial arrival on board the ship, with a few rare and short exceptions, I hadn't been able to get her off my back.

"To them, we are," Frances replied.

The gash on her face wasn't too bad, but I'd still bandaged it with what I could to avoid infection.

"What are they going to do to us?" asked Lillian, mother of a teenage girl and two boys who were sleeping in her arms.

The walk had exhausted them, as it had all the children with us. We took turns carrying the youngest on the way. Fortunately, a Japanese soldier had let the men help us. We had no food or water left. What would happen if tomorrow we had to walk again under the blazing sun? Some would die.

By mid-afternoon, the oldest in our group had sat down and refused to move any farther. We tried to cajole him into getting up and moving a bit more, but he was too stubborn and ignored us. As the soldiers passed him, they shot him without batting an eyelid. I remember his stunned expression as the bullet pierced his heart. He had gambled on the humanity of our guards and lost. This was the guy who had almost told me to shut up at the beach.

"Do you think Albert made it?" I asked Ruth in a low voice.

"Who?" Ruth whispered too. Nobody knew if any of the Japanese spoke English.

"Albert, the petty officer. The one who wanted to find bananas yesterday morning. Don't tell me you've forgotten him already, Ruth."

I felt really comfortable with her and her common-sense attitude.

"I'm not senile yet. Of course I remember him. I hope he made it. Maybe he'll be one of the lucky ones to escape."

"Is that food?" someone shouted as a hubbub arose among the prisoners.

Heads turned together to see natives carrying two large buckets coming toward us. We stood up immediately, ready for anything.

Rice and water were in the two containers. Without anyone asking, a silent queue formed. We didn't have enough glasses or plates, so most of us drank before passing the cup to the next person and took the food in our hands. The sickly woman who served me gave me a pitying look that made my heart ache. She whispered a word that I hardly recognised, "Sorry." As I sat down to enjoy my portion of rice, I noticed that the Dutch prisoners had joined the queue, but with plates and glasses.

"If they don't give us more to eat, I won't worry about my waistline anymore," joked Ruth.

I hid a smile. She was a bit…on the plump side. Frances, who was thin like me, laughed openly. Off to the side, Lillian scoffed. "If the four-star service stays the same, we'll have to find a container to eat from."

She was right. It was a priority.

"If I eat only this much food from now on, I'll disappear." Another dismayed voice sounded. "Let's hope that where we're going, it gets better."

Clara, still holding the rice she'd received, was crying. Her life of luxury was crumbling before her eyes, and she couldn't get used to it. If she wanted to survive, she would have to adapt. Quickly. Like all of us.

Knowing that the human organism could survive for a long time without food, I remained silent. I licked my hands so as not to let a single grain escape and thought of Joan. She loved my body. The right shapes in the right places, she always said, caressing my skin. That night, sensing her deep inside me, I sang "But Not for Me."

Chapter Thirteen

With my group I had been confined to an old cinema in Muntok on the island of Banka. We slept on empty pepper bags. The conditions were terrible, and in these circumstances, I used my nursing skills more than my voice, even though I had little or no medication.

We had only what each of us had been able to salvage from the shipwreck. Every day, we had to wait in long queues to fill scavenged drinking vessels. An old tin can or a piece of coconut shell found in a rubbish heap was a treasure. The food—poor-quality rice with a few tiny shreds of vegetables and meat, in most cases spoiled, when there was any—arrived in large, messy buckets. The first few days, the smell was so pungent some of us didn't even want to go near the pot. I was very reluctant too but couldn't stop thinking about Joan. I could hear her sweet voice in my head saying, "Eat, my love, eat. For me." As my stomach screamed its hunger, I overcame my distaste for the vile concoction and went to get my small portion.

"We have to forget our old life," Ruth insisted once again to our group.

Sitting next to me, eating from her makeshift plate—a crude piece of wood—as distinguished as if she were in the Raffles dining room, she persevered. "We have to prepare for the duration," she said.

"What do you mean?" asked Frances as she sat down next to us with her split coconut bowl. "What kind of organisation are you thinking of?"

"We may be here for years…"

All the women, hearing her, gagged. For years? I didn't even want to think further than the day itself.

"We can't sit here and do nothing."

"Why would they keep civilian prisoners for years? We're not a threat to them."

"Especially the women and children," Frances added. "That would be stupid."

"It doesn't matter to them. We are at war. Look at the men. They've already organised themselves. They're making junk furniture or whatever to keep themselves busy. At least Evelyn is nursing some of the sick, but us? What do we do but sit on our butts and sulk about the easy life we've always led?"

We quickly swallowed the little food we had but kept talking. We had nothing else to do.

Around us, many women were silently listening to our discussion. Some nodded, and others put on airs and pursed their lips in disapproval.

"The young people need to be educated," Ruth insisted confidently. "I can teach. Maybe others can too."

"We have no paper, no pens," Lillian insisted, desperation in her voice.

Her three children were sitting in the dirt nearby, with others of varying ages. Ruth watched them play for a while before a smile lifted one corner of her mouth.

"Look at them. They're smarter than we are. They've solved the lack of pen and paper."

The children were drawing in the dust directly on the floor, using their hands to clean up their "paper." I smiled back at Ruth. A small voice broke the silence.

"I'm good at math. I'm sure I could teach them something."

All heads turned to the frightened and very taciturn young woman who had just spoken. I had never heard the sound of her voice before. She seemed to shrink a little more before our eyes and hugged her knees to her chest. Since we had arrived here, she had been moving around with everyone, never saying a word or engaging anyone in conversation.

Enthusiastically, Ruth smiled. "That would be wonderful, dear. Heather, isn't it? Calculus isn't my forte. I'll teach English. Anyone else want to help us?"

Two hands went up. Happy to have so many volunteers, Ruth nodded. "So, ladies, we're going to design a lesson plan." Ruth's thoughtful gaze lingered on me. "Evelyn, do you want to teach them music?"

Me? Teach children? I'd never thought of that possibility. Adults, no problem, but unruly children? "I'm not a music teacher, but I could teach them to sing." Why did I agree?

"That's even better. No bawdy songs, of course."

I blushed. How could she think for a second that I could...All the women around us giggled. I understood. Ruth had a way of making a bad mood disappear in the blink of an eye. After this discussion, our compatriots walked away with a lighter step.

We knew there were other prisoners elsewhere, including soldiers. We could often hear them walking along the walls but rarely saw them. The only things the Japanese asked us when we arrived here were our name, date, place of birth, and nationality. They wrote it all down in a big notebook and then said, "Next!"

As the days passed by, everyone's spirits waned, but Ruth and Frances did their best to plan fun activities. Ruth's school was good for the children and the teachers. Following our example, little by little the women became organised. Some did the cleaning, and others helped the men collect anything that might be of use. Everything was useful to help us keep busy. Some made toys from what little we had, not thinking about the past but hoping for a better future.

The weather didn't help, and most of us napped during the hottest hours of the day. The mosquitoes were the worst, and malaria was rampant.

From the beginning, Clara had sulked in her corner, ignoring most of the solicitations. She wasn't the only one with this attitude, and although I didn't like her very much, I was worried. To survive this brutal treatment, each of us needed a goal. Mine was obvious: my beloved was waiting for me in Australia. I sang at night and nursed during the day. My time was full, even if my nights remained lonely.

Each night, as promised, I sang a song for Joan, the children, and those who listened. For many, this was the best part of the day because it gave us a taste of home.

❖

After we spent almost a month in Muntok, one day, suddenly, the order to move came. At the end of March 1942, the Japanese forced us to walk to the long jetty and put us in small boats. We didn't know where we were going. They just pushed us with their guns to make us move faster.

At least I was still with my group—nobody had died—and we tried to stay together. The twelve hours of transport under the sun, without food or drink, were a real hell. Our hats weren't large enough to fully protect us from the aggressive rays, and those with fair skin got blisters and burns. The toilet, which consisted of a wooden plank suspended over the water for all on board to see, was an absolute horror. If a woman had to go, we tried to protect her privacy with pieces of clothing. In addition, except for the pilot and the guards, we all looked down during these moments.

Within a month Ruth and Frances had become my best friends, and we spent most of our time together. Clara was very much present, constantly complaining, always clinging to one of us. She wore us down, but we couldn't turn her away, could we?

As soon as the boat docked, the Dutch captives who knew the area well told us that we were in Palembang, in the southern part of Sumatra. Arriving at an old school in Bukit Besar, near the centre of town, we were both amazed and pleased to be mingled with the British and Australian soldiers, who, knowing of our arrival, had prepared a wonderful surprise: a hot meal, the first proper food we'd had for weeks.

For several days we stayed together—talking, sharing information about the war, asking about acquaintances. Most women, even those with children, tended to stay together. However, some of the single women quickly became very friendly toward the single men. Was that why, after our arrival in the new camp, all the men were sent to another one? The separation was difficult for everyone. Some women lost their husbands or teenage sons. They were crying, and we tried to comfort them as best we could. We all felt helpless.

The walk to our new camp didn't take long. This time there were no walls to block our view, just a row of colonial houses surrounded by barbed wire. A sentry box stood at each corner and a guard post at the entrance. According to some of the women, the houses were built in a

Dutch style, and we were still in Palembang. The soldiers pushed us or, rather, crammed us ruthlessly into the accommodation—I counted at least thirty of us inside—and we weren't allowed out until further notice. No one dared disobey. The guards all had flexible rattan canes and were quick to use them. I'd had a taste of one in Muntok when I wasn't moving fast enough, and I didn't want to feel it again.

"We need to get organised," said Frances, standing in the centre of the house.

I almost smiled. In Muntok, she had played the same music for us, and even the most reluctant had ended up participating. Frances was the one who always demanded order and efficiency. I couldn't blame her because she was right. If we hoped to survive here too, we had to be resourceful and work together.

"Why? What's the point? Those who died when the ship went down were the lucky ones."

I knew that voice. We all did. Vera was the worst kind of defeatist. Like Clara, she was dangerous to morale. We didn't need that kind of thinking here.

Before anyone could respond, Ruth grabbed her arm and shook her. "If you ever say that again, or anything like it, I'll kill you myself. Do you hear me? We have to keep our spirits up if we want to survive this war, and survive we will! You can kill yourself if you want to, but don't discourage others!"

I had never seen Ruth so angry. No one was moving. There was total silence. Even the children weren't crying. After more than six weeks, they had accepted that nothing would be the same. It was harder for the adults. Maybe a little less for me, who had already left everything behind once. But Ruth was right. We needed hope.

For the first time since the guards had locked us in here, I really looked around. Something caught my eye. "Hey. I see some things the owner of the house left." I stood up and leaned into a corner. A chipped bowl. I clutched it to my chest. After eating out of a broken coconut shell for over a month, I considered it the most precious utensil I had ever seen.

Suddenly, all eyes were on me, or rather on my find. In an instant, the women jumped to their feet, and a fury of activity erupted. They searched the house from floor to ceiling, and even the chipped plates were a treasure for those who had nothing.

When we were finally allowed out for the first roll call—or *tenko*, as the Japanese called it, on the dirt esplanade, our numbers surprised me. Counting everyone was impossible, but there were hundreds of us. At each tenko, we bowed to our masters. Those who weren't fast enough learned the lesson the hard way by being beaten with a rattan stick.

That first tenko lasted more than an hour as we stood under the hot equatorial sun listening to a speech in quite good English.

"If I have to hear one more time that we are a dishonoured race because we should have killed ourselves instead of being captured, I will kill someone!" Grace spat.

She was the oldest of our group, but her stubbornness had already earned her a few strokes when we were in Muntok. They hadn't made her any wiser, only more careful, and thank God she hadn't lost her outspokenness. I smiled. I so wished I were like her.

"How many of us are there?" Frances suddenly asked as she watched all the women return to their homes.

"About two or three hundred here at Prinses Irenestraat," Sally replied immediately. "I tried to count the houses in this row. Eight are occupied, at thirty per house…"

Sally liked numbers. She had been an accountant for her husband's company in Johor.

"Some are still empty, if I'm not mistaken. Maybe there will be new captives."

"What did you call it?" asked Frances, frowning. "A Dutch name?"

"Prinses Irenestraat. That's the name of the street. Gretchen told me. She lived in Palembang before the war."

Sally pointed to a blond woman who was chatting in Dutch with her compatriots. She was part of a small group that had joined us in Muntok three weeks earlier. Only a few spoke English.

We had all forgotten that Sumatra was a Dutch colony and that these women knew more about the region than we did. Frances sighed.

"We need as much information as possible about this place. At least there's enough space for the children to play outside. Maybe we can grow a vegetable garden if we can find some seeds. I'm going to talk to the women in the other houses. Does anyone want to come with me?"

I don't know why, but I volunteered. Maybe I wanted to explore, to move around. Most of the women prisoners were the same as in Muntok. However, our morale was better with the much-nicer accommodation.

From the beginning Frances was the leader of our little group, the one who kept us organised, who talked to the others. As we walked along, we saw other houses a little farther on, also surrounded by barbed wire. More prisoners? But how many were we? Frances stopped.

"More women, you think?"

I squinted in the sunlight to see more details. "I see children."

Watching them, we remained silent for a long time before moving to the nearest house. It took us almost the whole morning to finish our tour. At each of the houses, even the two occupied by the Dutchwomen, Frances asked them to choose a representative and make a list of each one's capabilities. Later in the day, the Japanese commander demanded that he speak to only one spokesperson. We had until tomorrow to choose one. I knew who I wanted to represent us and crossed my fingers.

By the end of the evening, we were dirty, dirtier than usual, but our house was clean, and we still had tea to sip. Some of us had even found some usable old mattresses. Still hungry—nothing new about that—and in low spirits, I started a cheerful little song called "Cheek to Cheek."

As soon as I said the first line, "Heaven, I'm in Heaven," sarcasm in my voice and touching the crumpled, filthy clothes we were all wearing, the women burst out laughing. Ruth suddenly took me in her arms to dance while I sang. Fred Astaire and Ginger Rogers, London-slums version.

"You know how to cheer up the troops, dear," Ruth whispered in my ear before letting go. "Good work."

Chapter Fourteen

Early 1943

The tinkling of the bell roused me from a restless sleep. Since the shipwreck, I had been waking up with a start several times a night and had trouble falling back to sleep despite my exhaustion. The bloodsucking mosquitoes and the humid heat didn't help me get a peaceful night's sleep, especially as my fellow wretches also had their own demons rising in the darkness.

Ruth shook my shoulder. "Come on, Evelyn. Get up."

"Tenko! Tenko!" a man shouted outside.

How I cursed that word! We all hated this gathering three times a day where we had to line up and bow to our "masters." Several of us had been caned for not bowing fast enough or long enough. Once Grace, our oldest fellow prisoner, even had the audacity to refuse to bow. Months later, she was still suffering the consequences. Those cowards had beaten her almost unconscious. Only children under the age of ten escaped. Our executioners apparently loved children.

"Come on. Tenko. You don't want to get hit."

No. I didn't want to get hit. I pulled my still-numb body from my mat and stood on my feet, slipping on some patched sandals. Most of the women were already outside, and I hurried on. The guards were waiting in the courtyard in front of the houses and didn't miss those who passed within stick reach. I swerved at the last moment and felt the wind from the rattan whipping through the air. Missed. Happy with this small victory, I took my place in the lineup, just behind Frances and next to Ruth. Frances had easily been elected our spokesperson, as no one else volunteered to face Captain Yotaki every day. She often came back from their meetings frustrated, usually not getting anything—extra food or medicine.

The camp commander strutted in front of us every morning as we hunched over waiting for his pleasure. When he was in a hurry, to our relief, the tenko didn't last long. At first, few of us could stay in this bowing position for several minutes, and the Japanese clearly enjoyed watching us collapse in pain one after the other. We became gradually more resistant. Even that day, during the count, we were not allowed to stand up. As time went by, I had learned the numbers in Japanese, and I noticed that once again the guards were not getting the right ones. Yet no one had died for several days.

The muscles in my back tensed. Around me, a few discreet moans or curses of protest suggested the desperation of my companions. Why were the Japanese doing this? What was their motivation? None of us had tried to escape since we arrived here. Making small, stealthy movements, I tried to release the pain in order to last as long as possible. Each house had a group of women bent over. The first one to give in would be beaten. We all knew that.

Escaping into my thoughts, I analysed our last few months in Irenelaan, as we had called it among ourselves. Even since our arrival and her appointment as camp leader, Frances had not obtained much information, but she had understood that we would be here for a long time. So we started to organise ourselves quickly. Three days before, because the number of sick people was increasing day by day, Captain Yotaki had authorised the conversion of the last house in the row into a dispensary. We had little medicine to help the sick, but at least they would be separated from the group. As I recapped what remained to be done before we opened our place of health, the order to get up came to my ears. Grunting, I struggled to my feet and rubbed my back. Two houses away, a woman lay on the ground, a guard beside her.

"You bastard," several women muttered. Whimpering in pain, she was one of our oldest. These savages had no respect.

"Quiet!" ordered Frances in a low voice as she saw a soldier approaching our group.

Immediately the whispering died down. Captain Yotaki stepped onto a prepared platform.

"Prisoners. Today your troops are surrendering en masse to the Imperial Japanese Army. The Americans have lost another great battle. Soon we shall be masters of the whole Pacific."

Every day demoralising speeches tried to make us give up what little hope of liberation we still had. It was impossible to know if what they said was true, but the weakest among us often went into a fit of defeatism after such speeches.

"But I have good news for you," Yotaki continued in English. He gestured, and the gates to the camp opened. "As a reward for organising a hospital, the Japanese army, in its great mercy, is providing you with medical staff and medicine."

All heads turned to the new arrivals carrying a few boxes. Some wore only a stained grey dress buttoned at the front, while others still had the little bright red cape over their shoulders, the sign of the Australian Army Nursing Sisters, the AANS. The last ones in line were dressed in rags like us.

I stared at the boxes. Medicine! I hoped there was quinine. With all these mosquitoes, many of us had been suffering from malaria. I'd had my first attack four days earlier and was still feeling very tired. My gaze fell on the only pair of trousers in the group as someone walked past me. A man among the arrivals? I looked up and almost fainted, unable to speak. Instinctively I took a step forward, but a hand on my shoulder stopped me.

"You don't want to be punished," Ruth whispered through her teeth.

I put my hand to my mouth to hold back a scream and, like an automaton, fell into line, not taking my eyes off the women walking away toward the still-empty house next to the new clinic. We were now complete. All the houses in Irenelaan were full. The bastard who continued his speech, which I listened to distractedly, had known he was going to have more prisoners and they would be medical staff. I was still in shock at what I had seen and could hardly stand still. Ruth called me to order several times.

As soon as the Japanese released us from the tenko, regardless of my companions, I ran toward the house the newcomers had entered. I could hear the voices of Frances and Ruth questioning me far away, but I couldn't wait for them. Breathlessly I opened the door and entered.

"Joan! Joan!"

My voice broke as soon as she appeared. The surprise in her eyes made me smile. She rushed forward as I ran toward her. Clutching each other, laughing, crying, we didn't care about the women who looked at us and whispered. The love of my life was in my arms. She was alive but a prisoner like me.

"I had dared to hope that you would be quietly at my parents' house eating mutton stew," she said between two sniffles.

How I'd missed her Australian accent! I sobbed. "I too imagined you with your family, even though I have no idea what an Australian sheep station looks like. How did they capture you? In Singapore? How long ago?"

Joan put a finger to my lips. "More questions later." Still holding me by the waist, she turned and pointed to her companions. "We need to get organised."

I heard coughing behind me. Frances and Ruth were waiting quietly. Frances stepped forward.

"Frances McBride. I am the camp spokesperson for Captain Yotaki. Despite the circumstances, we are happy to welcome medical personnel and medicine."

"Joan Cliver, medical officer. I'm the only civilian. All the nurses here are AANS."

"Ruth Carter. I'm in charge of running the classes for the children. If any of you want to teach biology, you're welcome to do so," Ruth said, always ready to take on volunteers. "I'm also trying to plan the recovery of materials to improve our lot. We have started to organise the house right next to yours as a dispensary. It should be finished today if Evelyn decides to get to work."

Ruth smiled softly as she glanced at my hand in Joan's. I blushed but refused to let go. Even though I would have preferred my beloved to be safe, knowing she was close to me made me feel better after all these months of fretting over her.

"We're going to organise our accommodation here, doctor," a woman in her thirties in uniform said suddenly. "Go see the dispensary with one or two of us. It's best to arrange things under medical advice."

The nurse looked down on me from her height. I was not small, but she was massive. However, I didn't back down and, letting go of Joan's hand, crossed my arms over my chest and held her gaze.

"Even though I'm not a qualified nurse, as I left a few months before graduation, I did my studies in London. And you should know that I have been caring for these women and children since our capture in mid-February '42."

My tone was icy. I could barely see the amusement in Joan's eyes as this…woman had caught me off guard.

"Thank you, Wilma," Joan said. "I'll go see the dispensary with Laura. I'm sure Evelyn will have done very well. She's quite organised."

Without waiting, Joan led me outside, then slowed down and looked around. Ignoring us completely, Ruth, Frances, and Laura passed us and headed for the last house in the row.

"No soldiers?"

Joan pointed to the area in front of the houses. Indeed, only the women going about their business and the children sitting in the shade occupied the space.

"Captain Yotaki lets us run things as long as we have no incidents. We even manage to buy fruit and vegetables from the locals when we have money. Some of us have started a vegetable garden, and others are teaching a class. I'll explain everything in detail later."

Grabbing her arm, I led her toward our future clinic, but after a few steps, my heart pounding to be with her again, I stopped us in the middle of the field.

"I was so afraid for you. Now I am both reassured and sorry you are here." I looked around, but too many people were nearby. "I'd love to hold you."

"I'd love to hug you too. Where are the tropical bushes when you need them?" joked Joan, referring to our corner in the Singapore botanic gardens.

"Where's our apartment instead?" I replied.

"Our bedroom?"

"Our bed?"

Her green eyes glowed with a clear message. I immediately thought back to our nights of passion. "You can't put that kind of idea in my head here. It's not fair."

Joan burst into a loud laugh. God, I'd missed that laughter during the last ten months.

"And look at me. I'm so dirty...and my clothes...I've become a bag of bones..." I was a little ashamed of my condition, of my unkempt appearance.

"You're still the most beautiful woman I've ever met, my love," Joan murmured, suddenly very serious. "Even if you were bald and pustular, I would still love you." Her eyes sparkled with happiness, and she gripped my hand nervously. "I myself have nothing left of the dashing doctor who used to watch you sing." She pointed to her stained shirt, her trousers with a torn leg. "Show me my new domain before Wilma comes to remind me of my duties."

We resumed our walk side by side, often brushing against each other in a seemingly innocent gesture. A delicious shiver ran up my spine.

"How did you meet your nurses?"

"We were on the *Vyner Brooke* together on the evening of the 12th. You see, I left shortly after you. There were women and children, as well as my colleagues, the wounded, and over sixty-five AANS nurses. As I was the only female doctor on board, we talked. The captain of the ship was competent, but planes found us and finally sank us on the 14th. Some of us managed to reach the island of Banka by clinging to the debris. Some nurses were killed in the attack, but twenty-one of them..." Joan's voice broke. She fought back tears. "The Japanese shot twenty-one of them on a beach. They also murdered soldiers and civilians in the same place."

I couldn't believe my ears. We had heard of vile massacres by the Japanese in the camp, but I assumed these were just amplified rumours. I thought of our two executed sailors and of Albert. Was he still alive?

"How did you find out? We hear this kind of gossip every time a new prisoner joins us."

"Keep it to yourself, but one person survived. Vivian surrendered twelve days later, but she didn't tell anyone what she saw, of course. The Japanese would have silenced her. She informed only Major Tebbutt at Muntok prison, where we were held. We were sworn to secrecy to protect her. Her testimony will be important after the war."

Serious, Joan looked me straight in the eyes.

"I won't say anything. I promise."

A weary smile stretched her lips. "Now show me this beautiful hospital of yours."

When night fell, except in emergencies, we were not allowed to go out. Knowing that my beloved was three houses away, I turned over on my mat, trying to figure out how we could stay together.

"Joan could come live here," Ruth suddenly whispered, propping herself up on one elbow, "although I don't think it would do you any real good."

She giggled. I blushed. I was surprised that she and Frances hadn't commented all day. My first reaction had been so demonstrative I couldn't say that Joan was simply my best friend. I was dying to hold her in my arms, to sleep against her, but we could never go any further. Even here, during daily suffering, well-meaning women would always judge and condemn us. What would the Japanese do if they heard about us? Nothing? Separate us? Execute one of us? Or both? The possibilities made me break out in a cold sweat. I sighed.

"You're right. It's not an option. I don't want to put us at risk." With a heavy heart, I turned onto my side and hummed "Only Forever."

Chapter Fifteen

Joan's lips against my neck, her warm breath, sent waves of desire down my loins. I stroked her back with my fingertips, cursing the thin fabric of her shirt. Her hand slipped between my legs, and I threw my head back. Joan's mouth caught mine and swallowed the moan that rose from my throat. I clutched her to me in that final moment just before the tension drained away and gave way to that sweet, soothing afterglow.

"You have to be more discreet," Joan murmured, nibbling my ear. "The patients might hear us."

I tenderly caressed her perfect little breasts that fit in the palm of my hand. With a smile, I teased her. "You'll just have to say that you don't have a soft hand and that you were hurting me."

"You want to ruin my reputation," she replied, not in the least concerned.

She closed her eyes, savouring my teasing fingers as they slowly pushed aside the flaps of her shirt. I was very careful not to tear it, as whole garments were becoming scarce.

Joan was sweating profusely. The humidity here was worse than in Singapore, which benefited from the proximity of the sea. Slowly, I went after her trousers, which, with the passing days, had become shorts that stopped at mid-thigh.

"You must be hot in those. Let me air them out a bit."

My breath caressed her ear. Her green eyes looked into mine for a moment before closing abruptly as soon as my index finger located the sensitive spot. She found my shoulder, and I felt the pain of the bite, yet I gritted my teeth and suspended my back-and-forth movement only when she grabbed my wrist.

"What a great idea…this room being used as an…office…"

I smiled. When I had created it, I wanted this place all to myself so I could write down in peace the names of the patients and the care they received.

"Dr. Cliver?"

Frances's voice made us start furiously dressing to conceal our activities.

"Just a moment, please," Joan replied professionally as she struggled with the edges of her shirt.

I laughed. For this kind of exercise, a simple dress was much more useful. I settled for smoothing the folds of an old faded dress. I had only two outfits left, but they were deteriorating rapidly. No matter how much we sewed and darned, the constant washing, the sun, and the sweat were damaging the fabric. Even freshly cleaned, their smell had become horrible, but we had to get used to it.

Joan opened the door, and Frances came in. If she was surprised to see me and Joan together, she didn't show it. I liked this trait. Nothing seemed to faze her. She kept her cool under any circumstances. Very British. The slight smile she gave me indicated that she was not fooled.

"I saw Yotaki. He agrees that we can have night shifts here if patients are in hospital. Two people maximum. Tenko is not compulsory for the patients or for the nurse in charge at the time of the count. However, the number and identity of patients must be kept up to date and given to his secretary in the morning and evening."

"This is a good thing. These women are in no condition to stand around waiting for the masters' whim." Joan almost spat out the last word. "They are nothing but torturers and murderers!"

I had never heard her express such resentment openly. She had told me about Vivian witnessing the massacre, but I sensed something else we hadn't had time to talk about. Clearly trying to control her nerves, she turned her back to us and took several deep breaths.

"We were at Charitas Hospital before we were transferred here," she said in a voice choked with emotion, "helping all the prisoners, but the Japanese brutally closed it down, saying we were spreading anti-Japanese ideas." Joan burst out in a joyless laugh. "As a woman

I was lucky, for the Japanese never considered me a full-fledged doctor. They executed everyone else, beheaded Dr. Ziesel and his nine colleagues."

Joan turned to us in tears. I wanted so much to help her, to hold her in my arms.

"I'll never forgive them," she added breathlessly.

Refusing to imagine that I could have lost my precious Joan without even knowing it, I wiped the tears from my cheeks. Frances, clearly touched, sniffed loudly before saying, "Sorry. I left my embroidered handkerchiefs at home when I rushed away."

The incongruous answer provoked a huge burst of laughter, which we struggled to quell quickly.

"Thanks for the good news. I'll take what I can get at the moment," Joan said, once our laughter had subsided.

That evening, on duty in the clinic, positioned in my sweetheart's arms, at her request, I sang "You Are My Sunshine."

Chapter Sixteen

September 1943

A beautiful day with a beautifully blue sky. So rare in the tropics. My pupils were attentive, sitting in a semicircle in front of me on the dusty floor. If it weren't for the barbed wire, our clothes, and the hollowed-out faces of the children, we might have thought we were free. Elsie stood singing the famous Judy Garland chorus "Somewhere Over the Rainbow," or trying to. I helped her with the most difficult parts. Elsie was one of the best, but she was already thirteen and had been taking music lessons for several years. Each student had chosen a song. Twice a week we practised breathing, blowing in controlled bursts, vocalising to warm up, and doing solfeggio scales before we even started. The children laughed a lot during these exercises, and I encouraged them to do so. Laughter and humour would save us. Those like Clara who gave in to despair and depression had already left us and were now resting in the little cemetery.

After class we would take ten minutes to rehearse the few notes that the volunteers had to work on. Norah and Margaret, who had been with us almost from the beginning, had been right to form the choir. Their idea was brilliant. Most of the girls had insisted on being part of the secret concert. They were fearless and I admired them. At first, most of us thought they were crazy, but they had given us something motivating and beautiful to do and, above all, a way to resist our oppressors, who had banned music in the camp. These two women had not been deterred by the task of rewriting from memory the scores of classical music with its various instruments into scores for voices. Each of us had to hum one sound and one sound only to the requested rhythm. My job was to help them find the right tone and keep it. We had no need to sing words, so even those who didn't speak English could participate. The process was slow, but it was fun and gave us hope.

I was helping one of the boys with his song when Lillian rushed over to us.

"We're leaving the camp in an hour! Elsie, go get your brothers," she ordered her daughter.

"What? Who's...?"

"Frances has just received news from Yotaki. We have to leave everything behind except our clothes."

Stunned, I looked at her and shook my head. This was absurd. We had organised ourselves well here, and despite the lack of food and medicine, things were going smoothly.

As my students scattered in all directions, I rushed to the clinic, where the nurses were already packing up. Joan was in her office sorting through the few remaining remedies.

"How can I help you?"

She looked at me, frustration filling her eyes.

"End the war?"

I laughed out loud, and she couldn't help but smile.

"Take these drugs with you and hide them against your body. They don't want us to carry anything with us, but I don't trust them."

She quickly gave me some small papers or packets of leaves closed with a wooden pin.

"Share them among the other volunteers in case they search us. Go get your things ready."

"I'll come back here to help the sicker ones."

"No, you won't. I have enough nurses. Can you pack my stuff while you're at it?"

"Of course. But I'll be back here anyway. I want to be by your side in case they get the crazy idea of separating us and putting us in different camps." I took two steps and kissed her—for the future and because I could still do it. I quickly left the clinic and hurried toward the place where I lived.

It was a real madhouse. Women were packing and crying. We, the survivors of the shipwreck, didn't have much—a piece of a coconut shell, a few sandals made from wood and fibre, bits of hard-earned cloth. I didn't know how the Dutchwomen would manage with all the stuff they had when they arrived. I often felt bitter toward them. They had more money and used us shipwrecked survivors to do the work for them. These few hard-earned pennies allowed us to buy food from local traders who were sometimes allowed into the camp, or by taking great risks with the illegal ones who haggled beyond the barbed wire. Proud of myself, I had negotiated a few coins a week to teach the two Dutch children I admitted to my singing class. What choice did I have?

Frances was passing by. I stopped her. "Where are we going?"

"I have no idea. Not far, according to the captain."

I handed her a small package. "Medicine. Hide it on you."

She took it and went on her way.

With my things packed in a bundle, I went out to look after Joan's belongings. The women were already starting to gather in front of their houses. I had to be quick.

I had hardly reached Joan when the tenko bell rang. Once assembled, the long column began to move. The nurses were helping the sickest, and we were all silent. At a glance, I noticed that the garden had been pulled up to retrieve all the vegetables. Passing the graves, I said a prayer to my fellow prisoners buried on this piece of land. Clara was there, with twenty-three others. I didn't like that selfish woman, but she didn't deserve this fate. None of us did, not even the defeatist Vera, who had died six months earlier, tied to a pole in the sunlight for all to see. She had gone mad and insulted the guards. The captain had no mercy on her.

The camp gate opened, letting us out for the first time in almost a year and a half. I was scared, but Joan was by my side. I took a deep breath to calm my trepidation. Gently, she brushed my hand.

❖

After less than an hour of walking on a dusty road, our convoy slowed. The women whispered, and the news of our arrival spread quickly. Using their rattan sticks, the guards forced us to enter the new camp. To our dismay, huts made of bamboo and palm leaves in poor condition awaited us. We had left cramped but real houses for this primitive camp? Some were crying, and others were growling insults.

When I felt Joan's hand on my back, I realised that I had slowed down. What I saw before me looked insurmountable. I shook my head.

"I won't survive this," I muttered.

"You will," Joan said in a low voice, "and do you know why?"

With tears in my eyes, I stared at her in despair.

"Because we're together, and I love you."

Tears began to roll down my cheeks. Her words were always so sweet. Even in this camp of woe and death, they filled my heart with tenderness. As we walked, she put her arm around my waist, forcing me to stand up proudly and move forward.

The hut we entered was filthy. Many things were broken. I noticed a few bamboo bunks, but most of them had a hole in the middle.

"Let's look at it positively," Frances said. "There's a lot more room here than in the other camp. The houses are bigger and better ventilated."

She pointed to the holes in the walls and roof, and some of our group giggled.

"I'm glad, because I have a feeling there'll be more of us," one of the women said with a pout of disgust after straightening up a shelf of some sort.

She pointed outside, indicating two trucks that were unloading more prisoners. Grace, as usual, grumbled.

"Where did they come from, these ones? And how are we going to feed them? Do you think these savages will give us more of their vile rice with their tasteless water spinach?"

"We have to clean up first," Joan said. "In the long run, disease is our main concern, far ahead of malnutrition."

The forty or so women present sighed in unison. "We know that, Doc. You don't have to tell us what to do."

"Scrub, clean," sang Elsie, her younger brother Chester in her arms.

"And we'll stay healthy," the women finished in chorus.

"I'll go and see the new arrivals," suggested Frances. "Explain to them how we work."

"Our patients are lying outside. I'll help my nurses set up a hospital somewhere. I'll leave you to fend for yourselves here," Joan said.

As Frances was leaving, she stopped and spoke to Joan.

"Maybe it would be good to have one or two nurses per hut to identify symptoms quickly?"

"I'll check with Wilma. They're so used to being together that I'm not sure they'll accept such a change."

While I was wondering where to start, the math teacher, Heather, always very quiet, had somehow created a broom with twigs. Silently, she set about cleaning the floor. Others, following her example, started removing broken bamboo on the bunks, while two women dismantled one at the end of the line so they could have some material for repairs. After all these months together, we knew our strengths and weaknesses. Lillian, not very good with her hands but excellent at salvaging, took her three children and the other five in the house outside to look for building materials. As usual, she would turn the search into a game. Although the children weren't fooled, they enjoyed joining the survival effort.

Just as our hut was starting to look inhabitable, and I was thinking about taking a well-deserved rest, Norah and Margaret, the two who had formed the choir, came in.

"Nice!" said Norah, looking around. "You should see ours."

"Very stylish!" added Margaret, adopting an upper-class accent. "I love the stripped-down, local feel."

Most of us giggled. These two were incredibly peachy. As well as making us hum along, Margaret had even managed to construct card games using old photographs and was having wild gin games with grains of rice as the stakes. The winner would eat the stake.

"We need hands to clear the well," Norah said.

Margaret continued the theme. "I know everyone is tired, but no well, no water."

Like many of us, I grumbled but volunteered with the hard-working Sally, who liked numbers as well as Heather did. Although we were thin, we were healthier than many others.

"From what I understand, the men were here for several months, and they broke everything when they left," Norah told me. "One of the guards who speaks English couldn't help but try to make us angry at our countrymen. What they did made him laugh."

Walking beside her, I asked in a low voice, "But why destroy everything?"

"I don't think they knew we would replace them, and our brave soldiers in the imperial army were careful not to tell them." Margaret spat. "Here is the beast of a well."

Several women were already trying, in a well-organised chain, to clear the debris that had been thrown to the bottom of it. Two of them were inside and had to lift bamboo and pieces of wood. Farther on, I saw Lillian with four other women and the children sorting out everything that could be salvaged. Immediately, I moved closer to the edge to help the first in line pull out a broken plank. Without a word being exchanged, the new arrivals joined in to double the chain. Every ten minutes, those at the bottom of the hole were replaced by others a little less tired. We needed water. If a well had been built here, no stream was nearby.

We had been here for two months, and despite the difficult conditions, the ubiquitous rules to follow, the twice-daily tenko and the constant surveillance, we managed to re-establish a social centre. The women hummed the music quietly, and Norah planned to give our first concert just after Christmas. As the date approached, the murmurs grew louder, and the mood improved. I shared my bed with Joan in a tender way. Neither of us had the strength or inclination to make love in a squalid corner. I knew that some women were whispering behind our backs, but they couldn't see anything because there was nothing to see. Other women, in a similar search for affection, had also come together and formed inseparable couples that only death sometimes tore apart.

Lying on my bed, in Joan's arms, I listened to the rain falling on the roof made from *atap*—palm leaves the local people used as thatch. Although repaired as well as possible, it was not very watertight, but we had managed to channel the leaks to fill all sorts of containers. This, at least, provided clean water, unlike the well water, which was constantly muddy and needed to be boiled before drinking.

I thought of the two young teenagers who had been taken away that afternoon while their mothers were crying after them. Once a month, during the morning tenko, in front of everyone, the guards would pull down the shorts of all the boys to check those who had reached puberty. They were separated from the others and then moved to another camp. From what we had learned, they were sent to the men's camp nearby. Some were only twelve or thirteen years old, and we hoped someone would take care of them. Each departure cast an ominous shadow over the atmosphere of the camp.

Thinking of them, with Joan's arm around my abdomen, I hummed "The Muffin Man."

At the end of the first sentence, *Do you know the muffin man, the muffin man, the muffin man? Do you know the muffin man, who lives on Drury Lane,* I was surprised and pleased to hear Joan singing softly: *Yes, I know the muffin man, the muffin man, the muffin man. Yes, I know the muffin man, who lives on Drury Lane.* Just next to us, as soon as Joan had finished her sentence, Frances continued the part about the ice cream man. The person next to her replied. And so on. Quietly, all the women sang the children's song. It was so comforting. The sadness for those children separated from their mother faded a little from my heart.

Chapter Seventeen

25 December 1943

It was Christmas Day, our second in captivity. The children were excited with all the activity. Like last year, everyone had combined their resources to prepare a special day. We had made presents for our loved ones and those who had no one. While the usual meal of white rice was ready, we all started to pile up the presents on the wobbling table near the entrance. I could see an unusual activity at the back of the kitchen. The big cooking pots were hanging over the wood fire. For almost two years we had eaten the same thing over and over. For several weeks, Joan had enrolled us to dig for worms and other insects to add to the daily meal. I found it disgusting to catch them and include them in our food, but they provided protein and vitamins. Anyway, I preferred this task a hundred times over to using coconut shells to transfer the excrement from the trenches into buckets, trying to reduce the risk of flies and disease.

"You look like you could use some company."

The soft, velvety voice with an Australian accent rolled in my ear. I would never tire of hearing it, even if I lived a hundred years.

"Yes. I was thinking about worms and excrement," I replied.

Joan laughed out loud, drawing all eyes in our direction. I smiled fondly. "Do you think the Japs will give us a good Christmas pudding this year?"

"In your wildest dreams, dear," Ruth replied in Joan's place, her empty wooden plate dangling from her fingertips.

Many women were arriving, the queue was forming, but it seemed the kitchen wasn't ready.

"What are we waiting for?" asked Wilma, the head nurse, just behind us.

"I think it's coming." Norah's voice sounded cheerful, much more cheerful than usual. Did she know something we didn't?

The cooks entered from behind and took their places by the first pot, but none of them started to serve. They waited without flinching, hands behind their backs, smiles on their faces. Everyone's impatience was growing. Suddenly, two women arrived, carrying a large object between them. When I recognised what it was, my mouth fell open, and I let out a short moan. The children shouted with joy. Bananas, a bunch of bananas! My mouth watered. I could already taste them. How did they do it?

"I'm glad our little surprise is so well received." Frances's voice overshadowed the noise, and soon everyone was listening. "Many thanks to Gretchen, our Dutch friend, who sold some of her belongings and decided to prepare an unforgettable Christmas meal for us. Each of us won't have a whole banana, of course, but we will all have a piece."

The applause rang out with "Long live Gretchen!"

As soon as I was served, I went out with Joan and sat on the edge of the terrace. I was still staring at the piece of banana on my plate next to my spoonful of rice. Joan pulled something from her pocket and topped my rice with it.

Frowning, I looked at her, but then astonishment overwhelmed me. "Is this what I think it is?"

She smiled and replied with a simple "Merry Christmas."

"The best," I murmured, a tremor in my voice.

My love had just sprinkled little cashew chips on my plate.

Ruth, sitting next to us, exclaimed enviously, "Wow, that's a nice gift." More discreetly, she added, "For this reason alone, I regret not being married today."

I put one of the pieces in my mouth and chewed it gently. It tasted delicious.

"I can see that someone is lucky," Frances said as she met us again.

Soon, as usual, Lillian and her children joined us. We had formed this habit as soon as we arrived at the Atap camp, as we called it. The dining hall was large and could hold many people, but we had no privacy. We often used this time to talk about positive things, to force ourselves to be less depressed.

On her way out, Norah left her friends for a moment and approached us. With a conspiratorial expression, she leaned over and whispered before heading off to another group, "The day after tomorrow, at dusk."

Suddenly my heart beat faster. The date of our first concert was set.

On 27 December 1943, all the prisoners were discreetly preparing to attend as singers or spectators in the event that was to take place outside. We were all afraid of the guards' reaction, but we were so excited by the prospect of something new that nothing could stop us. Dressed in the nicest clothes we could find, we moved slowly, in dispersed order, toward the rallying point. Some of us had even picked up a bit of lipstick from who knew where. Elsie, like many young women, had added a ribbon to her hair, of course to make her feel pretty.

Before we got into position, we started humming to warm up our voices. Once the whole choir was assembled, Norah quickly took her place in front of us, while Margaret joined us. The guards, who were not expecting anything, appeared stunned, but soon orders came in Japanese as the audience sat down on the floor in front of us.

The Japanese did not like large gatherings and were usually quick to intervene. Before things could get out of hand, Norah gave the signal. Each of us, with fear in our stomachs, expelled the notes we had been learning for weeks. Anticipating being beaten at every second, but unable to stop, we hummed for our lives, for the beauty of the music that rose from our throats and into the middle of the horror camp. It was our act of rebellion.

The imperial army had banned everything beautiful. They had starved us more and more every day, but our spirit was still free. Even from the depths of hell we could show our tormentors that they would never win.

Classical music rose in the air. To our surprise, the guards stopped dead in their tracks to listen to us. They seemed as charmed by the beautiful music as the spectators were. Some of them sat on the side until the end of the concert. When the last note was played, we embraced each other with pride at our achievement. That evening the soldiers sent us back to our huts with, it seemed to me, less harshness in their voices and more awareness of us as human beings.

❖

"Walk with me." Joan took my hand and wrapped it around her arm. For a few seconds I was back in Singapore, strolling in the park with my lover by my side. It was something we tried to do once a day at dusk to be together, alone.

The barbed wire in front of us quickly reminded me where we were. The illusion never lasted very long. Usually Joan did her best not to walk along the fence, so today I was surprised that she had dragged me there.

"Be patient with me. I want to show you something," she whispered in my ear, checking around us. "Watch the guards."

A little bewildered, I did as she asked while she leaned close to the fence and seemed to dig. We were well hidden from the guards' house, but this place was well known. When women wanted to get something from the Japanese, they came here. Usually they would exchange sex for cigarettes, food, or medicine. Some of us criticised them, and at first I was among them, until Joan showed me some tablets that one of them had acquired and given her.

With a small smile, Joan stood up. She looked down at her open hand, and I followed her gaze. A thin, dust-covered package was in her palm. She quickly hid it in her shirt.

"What is it?"

"Do you remember the cashew nuts?"

What a question! My best Christmas present ever. I nodded, unable to see what she was getting at.

"They were on the floor right there. When I recognised them, I bent and picked them up. I was intrigued because there are no cashew trees around here. As soon as I held them, someone threw a new one from the other side of the fence, and I saw an Indonesian man in the bushes. He pointed to this place under the barbed wire, and, looking around, I found a piece of paper."

Joan paused. The suspense was slowly killing me. Impatient, I shook her arm. She laughed.

"Come on. Let's go back. I don't want to draw attention to this place." Slowly, she started walking toward our hut.

"Tell me the rest. What was written on that piece of paper?"

"You're so curious, love."

"You're a tease, my beloved. Someday…"

"Yes. Someday." Her eyes on mine, Joan squeezed my hand hard before releasing it.

"And what did it say?"

"It said, 'What do you need'?"

I was so surprised that I stopped short. "In English?"

"Yes. In English."

"What did you do?"

She was taking the long way around to tell me everything, and I wanted to shake her until she spilled the beans. Her little smile told me that she was enjoying our verbal exchange.

"I immediately replied on the back of the message, of course, and asked for medication. After all, I am a doctor."

"And?" She let me stew for a few seconds. I nearly exploded.

"The answer is in that package."

"We have to open it!"

Again, Joan laughed. "Of course we'll open it. Where do you think we're going?"

With her chin she pointed to the hospital. I was so engrossed in her little story that I hadn't noticed where we were headed.

The nurse on duty was busy, and discreetly, so as not to disturb the patients, Joan led me into the doctor's office, just a modest space separated from the main room by bamboo. It was getting dark fast at this latitude, and only the light from the fence allowed us to see anything. Joan pulled the packet from her shirt and opened it. Pills, many pills, in small, folded papers. By candlelight Joan read the names on them: thiamine, yeast…

"Oh, my God, Evy. These will save so many people!" Immediately Joan called the nurse and gave her instructions. She took the yeast with us. "We have to give it to the cook tomorrow so she can put it in the food. It'll help us all fight beriberi."

"Who do you think they are?" I mentally speculated as we walked to our hut.

"I don't know, and I don't care, as long as they get us medicine. We will have to discreetly check the place every day or two. I'll ask for specific remedies and see what they can provide."

"We'll need help. Do you want me to tell Frances?"

Joan shook her head. "No, just you and me. I don't want to risk anyone trading information with the Japs for favours."

Surprised, I forced her to stop. "You don't think Frances…"

Joan looked sad.

"No, but I want to be careful. Some women will do anything for a little food. I'd rather nobody else knows about it but you and me. Let's hurry to our hut. We don't need the guards to punish us."

Joan was absolutely right. Margaret had told me about her misadventure when she found some crates thrown in the corner of the camp and took them to use as chairs for us. Someone had reported her to the sentries, and, in order to avoid punishment, she had to carry them back, asking for forgiveness in Japanese and slapping herself repeatedly to prove her good faith.

I was sweating. It was unusually hot and humid that day. Most of us were lying around doing nothing, and I would have stayed like them, but I had a duty, along with one of the nurses, Betty, and two other women, to clean the toilets. For hygienic reasons it had to be done, and we took turns with this disgusting task.

Twice a day, four of us had to pick up the faeces in the trenches and scrub the primitive toilets. As I walked toward the area, I saw a slightly wobbly woman coming toward me. A smile stretched my lips. Lillian was getting out of the clinic. She had been staying there for several weeks because of beriberi. Elsie, Leo, and Chester would be delighted. As soon as she reached me, I hugged her. She had become so frail and still seemed out of breath.

"How are you doing?"

"I'm better. Thanks to Joan. I don't know where she got the medicine, but it helped me a lot."

"She has her secrets. Don't tell anyone," I muttered.

Lillian replied with a slight nod and a hard look. "Are you going somewhere?"

"Toilet service," I replied glumly.

She winced. I laughed.

"I agree with you. But don't stay in the sun. Go into the shade. You're too weak. Let me help you." I took her arm and slowly led her to our hut.

Almost there, she forced me to stop. Her blue eyes filled with tears. "Can you promise me something, Evelyn?" Her speech was slurred by her breathlessness. She needed to lie down, yet she didn't move and continued to stare at me. I didn't like her serious look at all.

"I'm listening."

"When I'm dead, could you take care of my three children?" Lillian swallowed hard. Her lower lip trembled.

I refused to accept the worst. "You haven't left yet," I said in a harsh voice. "You're just out of the hospital. You're getting better."

She squeezed my forearm and pointed to the swelling in her legs. "You know as well as I do that with beriberi I won't live long without medication, and I don't think Joan has much left. I'm only on borrowed time. I know that."

I wanted to tell her that she was wrong, that everything would be all right, but, defeated, I lowered my head. Having seen many die with the disease, I knew she was right. Her condition was too serious.

"Your girlfriend can work miracles, but she's not God," she added in a low voice.

My girlfriend? So we weren't so discreet after all.

"Promise me you'll take care of them." Lillian tightened her grip on my arm, clearly desperate.

"I promise you. If anything happens to you, I'll help them until the war is over."

With sadness in her eyes, she stared at me and shook her head slightly. "I didn't express myself very well. My husband has died, as well as my parents and his own. We have no close family. I want you and Joan to take care of them, even after the war. Could you do that for me?"

The sun was very hot, and I was sweating profusely under my leaf hat. What she was asking...My heart beat faster. What a huge responsibility. I was only twenty-five and Joan twenty-seven. Could we parent one teenager and two children? I had to refuse. My throat tightened, and words struggled to come out.

"Your children are lovely and well behaved. It will be an honour to be their foster mother." What had I just said? I put my hand to my mouth, ready to refute my absurd words.

Crying, she took me in her arms. "Thank you, Evy, thank you. I will die in peace. You and Joan. Thank you very much."

Tears welled up in my eyes. What had I done? Without telling Joan?

"Come on. You need to get onto a bed. Maybe the war will be over soon, and we'll laugh about this conversation."

Between her tears, she smiled. "A bed? Where have you seen a bed in the last two years?"

Now that she was relieved, her sense of humour was back. Lillian was our clown, together with Ruth. She could make us laugh with one sentence.

Grace was good too, but with a bit more cynicism, maybe because she was older. Once inside, I led Lillian to her place. Leo was the first to spot her and rushed to embrace her. Soon all three of her children were in her arms. I ran away more than I left so that no one would notice my tears. The bathroom chore wouldn't do itself. It would take my mind off the sad subject.

As soon as I grabbed the bucket from Betty's hands, I began to sing "When I'm Gone." The other women, who had been waiting for this song, picked up the catchy chorus.

Chapter Eighteen

June 1944

Twilight. I loved that time of the afternoon when the sky turned all the colours of orange and purple to create a flamboyant picture. The water glided over my burning skin, washing away the sweat. What a wonderful feeling after this frustrating day. Yotaki, annoyed by who knows what, had forced us to do tenko for almost an hour in the morning, and then a big storm with impressive lightning and a downpour had poured uninterrupted streams all afternoon, leaving us wading in the mud.

It had been the same weather the week before, when Joan arrived at our hut, crying, and took me in her arms. Lillian had just died.

Telling the children about the loss of their mother was the hardest thing I had ever done. They were familiar with death now, but this was their mother, their last parent. They were orphans. All three of them had sobbed in our arms for a long time before Elsie dared to articulate their fears. Who would take care of them?

I explained to them the promise I had made to Lillian. Their grief too raw, Elsie and Leo just said thank you and hugged us some more.

I was alone in the hut that served as a bathroom. It didn't happen often, but tonight I needed to think, and I didn't rush to follow my friends to our home. I paused. When had the dilapidated bamboo hut become my home? I couldn't remember. We had been captive for two and a half years, and our health was deteriorating very fast now. The number of deaths was increasing. We were all so thin. I didn't know where we got the energy to wake up each morning, let alone how we managed to do our daily tasks. More sick, more dead, almost every day. A shallow grave to dig, often in the mud, with a body hastily covered. Yet laughter persisted, and caustic humour became the norm.

I could resist no longer and scratched my scalp furiously. The lice were driving me crazy. No one could escape them, but only a few people had dared to shave their heads. Three weeks earlier, Joan had taken the plunge, saying it was more practical and at least she didn't feel like a pantry anymore. We laughed. Every time I washed, I checked myself from every angle. Hygiene was of the utmost importance, even if no one would survive if the war went on much longer.

I was wiping myself with a piece of cloth when I heard a scrubbing sound. I froze. Was anyone else here with me? Suddenly the hut seemed too empty, the silence too deep. Even the frogs seemed to have fallen silent. I should have left with my friends.

I dried myself hurriedly and grabbed my clean dress. Footsteps behind me. Holding my clothes in front of me like a piece of armour, I turned around. A uniform. Lowering my head, I took a step back, muttering apologies in Japanese. Without speaking, the soldier hit me in the face. Stunned, I dropped my dress and fell hard to my knees. With one rough hand, he knocked me backward, forcing me to lie on my back. I tried to crawl away on the wet floor, screaming, but he pulled me to him with a firm grip. I was too weak to push him away. God knows I tried. His hand over my mouth to stop my yells, he lay on top of me. As he roughly pushed my legs apart, I closed my eyes and thought of my sweet Joan, of her infinite tenderness. Feeling like I was split in two, it seemed like what my body was undergoing wasn't happening to me. It all took place so fast that he was gone before I even realised it was over. Still groggy, I straightened up against the bamboo wall and, crying, hugged my knees. I couldn't feel anything, I couldn't move. Except for Joan, no one had ever touched me…until now.

"Evy?"

Joan's voice.

"Evy? Are you there?"

It was dark, and she couldn't see me, cowering in the corner. I cried her name, and she ran to me. Tenderly, she hugged me.

"Evy, what happened? Did you fall?" The tremor in her voice made me sob harder. "Talk to me."

At my silence and my tears, she panicked. My kind, cool-headed doctor was shaking. I couldn't stand it.

"I'm fine," I whispered. "He just attacked me and…raped me." Her arms tightened around my back. "Who?" she growled.

"It was too dark. I don't know. He hit me and then—"

"We have to talk to Captain Yotaki." Joan helped me to my feet.

"No. Did you see what they did to the women who accused a guard of raping them? They were punished until they withdrew the accusation. I don't want to be tied up under the hot sun for an offense one of those savages committed."

I clung to her desperately. We could say or do nothing against the soldiers of the great imperial army. Moaning because she was helpless, Joan embraced me, kissed my forehead. Even in the dark I could see she was crying.

"No, my love. Don't let them win. You and I are stronger than they are." As I said this, my inner strength began to return. "Help me clean myself up."

My busted lip was beginning to swell. Strangely, the taste of blood in my mouth had a calming effect.

"I couldn't even protect you from this infamy," Joan sobbed, overwhelmed. "You're the woman of my life and…"

"Stop it, Joan. Please."

Her guilt hurt me intensely. I couldn't let her go down that road, for it would destroy her and me.

"Look at me. We're luckier than most women here, because we're together. Most of them don't know if their husbands are dead or alive. Some have lost their children, and some have lost their mothers. You and I have a promise to keep." Determined to finish this conversation, I clenched my fists. "For us, for Lillian's children, we must fight and survive this misery. Now I have a split lip, and you are a doctor."

Even in the dark, without seeing them, I could feel Joan's eyes on me. I cradled her head in my hands and pressed her forehead to mine. "I'd like to kiss you to erase this horror, but my lip is too sore."

"I…"

I put the tip of my index finger to her mouth and wiped her tears with my fingertips. "Come on, Doc. Do what you do best. Heal me."

With Joan's help, in the darkness, I washed again and dressed quickly, being careful not to get any blood on my dress. We were walking toward the hospital when a guard, out of nowhere, stopped us.

"Why you outside?"

Taking off the rag, I showed him my split lip.

"Hospital."

Was he the soldier who had raped me? Was he waiting for me to come out? I shuddered. I couldn't start thinking like that—wondering, doubting.

"I'm the camp doctor. I have to fix her lip."

Even though she guessed he didn't understand, Joan used long sentences. She knew it annoyed the soldiers, and she did it on purpose.

As the seconds ticked away, I was sure he would refuse to let us go and send us back to our hut, but surprisingly he went with us, even using his lantern to light our way. After more than two years, I still couldn't understand the Japanese. They would treat us like dogs and beat us, and then the next day they would help us.

"*Arigatô gozaimasu. Thank you.*"

Thinking he was going to leave us, I thanked him profusely when we arrived at the hospital. To our surprise, he entered and waited, his lantern raised, for Joan to clean my lip. The nurse on duty, Vivian, the one who had witnessed the massacre on the beach, became very nervous when she saw the soldier, fear in her eyes. After that atrocity, she wouldn't trust any of them.

"More light, please," Joan asked, pulling the lantern with her hand. The guard complied.

"I'll have to put in some stitches. I'm sorry. You'll have a scar on your beautiful face." She whispered the last words.

"Will I look like a pirate?" I joked as she held the needle over the flame to sterilise it.

For the first time since she found me in the shower room, Joan smiled.

"I suppose so. It depends…whether I'm good enough or not. I don't have anything to anaesthetise it, though. It'll hurt."

"Will you kiss it after? To make the pain go away?"

Needle and thread ready, serious, she said, "Of course. You know I'll do anything to make my patient feel better."

I wanted to smile, but it was too painful. I lifted my head a little so she could begin. Oh! Just her fingers bringing the wound together hurt.

"Don't move."

I clenched my fists and gritted my teeth. Joan finished in less than a minute, and I could breathe again. Still silent, the guard escorted us back to our hut and left us there. I suspected that he was the one who had…why else help us?

As soon as we entered, Elsie, Leo, and Chester threw themselves into my arms. Elsie was crying.

"We were worried, Aunt Evy."

"What happened?" asked Frances.

"We heard the guard," Ruth said. "He didn't beat you, did he?"

"I slipped and fell in the shower room, that's all. I just split my lip, and Joan had to put some stitches in it. Now I'm very tired. So if you'll excuse me, I'd like to lie down."

Without waiting for more questions, I walked to my bunk carrying Chester, Elsie and Leo still clinging to me. Since their mother's death, they seemed afraid I would disappear too.

I could hear women whispering, but I didn't really care. After a few minutes, Joan came and lay down beside me. "How are you? Really?"

"I want you to shave my head tomorrow" was my only answer.

That night, for the first time since I boarded the ship leaving Singapore, I was unable to sing. Joan hugged me, and I wept silently.

"What did you say?"

I couldn't believe my ears. I leaned against the wobbly table to keep from falling over.

"You're pregnant," Joan whispered darkly.

KADYAN

I almost asked how, but I knew. We knew. I hadn't had my period in the last two years, so I'd forgotten about the horrible possibility after that night. I hadn't even dared to think about it.

I looked around to make sure no one could hear. We were alone in the examination room, but the bamboo walls and the piece of rag that served as a door weren't exactly soundproof. Scared, I grabbed Joan's hand. I wanted to scream but only had the strength to whisper, "What should I do?"

Her green eyes filled with tears, Joan shook her head. Neither of us had thought of this possible consequence. Panic was creeping into me.

"Your choices are limited," she said.

I interrupted her in a firm voice. "Our choices."

Surprise flashed across her face.

"You're not my doctor right now. You're my lover, my partner, for better or for worse, you once told me. Do you remember that? The worst is here. We have to make all the hard decisions together."

She sighed, pulled up a rickety stool, sat across from me, and clasped my hands in hers.

"The risks are too high for an abortion. You could die."

She gently kissed my knuckles, stroking the backs of my hands. Tears streamed down her beautiful face. She didn't dare talk about the other option: keeping it. We both knew that could also kill me. We were already so weak that carrying a pregnancy on top of that liability was very dangerous. Some women in my condition had survived, but others had not.

What were my options? Either way could kill me. But with an abortion, Joan was taking the risk of killing me herself, and I couldn't leave that to her. The baby was lost anyway, and I knew that a backstreet abortionist was operating in the camp. Squeezing her hands, I took a deep breath.

"Even if I go to full term, they'll kill the baby."

Every time a woman gave birth, the guards murdered the child. Since Muntok, apart from them, we had no men with us. I had wondered if that was why they removed the boys as soon as they reached puberty. That way they knew that the babies who were born were automatically their own bastard children, their sin visible to everyone. To kill them was to remove the fault, the proof, for the glorious imperial army could not have rapists in its ranks, could it?

"We could…"

Joan paused and shook her head. My Joan didn't doubt herself.

"What?"

"It's a stupid idea." She released my hands but sat still.

"I'm listening."

Joan looked around, then grimaced. She stood up and invited me to follow her outside. The conversation we were about to have needed no witnesses. We walked quickly away from everyone else. But even then, Joan was whispering. "What if you escaped? I could send a message to our friends outside, asking them to look after you."

"Are you crazy? If I escape, the Japanese will starve and beat you all. Did you see what happened at the beginning, when the Dutchwoman ran away? We had nothing to eat until they found her. They left her to die in the sun, tied to a pole. I wouldn't trade my life and the baby's for yours or any of the other captives. No way, Joan."

The blood was pounding so fast in my veins I felt like I might pass out.

"Keep your voice down," Joan pleaded. "I don't want to starve, at least not any faster than I am now." Determined, she stared at me. "What if you die and we bury you? The guards won't be looking for you, will they?"

I opened my mouth to object but closed it again. What had she said? Playing dead? Would that work? Each of us lost in thought, we moved forward in silence. I held her arm like a damsel with her beau. Without the barbed wire, the starvation, the mud…the illusion would have been perfect.

"Trust me. It would work if our friend on the outside takes care of you."

Joan was waiting for my answer and was getting impatient. The hospital had run out of medicine for several weeks, and many patients, including Lillian, hadn't been able to resist the beriberi.

"We haven't had any contact with them for four months, love. You don't think they were killed? There's Mild…"

"We have to try something. I can't let you die. And forget Mildred. No way am I leaving you in the hands of that woman."

Of course, my Joan had considered the abortionist's solution too. Apart from her dislike of the woman's illegal and dangerous activities, Joan hated the unscrupulous individual who charged for her services.

"I don't want to run away and leave you here with the children. I promised Lillian."

"We'll manage. If you're dead, you can't keep your promise anyway."

Joan looked desperate. She made argument after argument. Our silent walk had paid off. I wasn't going to win this game. I had to digest the news and consider the pros and cons at my leisure.

"If we make contact, I'll think about your proposal."

As she continued walking, Joan nodded. Knowing me, she also realized that she had not completely won the game yet. In a low voice, as if to reassure her, I hummed "We'll Meet Again" just for her.

Chapter Nineteen

4 November 1944

"The Japs are moving us tomorrow!" Grace entered the house, breathless.

"What? Again?" came several voices. "How do you know that?"

"These people are maniacs. Why do they make us run from camp to camp every twelve to eighteen months?"

"This one was already worse than the last one. What will the next one be like? A dumping ground?"

Everyone was talking at the same time. Fear gripped me. I grabbed Joan's hand and squeezed it hard. In my condition, I wasn't sure I could change to another camp, especially if I had to walk far. Without proper food for years, most of us had become very weak, so with a baby growing inside me, I felt that either it or I wouldn't survive another ordeal.

With no choice left, I had taken Frances and Ruth into my confidence about the rape, the baby, and our outside contacts. Frances had spoken to one of the cooks on my behalf. Knowing my condition, they were giving me a bit more food, but what for? As soon as my baby was born, the guards would kill it. That spoonful of rice, that piece of vegetable—that was food my companions didn't have. I felt guilty for literally taking the bread out of their mouths.

Someone had picked up Joan's message two weeks before, leaving a few tablets in exchange, but that was it. Since then, nothing.

"At least you're in luck. The Japanese will be too busy with this move to care about us. Let's go to the hospital. You're dying."

Shocked, I stared at Joan for a moment. "What are you talking about? I feel fine..." Suddenly I understood. Joan had returned to her original plan, an impossible one, in my opinion.

"We didn't get an answer from the outside," I argued. "We have to prepare better. You can't—"

"Tomorrow morning, you'll be dead and buried," Joan said in a low voice, but not so low that Ruth couldn't hear.

"You want to go through with this crazy plan? In her condition? Without knowing if anyone will take care of her on the outside? It's madness."

"Let's not talk here," Frances whispered.

Elsie watched the four of us walk out, but with a look I told her to stay with Chester. This was a discussion for adults.

Joan clenched her jaw. I knew that defiant look. She was ready to go into battle.

"We don't know where we're going or if there'll be another opportunity. If we want the baby to live, and especially if we want Evy to live, this is the only way. We have to get a message to the usual place right away so our friends can help Evelyn after we leave tomorrow."

Incredulous, her lips pursed, Ruth stared at Joan without saying anything. All along I had noticed a bit of jealousy between them about me and had always wondered if they would ever confront each other. Yet, to my astonishment, Ruth took a deep breath and nodded, leaving me stunned.

"Have you both lost your minds? If no one comes, what will she do? Survive alone in enemy territory? Five months pregnant?" Frances asked.

She was right. If no one was there to help me, what would I do? A little voice couldn't help but whisper in my ear, "But what if someone comes?" Hope is a nasty thing sometimes. It makes you take every risk in its name.

"If no one comes, I will go to a Japanese soldier. I will explain to him that I was not really dead, and that I woke up in my grave."

Within minutes I had convinced myself that this was the only acceptable solution. But leaving Joan and the children behind, not knowing if I would ever see them again, tore at my heart.

"Like this? And you think they'll welcome you back with a smile?"

With her arms flailing, Frances stared at us, her three friends. So far we had survived everything. Many had died, but we had stayed together, cheering each other up, stealing when possible to make things more bearable. She recognised the determination on our faces and sighed.

"How can I help?"

The shadow of a smile crossed Joan's lips. "Write a message for our friends outside and drop it off at the usual place before sunset. Ruth will help you keep an eye on the guards. Evelyn will start playing sick now so that she can spend the night in hospital and die there in the morning."

"Japs," I whispered as a soldier approached us.

I took two steps forward and, pressing my stomach, fell to my knees. Joan came to my aid and pretended to examine me.

"We have to get her to hospital," she ordered in her doctor's voice.

Ruth rushed over to help support me. As soon as the guard left, I smiled at them. "Now we have a good excuse for the hospital. Frances, write the message and put it up. Let's go."

"I'll do it, but I still think you're all fools," Frances said.

This was no time to back down. I took a deep breath and stared at her with determination. "This is my decision, Frances." I was so scared I didn't know how my voice could stay steady.

Seeing Joan helping me, the two nurses on duty immediately came over to give us a hand, but Joan shook her head, and they returned to their patients. Some were shaking with fever, dying slowly from beriberi or diarrhoea. The moaning was constant.

Joan refused to leave me. We talked, cried in each other's arms most of the night.

"Promise me you'll survive at all costs," I said, sniffling as dawn approached. "The baby and I will need you after the war."

She placed a soft kiss on my lips. The last one.

"I promise, if you promise to take care of yourself too. You are my life. Without you I am nothing. We will survive, and we will meet again when the war is over."

Hope swelled in my heart for a moment. I had to believe that this nightmare would soon end and that we could live together again.

"Where?"

She thought for a few seconds.

"The Raffles. Two p.m. I'll wait for you every day until you come."

Neither of us asked what would happen if one of us didn't show up. Neither of us dared to even think about it. We were soul mates. In this life or the next, we would be together again. Nothing could change that. We would survive. There was no other way. Torn, I hugged her to me until dawn.

A hand gently shook my shoulder. I must have finally fallen asleep at the end of the night.

"It's time," Joan whispered in my ear. "You're dead, and we have to bury you before they move us. I can already hear activity nearby. We have to hurry. Dawn is almost here."

True to my role, I didn't move a muscle. When Ruth and Frances arrived, Joan asked, "Any news of our friends?"

"None," Ruth replied, "but the paper is gone."

The pressure in my chest eased a little. At least they had received the message. Frances brought the bamboo stretcher, while Joan put a cloth over my head. Together they carefully laid me on it.

Joan knelt beside me. "You have to stay completely still. You understand me. Breathe slowly without moving your chest."

A second later, the stretcher was lifted and moved. As soon as they left the hospital, I heard "*Tomatte!*"

The voice of a guard telling them to stop. My heart missed a beat. Of course they didn't want us wandering around the camp as they were trying to organise us for departure. We hadn't thought about that.

"My friend is dead. I want to bury her," Joan said.

"No. Today, go another camp. All women inside." As usual, the guard shouted, sounding angry.

"Please. I can't let her rot inside the hospital. Please." Joan pleaded, refusing to back down.

Another voice spoke not far away in Japanese. I thought I recognised the sergeant in charge. He was not a bad man, and I hoped he would allow my friends to bury me. I was terrified, but I couldn't allow myself to shake or cry, so I concentrated on staying still, very still.

"Please, Sergeant. We'll make this quick."

Frances's voice. Barking orders. The stretcher moved again.

"*Arigato*, sergeant."

Ruth's voice.

"*Hayaku! Hayaku!*"

He was rushing them. My friends sped up as much as they could. I felt guilty for exhausting them further. I was ready to get up, but I thought of the punishment we would all receive. Before I knew it, the stretcher was roughly placed on the ground, and my friends slowly dug in it with coconut shells. I could hear the Japanese guard mumbling to himself, shouting at them from time to time to go faster. When they grabbed me and laid me on the ground, I kept my eyes closed. Immediately the cloth was removed, and a thin layer of earth began to cover me, leaving only my face free.

"Breathe through the bamboo, my love, and be still until tonight," Joan whispered through her teeth. A hard piece of bamboo was slipped between my lips as the earth covered my face. "I love you, Evelyn. Take care of yourself."

My heart bled for not being able to respond or react to my beloved. As soon as they had finished, I heard the soldier scold them and push them unceremoniously toward the camp. I had been very lucky. He was in a hurry and hadn't even checked their work. Their footsteps disappeared, and suddenly the loneliness hit me so hard that I wanted to get up and join them. Focusing on my unborn baby and Joan, I forced myself to stay still. Dawn was just coming. The birds were calling, and I remembered their cries when I was waiting for my beloved in the botanic gardens. To distract myself, I let the anecdotes rise in my memory. Most were about Joan, but some were about England with my sister and family. Would I ever see Dorothy again? The hours passed. The earth that covered me protected me in part from the heat.

When I felt a slight chill, I knew that the worst of my waiting was behind me. However, dusk still seemed far away, and my composure was tested to the limit. After a while I couldn't take it anymore. Slowly I shook my head and opened my eyes. Big grey clouds covered the sky. It was still daylight. I cursed my impatience for a moment. If anyone was around, I was sure they would see me. I was so afraid that I listened to the slightest noise while remaining motionless. Birds, insects, the sounds of nature, nothing else. No voices, no screams. Had they all left in one day? Moving five hundred people so quickly? Was it possible? To go where?

I was dying of thirst. Before departing, Ruth had whispered that she was leaving water nearby. This information obsessed me, and my thirst increased by the second. To forget, I sang in my head for me, just for me, to ward off my fears, my thirst. I didn't feel hunger anymore after those months of starvation.

The sky was getting darker and darker. The clouds were growing bigger, showing every shade of grey almost to black. Night wouldn't come for an hour, but I couldn't wait any longer. With the rain, everything would turn to mud, and I would leave too many tracks. I had to get out now. Slowly, I rolled to the side, the earth flowing around me. I tried to build up the grave into a mound so no one would suspect the deception. Out of the corner of my eye, I saw the tin that Ruth had put down and eagerly moistened my parched lips with my tongue. I crawled a few feet and grabbed the precious can to drink what was left after so many hours in the sun. Taking the now-empty can with me, I made sure no one was watching before dragging myself to the bushes bordering the cemetery. No sooner had I settled down than the rain began to fall. First a few heavy drops, then more and more heavily. I was as thirsty as ever, so I opened my mouth to catch some water before thinking of using leaves to direct the water into the container as we did in the camp. Soon the can was full, and I could happily drink my fill.

A flash of lightning lit up the sky just before a tremendous thunderclap filled my ears. I was soaked, but I was free. I didn't know what tomorrow would bring, yet at that moment nothing mattered. Would someone come? If not, what would I do? Could I hide in the jungle and survive until the war was over? Were we even close to the end? We had no news in the camp, only false information from the Japanese from time to time. Each time they told us they were winning, but was it true? Could they really be? I refused to believe it. Not with the Americans in the conflict.

Because of the storm, night fell even more suddenly than usual. The clouds were becoming fewer, and the stars were slowly coming out. Doubt crept into my mind. Even if no one came to get me, I couldn't surrender. I had decided to leave the place when I heard a slight whistling sound. My heart raced. For me? Slowly I made a frog sound. A minute later, a bent man came up to me.

"Come. Silence."

From his accent, I knew he was a native, not an Englishman as I had expected. But he was there, and I trusted him. What choice did I have?

From the start, he was very careful. We were near Palembang, and Japanese soldiers were everywhere. For an endless time, we walked, stopped, crawled, walked. When he finally straightened up and continued quickly, but normally, I knew that the most dangerous part of our journey was behind us. After what seemed like hours, he stopped in the middle of the jungle. I was out of breath and so tired I almost collapsed on the path.

"You rest and eat, *ibu*—madam," he said softly.

"Eat? Eat what?"

It was dark, but I could see something in his hand. Like an animal, I pounced on the food. The coconut pieces were hard, but they were full of energy. Every time I finished swallowing, he gave me another one. I couldn't make out his face in the dark, but I could tell he was smiling.

"You, papaya, *ibu*?" he asked in his limited vocabulary.

I explained in my poor Indonesian that I liked papaya. I had learned a few words in Singapore and some in the camps, but my conversation was very basic. However, he seemed satisfied with my answer and gave me half of the papaya he had just cut with his jungle knife. My taste buds were in heaven. The taste was sublime and sweet. Tears welled up. For the first time in I don't know how many months, I felt full. What a wonderful sensation.

After a few minutes, he helped me up and continued along the small path.

I asked him where we were going, but his answer in his language was too complicated for me to understand. Only a few words made sense to me: madam, go, and tomorrow. Did he mean we would arrive tomorrow? Regularly, he stopped to make me eat and drink. Always coconut, some bananas, and even a handful of cashew nuts. I was exhausted but in food heaven.

Once again, he took another path as the jungle closed in on us. I couldn't remember how many times we had changed direction. I assumed he wanted to cover his tracks and escape the Japanese patrols. The wet ground was very slippery, and I had fallen many times, but each time the man helped me. Gentle words in broken English or in his own language encouraged me to take another step. Each time, his kindness brought tears to my eyes. Like in a zombie film, I moved forward thinking of Joan, the children, and my friends at the camp. For them, I took another step and another.

"*Rumah!*"

Home? I looked up, trying to follow the pointing finger. My guide was smiling. The word filled my heart with joy. Home. Had we arrived? I was so tired I didn't dare to hope. Yet a new energy flowed through my veins. My poor clothes, already in bad shape before I escaped, now looked like muddy rags. But I didn't care. I straightened my back to take those last few steps, within my head the music of "I Got Rhythm."

Chapter Twenty

The little bamboo house was well hidden in the jungle foliage, and I could see it only when I was very close. As soon as we came into view, two more men, with rifles on their shoulders, appeared after a high-pitched whistle imitating a bird. The door of the hut opened, and a white man stepped out onto the threshold. Moving closer, I couldn't believe my eyes.

"Albert!"

If I hadn't been so tired, I would have run to him. He was alive. And free.

Although he seemed surprised that I knew his first name, he didn't recognise me. I was much thinner than I had been then, wearing rags and sporting a shaved head. I could understand.

"I am Evelyn Baker. We were in the lifeboat together..." Because of my emotion, my memory failed me for a moment. "A long time ago. You had gone to get bananas."

Immediately I saw in his blue eyes that he remembered. He smiled. "You were with..."

"Ruth. We wanted to cook breakfast. I'm so glad you're alive. Have you been hiding ever since?"

He shook his head and held up his hand, ending my questions.

"We'll talk, but come in. You must be exhausted. The way here is not easy."

He spoke a few words to his men in their language. The hut was very spartan, but in the middle of the jungle I couldn't expect

KADYAN

anything else. Still, it was better than what we'd had in the camp. Everything was made of bamboo: two tables, two benches, a bed, and a stool. A radio and some papers were placed on the side table. A second door was at the back.

"Please sit down. It's been a long journey, and you need to rest. One of my men will bring us food and boiling water for tea."

Albert pointed to one of the benches and sat on the other, facing me.

Food? Tea? Tears welled up in my eyes. In a trembling voice, I explained quietly. "They starve us in the camps. So many people have died from minor illnesses, beriberi, septicaemia, malaria. We have nothing. Even the Dutchwomen, who came with a few possessions at the beginning, now have no more than we do. You helped us a lot with your medicines, you know. When we didn't hear from you...we were afraid you had been captured or killed."

"We had to move to another place. The Japanese were on our trail. It took us a while to get organized again and receive supplies. I'm sorry we couldn't help all the camps more. The military are suffering a lot, you know, and they are more difficult to reach than the civilians. The Japanese treat them..."

Albert paused. He clenched his jaw. I so understood his sense of helplessness. He took a long breath before continuing. "I got your last message, but I didn't know what to do so I asked for instructions..."

Avoiding my gaze, Albert stared at the radio without adding anything, and I understood.

"They said no, didn't they? They told you not to help me."

He nodded in shame. I frowned in bewilderment.

"How come someone was there?"

Before he could explain, one of his men entered with a tin pot and a small bowl of food. He smiled at me, put it on the table, and left. The aroma was wonderful. I hadn't smelled such an delightful smell for so long. My mouth was watering.

"What's the date today?"

"Five November 1944. Eat, rest. We'll have time to talk later. I'll tell you my story, and you can tell me yours."

He gently pushed the bowl in front of me. Tears filled my eyes as I grabbed the spoon and tasted the grilled meat on skewers and the sweet potatoes boiled in coconut milk. The taste, the flavour…The tears were streaming down my cheeks.

The same man returned with a bucket of water and clothes under his arm. He went to the back door and put everything inside.

"It's for you," Albert said, "but finish eating quietly, and then you can wash up and change your clothes. After what you've been through, you must eat little, but often."

Shamelessly I scraped every last crumb from my bowl and licked it clean. It was my first real meal in two and a half years.

"Rest on my bed until the boys build you one. I have to talk to them, so the cabin is yours."

I was so tired I could hardly stand, but the thought of cleaning myself up and getting decent, fresh clothes helped me find the strength. Fed and clean, I was in heaven.

Eating, drinking, and sleeping were my main tasks for two days. I listened to Albert talking in Indonesian with his men, watched people with guns or supplies come and go. Everything seemed so unreal. I couldn't believe that I was saved.

On the morning of the third day, I got up fresh and ready from my new bed with its mosquito net. Albert had apologised that I had to share the hut with him and put up with his snoring, because for practical reasons it was not possible to build me a separate hut. I brushed off his excuses, especially as Lutfi, the man who had brought me my first meal, had stretched a string in front of my space and hung up a sarong to give me some privacy.

Sitting in front of the radio with a cup of tea in his hand, Albert smiled at me as soon as I pushed back the cloth.

"Hello, Evelyn. Tea is ready."

With a twinkle in his eye, Albert pointed to the kettle on the table and the plate of *nasi lemak,* a local breakfast dish. I salivated when I saw the mound of fragrant rice cooked in coconut milk. I refrained from pouncing on the food, however, and helped myself to the hot drink while sitting on the bench. As I began to eat, Albert sat down opposite me and grinned.

"You can't stay here. We will evacuate you to Malaysia. From there, the special services will try to send you to India, then maybe home."

I felt overwhelmed. *To India? To Europe? But why?*

"I don't want to go back to England. Before I left the camp, I made an appointment with my friends to meet them in Singapore after the war ends. And it will soon be over, won't it?"

Albert sighed and ran a hand through his short hair.

"We are winning on all fronts, that's true. The Allied forces landed in France on the 6th of June this year, pushing back the German armies. The Americans and Australians are doing the same in the Pacific, retaking island after island. But no one knows when the war will be over, Evelyn. England is a safe place at the moment."

As he watched my reaction, he added tea to my cup.

I didn't want to lie to him, so I told everything. "I'm pregnant by one of those bastards. I was raped five months ago. They kill the babies as soon as they are born to hide their guilt. My friends helped me escape. They took huge risks, but they had to stay in the camp. I can't abandon them. I can't leave."

Albert's eyes widened. I was so skinny that my pregnancy wasn't noticeable. For him, it would be all the more reason to evacuate me as soon as possible. How could I make him understand how I felt?

"I left them knowing what could happen to them. It's the worst thing I've ever had to do. I don't even know if I will see them again. Most women who give birth die. They are too weak. When we heard that they were moving us again, urged by my friends, I decided to take a chance, even after not receiving any response from you. I had no other option…"

Clearly touched by the sob in my voice, Albert looked at the liquid in his cup for a long moment and then sighed before confessing. "My superior didn't give me permission to help you, but I assumed you were desperate to escape, so I let one of my men watch your camp. You can't have your baby here. It's not a safe place. There is no doctor. Anyway, we'll soon move to another location. We've been here too long already. The Japanese know that, and they send patrols all the time."

Patrols? I swallowed the sip I'd just taken. Could they capture me again? A pure nightmare. Instantly, guilt came over me. Here I was, with a full belly and a cup of tea in my hand while they were... Joan was...I didn't want to think about it. I couldn't.

"You never told me what you did after we were captured," I asked suddenly. Albert looked surprised.

"I know." Clearly troubled, he looked down.

"I waited in the bushes while the soldiers seized you and killed my fellow soldiers. After a few days, I met two other survivors. A fisherman helped us, and we finally left for India, but I couldn't stay there. I didn't want to leave you and the others behind, so I asked to be trained and to come back to gather information. What I saw..."

He wiped his eyes before continuing. "I felt so helpless. I couldn't do anything—just report or deliver medicine. So when some of the prisoners escaped, against my orders, I told my men to help them as much as possible. But you're the first woman to make a successful escape. I'm glad it's you, you know."

I smiled shyly. "I'm glad it's me too. You can use me here or elsewhere, but don't send me away."

Albert seemed reluctant so, despite my ragged appearance, I played up my feminine charms a little. "I could try to make you a real English pudding."

Suddenly he laughed out loud. "You'll do anything to stay, won't you? Even corruption..."

"I'm a survivor. Don't forget that fact."

Teasing him felt really good. He swallowed the last of his tea quickly, but suddenly his face froze into a sad mask.

"I know it will be difficult for you, but I need to learn everything about the camps. I've already reported as many details as I can, but from the outside it's not the same. Can you help me? Do you know the names of some of the women who died? Or those of the survivors? I could at least radio this information so we're prepared when the armistice is signed."

My heart sank with pain. For a moment I closed my eyes and took a deep breath.

"If you give me food again, I'll sing the sixty-two names of the women and children who died in my camp from April '42 until I escaped."

From the way he looked at me, I could almost guess his thoughts. I smiled sadly.

"I'm not crazy. If you remember, I'm a singer. I wanted to learn all the names of the dead women to pay tribute to them, and I used a song for this project because it was easier."

Without waiting, I started to sing: "Elizabeth Roberts, Beatrice Telling, Regina Anthony…"

"Oh my God! Stop. I have to write them down."

Albert rushed to get some paper, and I began to sing again. As I had used a lullaby, the tempo was easy and slow enough for him. Nevertheless, I had to repeat my song three times. At the end I couldn't hold back my tears. Every time I sang a name, in my mind I saw a face or a grave. I didn't know them all because some of them weren't in Irenelaan, but in the Berhardlaan camp during the year and five months we were there, yet all of us had suffered together. We weren't soldiers, but in my heart we were sisters in arms.

"I'm sorry," I said, wiping away my tears. "I can't believe I'm here with food, and my friends are still there with nothing. Do you know where they sent them?"

"I'm still waiting for confirmation, but they put them on the boats going downstream, so I guess the women and children went back to Muntok. It seems they're still following the men by a few months. I'll know more when my guys get back here with information."

Muntok. I remembered that infernal transfer of several hours.

"They'll all die of starvation or malaria over there. We have no medicine, only what you gave us."

Oh, my Joan. I hid my face in my hands to help conceal the depth of my grief.

Albert looked at me blankly for a long moment. Then he rubbed his chin.

"One thing I don't understand. One of my men saw Red Cross parcels arrive in the camps, and I have it on good authority that they contain food and medicine."

I suddenly raised my head, my mouth open, astonished.

"But…but we never received anything." Rage erupted inside me. Indignation overwhelmed me. "They stole them? We were starving, eating bugs or whatever, and they didn't distribute the packages they got for us?"

The overflow of emotions threatened to choke me. In tears, I dropped to the bench like a dead weight. Unable to help me, Albert turned away, obviously trying to give me some privacy. Now that I was free, I had to find the strength to think about the future. I cried for my sweet Joan, the children, and my friends. I had to believe that we would meet again. We had a date, and I would keep my promise.

"I don't want to go to India," I suddenly cried, lifting my head.

My tears were gone. A new resolve filled me. I knew what I had to do. "I want to go to Malaysia, though."

Albert opened his mouth, most likely to argue.

"No. I promised my friends I would meet them in Singapore after the war, and I intend to keep that promise. I will wait for them there, whatever it takes."

Albert seemed a little sceptical but listened to what I had to say.

"I know it sounds crazy, but I believe in promises. Those who lost hope or faith died first. Joan, Ruth, Frances are my friends. Without them I wouldn't have survived. I want to see them again. There are also three children for whom I am responsible. I swore to their dying mother I would take care of them. So please let me stay in Malaysia. They must have freedom fighters there like here."

"I understand better the reasons for your stubbornness. I'll see what I can do. The best thing for you to do now is to continue to rest and regain your strength."

"I can help you…let me help you. I know you'll have to arrange my transport to Malaysia, and that will take time. In the meantime, I don't want to be a burden."

I could almost see his mind spinning. He had an idea but wasn't ready to spit it out yet. "Let me think about it, okay?"

"I could also make tea or cook, maintain this hut and your fighters' huts, if you tell me where to get water." I gave a sweet, innocent smile, which I knew the men weren't immune to. "I'm also a nurse, by the way."

Albert burst out laughing. Like Joan, he laughed with his shoulders. Such a reaction was the only thing that kept our spirits up in the camp.

"You know how to plead your case," said Albert.

"I was a professional singer. Part of my job was to charm men." I ran a hand through my extremely short hair. "But I've lost some of my appeal, I suppose."

"Don't worry. It'll grow back, and you're as charming as ever."

Although he tried to hide it, Albert gave a blush at his bold statement.

"Thank you. That's very kind of you. So, do you have a job to offer me?"

Albert laughed again. "Rest again today, and we'll talk seriously tomorrow."

❖

It was getting dark, and the mosquitoes were biting, but I sat outside and listened to the noise around me. Since arriving in Singapore years before, I had learned that the rain forest is never quiet. Day or night, with insects or other animals, there was no silence. Here, deep in the Sumatran jungle, the noise surprised me even more. Only a few bursts of voices from the men's hut covered it from time to time.

The rain had finally stopped, and I took a deep breath. I was so far from England, but that didn't matter. Even after all I had endured, my heart told me that I belonged here, in this part of the world, with my baby, Joan, and the children. Our survival was imperative; anything less seemed unimaginable.

"You should go back inside," Albert said gently, sitting down beside me.

He handed me a cup of tea. I took a sip and savoured the sweetness. "I like the smell after the rain and the little sounds that come up slowly. It makes a kind of soothing music."

For a long time, we sat silently side by side until we finished our drink. Albert got up but didn't leave immediately. "I need someone to look after the radio while I go with my men on a mission. If you want to learn…"

I understood the gift he had just given me. I was filled with joy.

"Good night, Albert, and thank you."

"Don't stay up too late. Good night, Evelyn."

For the first time in months, at a slower tempo than Gracie Field, I sang "Wish Me Luck as You Wave Me Good-bye" with all the strength in my voice. A promise to all those who were waiting to be saved.

CHAPTER TWENTY-ONE

Alone in the hut, I was reviewing Albert's instructions when suddenly the door opened and startled me.

"Quick, *ibu*. The Japanese are coming."

Robet, the man who had saved me, ran to the radio to pack it up.

Following Albert's instructions in case of emergency, I grabbed the papers and maps before running to retrieve my bag containing the few possessions I had acquired over the past three weeks. One last look back and I quietly followed Robet outside. The little path he led me down was well marked. Why he was taking it? The Japanese would soon guess that we had escaped that way. When I reached the river, I understood. My guide didn't cross it, but he went upstream, taking care not to leave any traces. Robet knew what he was doing. He was a native of the country and could move through the jungle even at night. After a long time, he gave me a break so I could catch my breath.

"Robet, wait." I asked where Albert was. He must not fall into the hands of the Japanese.

I didn't understand his answer and shook my head, so he slowly explained that he was in another house and that we had to be on our way again. I smiled. At first, I had tried to teach him English, but he had taught me Indonesian instead. He was right. It was more useful here.

After a few hours of sustained walking, I became tired. A devouring hunger gnawed at my stomach. I had been able to forget it for more than two years, but after those weeks of sublime meals, it roared back. The few short breaks to quench my thirst at a liana or a tiny spring weren't enough for me to recover. Yet, with fear as my fuel, I moved forward without complaining. Every time I thought about giving up, I remembered the camp, and my legs regained their strength.

At the bend of a hill, I was surprised to come across a small village hidden in the middle of the jungle. Children were running around staring at me. A few women sat on wooden benches and just looked at us. No one spoke as we walked through it. My presence, the presence of a white woman, had apparently rendered them all speechless.

A bamboo hut outside the village, hidden in the lush vegetation, came into view. I pushed open the door and entered. At the sight of Albert, smoking his pipe, I sighed with relief.

"You've escaped. That's fine. It was a close call. We stayed there too long. My fault. I'm sorry."

Warm with confusion, I realised that he had waited for me to regain my strength, and it had almost cost me my freedom. "Don't do that again. If we have to move, we move. I'm part of your group. Don't treat me any differently than you treat your men."

"But you're not—"

I shook my head. "Don't do that, Albert. Above all, don't do that. After what I've been through, I can handle anything but being sent back there. Next time, don't think about me. Think about us."

Seeming a little ashamed, he nodded and smiled before pointing to a plate of food. This guy knew how to smooth my feathers. I was angry, tired, but most of all I was hungry. The food in my mouth was a sweet nectar. The more I ate, the less my bones seemed to protrude, and my belly became rounder by the day. The baby was growing fast, and so were all my ambivalent feelings about it.

While I ate my fill, Robet was quietly setting up the radio in its new location. In a way, his presence was reassuring. For as long as I had known him, he had acted like a guardian angel—discreet but almost always within earshot. He and Ajin had taken turns watching the camp. Day after day they had seen us die of hunger and disease. I knew from the way he treated me that helping me had helped him too. Saving me was saving his soul.

❖

Placing my hands on the small of my back, I stood up. Washing clothes on my knees was deadly for those muscles. Almost every day the women of the village scrubbed their clothes in the river, and sometimes I joined them. The initial shyness had quickly vanished in the face of their natural curiosity. Laughter had punctuated my apprenticeship as a linen maid, but especially my use of their language. They all seemed to find it very funny to hear me talk.

I wore the same clothes as they did—a sarong, a matching tunic, and fibre sandals. These clothes were easy to clean and put on. I discovered the infinite uses of the sarong: clothing, blanket, towel, baby carrier…Very practical. The village midwife had given me valuable advice for my pregnancy as well as herbs to brew a potion she said was good for the baby. Maybe for the baby, but it tasted so bad that the first time I drank it I almost spat it out. All the women present had laughed, at least those who knew how bad it was. Nevertheless, the midwife kept pushing me to swallow it every night. What could I do but comply?

During these weeks, I had become quite good with the radio. We had to report every four days at a different time. Albert would write the scripts, and I would code them and send them. At certain predefined times, I would stay tuned for any message that might be intended for us.

Despite having my headphones on, I heard the door slam open. Albert, Robet, Ajin, and Lutfi were back. I smiled at them and held up a finger, asking for some silence while I listened and wrote in the little notebook.

"How did it go?" I asked after the radio was turned off.

Albert lit his pipe with a sigh of relief. Three days without smoking so as not to be detected couldn't have been easy.

"No problem. I'll write down the message with the information we got. You can pass it on."

With an affectionate gesture, he patted Lutfi on the back. "This boy, with his cat-like eyes, saved the day. A night patrol almost caught us, but thanks to him, we had time to dive into the bushes."

While they ate, they were all laughing and talking at the same time, like boisterous teenagers. Concentrating, I decoded the last message. Emotion overwhelmed me.

"The Americans landed in Luzon on the 9th of January."

I felt so drunk with joy it was as if I were floating. Albert consulted his maps and grumbled but didn't comment. I understood. The battle for the recapture of the Philippines wasn't yet won.

Robert grabbed a bottle of *tuak*, a palm wine of his own making, and they all toasted the Allies' success without hesitation. I settled for a coffee with palm sugar and a cinnamon stick that I used as a spoon. As usual, the men were friendly toward me, very personable, especially Robet and Lutfi. They smiled a lot and tried to talk to me despite the language barrier. Ajin was different. He kept everything to himself. I could often feel his dark eyes following me when he thought I wasn't looking. What was he thinking? Was it because of the half-Japanese baby growing in my belly?

The laughter and talk of the imperial army soon to be thrown into the sea helped me out of my troubled feelings. Like all of us, I was following the recapture island by island. The American troops were winning in the Pacific, but progress was very slow. The Japanese soldiers were fighting like demons, never surrendering, and the casualties were heavy. When would our soldiers get here?

At night, as usual, I was alone with Albert. After two months of living together, even though we had to move three times in the meantime, we had established a routine of having a cup of tea with a bit of conversation before bed. Tonight, however, I could feel something different.

"What?" I asked. "Say what you have to say, Albert."

Stunned, he stared at me, shaking his head gently. "You women…I don't know how you do it. You can always tell when men have something on their mind."

Amused, I chuckled but didn't let him turn the conversation away. "What's up?"

"We've got you a boat to Malaysia. You'll leave tomorrow with Robet and Ajin. It'll take three or four days' walk to reach the coast. I'll send a message by radio for someone to pick you up on arrival."

He spoke in a monotone. Still in shock, I remained silent. Leaving Sumatra meant leaving Joan. Even if we couldn't be together, I was close enough to her. But Malaysia? That would be across the Straits of Malacca, closer to Singapore. Closer to our reunion place.

"Evelyn? You know you can't stay here. We've been over this. Yet, believe me, I appreciate your presence."

Albert's voice was soft. Even though I hadn't admitted it to him, he must have sensed that I had left someone I loved in the camp.

"Yes, I know...It's just that...I don't know, I got used to being with you and your men. I dread going into the unknown again."

He smiled mysteriously.

"What?"

"After what you've been through and how you escaped, nothing will scare you anymore, Evelyn, although crossing the Straits of Malacca won't be fun. Many Japanese warships are patrolling the area, and you'll have to hide in a pirate ship."

I jumped to my feet. "A what?"

"You heard me right. Along with the fishermen, they're the only ones who dare to cross. You may even have to change boats several times."

Pirates? Anxiety overwhelmed me. In a dull voice, I asked the question that was terrifying me. "What's to stop them from selling me to the Japanese?"

"We're winning the war, and they know it. Besides, I've promised weapons if you get there safely. Don't worry. Robet will accompany you to the ship, and Ajin will go with you to Malaysia."

Albert handed me a strong cup of tea.

"Trust me, Evelyn. I wouldn't use them if I thought they'd betray me. You can't stay here anymore. The resistance is more organized in Malaysia. It'll be easier for the baby."

Yes, there was that. This thing moving in my belly. I had really mixed feelings about it. It was my baby, but it was also his. Yet I tried as hard as I could to forget its presence, chased away the images of his hands on me, of its...no, I had to not think of that, ever again. I sighed. Oh, Joan, how I miss you—your wisdom, your love.

❖

Ajin whispered urgently in Indonesian as he stopped next to me. He asked me to go downstairs quickly, but I didn't know why. The night seemed peaceful, and the sea wasn't too rough. After two days of playing hide-and-seek with the Japanese along the coast of Sumatra, I was glad to get some fresh air on deck. The smell in the hold was horrible. I resisted, but Ajin grabbed my arm and, despite my protests, pulled me along.

"A Japanese ship is coming. We have to hide...quickly."

I was so stunned to hear him speak English that I stumbled and almost fell face-first into the bilge. He held me back.

"You speak English? Why do you—"

"No more questions. We have to keep quiet. Everyone risks their lives if you are discovered."

We were not yet hidden when a flash of light flooded the deck. Fear immediately ran up my spine, grabbing my insides. Ajin pushed me ruthlessly into a narrow space between the fish baskets and, holding his weapon ready, pressed himself against me. A crewman came down after us and piled traps on top of us. He said only a short sentence in a low voice, and I recognised the phrase for "No talking."

Overcome with fear, I tried to breathe slowly. The stench seeping into my nostrils was making me nauseous, and I let out a soft, throaty noise. Ajin's hand came to rest on my mouth as the sound of boots on deck echoed. The Indonesian crew walked barefoot. Terror flooded me. I grabbed Ajin's hand and knotted my fingers with his. The Japanese were on board. The darkness, the smell, the water dripping from the basket above us—all was forgotten. Seconds became minutes, then hours. Motionless, barely breathing, I listened. The footsteps on the deck came down the ladder to check the cargo. A small light reflected between the gaps. I tightened my grip on Ajin's finger. The Japanese would find us, I was sure. I wanted to groan with fear. The idea of returning to a camp revolted me. Death seemed preferable. Joan's sweet face appeared before my eyes. Her mouth opened slowly, and she said, "See you in Singapore" repeatedly. I clung to the thought and closed my eyes. The sound of boots faded away. I heard the man climb back up the ladder, walk on deck, and then silence, followed by the rumble of machinery.

"Breathe," said a soft voice in my ear. "They've gone. The crew will release us when it's safe."

Time passed slowly in the cramped space. Before being in the camps, I couldn't have stayed there more than five minutes, but now I could have spent days without complaining. Fortunately, perhaps after an hour, the captain himself came to free us. He and Ajin immediately exchanged a few sentences in a thick accent, of which I didn't understand a word.

"Come. We are at the rendezvous point and will soon change boats," Ajin explained after the captain had left.

"Really?"

On the deck, breathing in the fresh air once more, I turned to Ajin. The darkness of the night prevented me from seeing his face. I didn't know if this transfer was planned. No one had told me anything before I boarded. I felt like a sack of potatoes being carried from one place to another.

"I suppose so. We have no choice."

If he wanted to reassure me, he failed.

"Why didn't you tell me that you spoke English perfectly?"

"I never told Albert. He would have felt betrayed if I had revealed this information when you arrived."

I didn't understand. "Why hide it?"

"I'm a communist, and you and Albert are imperialist colonisers. I want independence for my country, and working with the British is not what I would have chosen—"

"But you've changed your mind." I cut him off before he could develop his political discourse.

"The Japs are worse than you. I am of Chinese descent. What they did to my people in China, Singapore, and other cities, I will never forgive them for."

He was silent for a moment. I tried to peer into the darkness around us but could see nothing. How these crewmen could find their way across the ocean was beyond my comprehension.

"I heard you singing in Singapore, you know," he whispered uncertainly.

"You heard me? Where?"

"At the Blue Tiger, a few weeks before Singapore fell. You were the highlight of the show. I was with my brother. He loved your voice and wanted me to hear you. You were wearing a beautiful dark blue dress with a yellow ribbon."

I remembered the dress, a gift from Joan. Late 1941. A lifetime ago.

"Where is your brother now?"

"Dead. Killed by those bastards," he spat. "Him, his family, my parents, all dead because they were Chinese. I joined the resistance after that."

I heard the pain and despair in his words and hugged him. He stiffened, but I refused to let go.

"We have all lost a lot in this war. Look at me. Where is my beautiful dress? My hair? How do I look with a bun in the oven by the same bastards who killed your family? But you know what? We will survive because we have to. To free my friends, to honour all the dead."

I felt him relax and cry on my shoulder. I didn't really feel like singing that night, but my promise to Joan was stronger than my reluctance, and, thinking of her, I hummed "Night and Day."

Chapter Twenty-two

I thanked the captain in Indonesian as I disembarked his boat on two rickety planks. I didn't trust the rotten wood, but I would have faced worse to get off that boat. I was so happy to be back on the ground after four days on board that I didn't notice at first that nothing but jungle surrounded us.

"Now we have to walk," said Ajin.

I laughed nervously. He frowned. I laughed some more.

"Why am I not surprised? Of course we're going to walk. How could I expect anything else?"

Ajin's eyes reflected his incomprehension. The sarcasm of my comments escaped him. With my hand I pointed around us to the tall, green trees with their roots running through the muddy soil. A huge mangrove. "But where do you want to walk? There is no path."

Going deeper into the green hell would be our downfall.

"The guy waiting for us there will guide us."

Ajin pointed to a huge mangrove tree. At its foot, a native sat on his heels, waiting calmly.

How did he get here? How did he know we would arrive at this place? Apart from his sarong, the man was naked. He watched us with his dark eyes as we walked toward him. Only his hand holding a cigarette was moving. Ajin exchanged a few words without making him budge. Evidently, time didn't matter to him. Had he been here for hours, for days? Once he finished his cigarette, and only then, did he decide to get up. Without a word, he picked up the machete on the ground and began to cut a path. Ajin invited me to follow him as he stepped behind me.

Every hour, the man stopped so we could drink and rest. As I had surmised from the beginning, no paths existed, and he had to cut one with his machete when the vines became too dense. During the breaks, I was pleased to have learned to sit on my heels in the camps. The posture, although uncomfortable after a while, avoided putting one's buttocks on anything.

Our guide chose most of our stops well, without leeches. I hated those creatures. They were like mosquitoes—bloodsuckers wanting to feed on us. Sometimes, lying in the darkness, I imagined an army of those little vampires with big teeth drinking all my blood while the Japs laughed and cheered. My nights had been filled with terrible nightmares since I left the camp. Most of the time Joan was there, but I couldn't reach her, or she didn't recognise me. Each time I woke up crying.

Our guide got up and, with a sharp blow, cut the stems of a beautiful plant with huge thorns to create a narrow passage.

Walk, take a break, eat, walk, take a break, walk, eat, sleep... How many days? Four days? More? My legs were aching. My back... was it a back or an ocean of pain? I used all the methods indicated by the midwife I had met on Sumatra, but nothing helped. In one of the small villages I passed through, one of the women took pity on me and gave me a large bark belt to tighten around my belly to support the baby. The relief was immediate. But the fatigue only increased. Even though I had been free and eating properly for three months, I hadn't regained all my strength. I shook my head wearily. Who was I kidding? I had never made this kind of effort before. Strolling in a park, yes, but walking for days in the deep jungle, no.

"He told me we'd arrive tonight. We're almost there, Evelyn."

Ajin tried to encourage me as much as he could. Now that we knew a little more about each other, I found him reserved but friendly, despite his piercing gaze that sometimes made me uncomfortable. What a strange man.

When I saw the huts, I was relieved. We had arrived! That evening, Ajin explained that we would stay there for only a few days to rest. Our real destination was farther away.

In all, it took us two weeks and three different guides to reach the main camp, deep in the Malaysian jungle. Soldiers, mostly Chinese, heavily armed, patrolled the area.

"Who are you? What are you doing here?" exclaimed someone with a strong Scottish accent behind me.

I didn't have time to answer before he shouted, "Lieutenant, come and see."

"What is it, Sergeant?" asked an Englishman emerging from the nearest hut.

"A woman, sir."

The sergeant pointed at me, their manner amusing me. It gave me great pleasure to hear my language spoken in accents so different from my own.

The officer frowned in puzzlement.

"I see it's a woman, Sergeant. We've had several here. Why did you...?"

The sergeant moved closer.

"Her eyes, sir. She's not a native."

I was wearing local clothes, I had dyed my blond hair black, but I couldn't hide the colour of my eyes. I gave them my best smile.

"Hello, gentlemen. I am Evelyn Baker. Pleased to meet you."

The officer was so surprised he took a step back and blushed. Ajin and the guide had left, perhaps thinking that this was a matter for the English.

"May I sit down? I've been walking for a fortnight to get here, and I must admit I'm tired."

Reminded of his manners, or lack of them, the officer rushed to my side to offer me his arm and pointed to his hut.

"I am Lieutenant Stephen Aftertown. Sorry for the welcome, but what are you doing here?"

"I've just come from Sumatra. Petty Officer Albert Johnson must have told you I was coming, right?"

"I got a message that a man named Baker was joining us..." The officer paused and stared at me. His Adam's apple bobbed back and forth a few times. "What name did you give?"

"Evelyn Baker."

"You're a woman!" the lieutenant snapped.

"Last I heard."

Instinctively, I stroked my bulging belly. He followed my gesture with wide, astonished eyes as the Scotsman stopped beside us. "Sergeant Archer. Nice to meet you, ma'am."

The medium-sized but very muscular man held out his hand to me. His amused look surprised me. He might have been handsome had it not been for the ugly scar above his left eye.

"Would you like me to make some tea, Lieutenant?"

"Oh, tea, and perhaps something to eat, sir? That would be wonderful," I replied quickly. "I'm starving."

Regaining some composure, though still obviously annoyed, the lieutenant invited me into the hut.

"Come in and sit down. I don't know why you're here, but this is no place for a British woman, especially not in your condition. As you have seen, we have only bamboo and palm-leaf huts and not the slightest facility for a lady."

Stunned by his words, I stared at him and laughed. The sergeant returned with tea and a plate of biscuits. To my dismay, my laughter turned to tears. "Sorry, hormones," I said.

I grabbed a biscuit between two fingers and smelled it for a long time. It was a real English biscuit.

"Do you know how long it's been since I've seen a biscuit like this? Three years. I spent two years, seven months, and two weeks in a prison camp in Sumatra, where the Japanese starved us slowly, where we had no medicine, and our huts took on water with every rain. Don't tell me you have nothing for me here."

My hand shook as I bit into the biscuit. It wasn't as crisp as it should have been because of the dampness, but it tasted like home. I half closed my eyes.

Surely embarrassed, the two men looked at me as I drank, ate, and talked about the fall of Singapore, the shipwreck, the camps, my escape. A long silence followed my story.

"I am here to have my baby in a safe place, but I also want to help the war effort. My friends are still there, and the sooner this war is over, the sooner they will be free. Albert trained me in radio, but I'm also a nurse…and a singer."

I smiled at the last word.

"A singer?"

"Yes, Lieutenant, but I think a nurse might be more interesting for you."

"I should agree with you, but sometimes, when morale is low, a little entertainment would be welcome."

The sergeant smiled appreciatively. He was missing a tooth. This middle-aged man was certainly no rookie when it came to combat, whereas the officer looked like a fresh-from-school kid.

Finally, after much hesitation, clearly seeing that his choices were limited, the lieutenant extended his hand.

"Welcome to the camp. There is a room in the hospital for you to use. It's small, it needs cleaning, but you'll be alone."

Somewhere in the Malaysian jungle, 14 March 1945

Barbara was sleeping peacefully in my arms. She was a slightly scrawny baby, but to me she was beautiful and almost never cried. Was it because she was wrapped tightly in a sarong? I had been surprised to get her back like that just after she was born. Only her face was visible, her arms, body, and legs well confined. The women in the village had explained to me that the baby needed to feel safe after nine months of being compressed in my womb. Too much space was stressing her out. I knew nothing about babies, so I let the Malays teach me. Since giving birth ten days earlier, I had enjoyed being among women—laughing, cooking, talking about things other than war. I felt almost normal. My hair was growing, and I dyed it with henna at least once a week.

As I hummed a lullaby, Atit, the village midwife, rushed into the hut. We all looked at her with concern. She pointed at me and spoke quickly.

The Japanese were coming. I had to get away. My heart missed a beat. Before I knew it, she took my baby from my arms and showed me the door. As if by a miracle, Ajin was there, waiting for me.

"Come quickly, Evelyn. They'll be here in a few minutes."

I stood up and turned to Atit, who crouched among the women, Barbara lying beside her.

"My baby…"

"The Japanese won't even notice her with her black hair and complexion, but you…"

I finished the sentence for him. Up close, I could never pass for a Malay, and if I were captured here, the whole village would be executed.

Without waiting another second, Ajin grabbed my hand and dragged me off into the forest. The deep jungle immediately engulfed us. Walking carefully so as not to break an ankle between the roots and vines, I let myself be guided through the uneven, mossy terrain. It was so easy to get lost in this kind of nature. The sun couldn't penetrate the thick branches, and the paths, except for those used regularly, were almost nonexistent. The Japanese wouldn't find us in here.

"Stop," I ordered him. "There's no point in going any farther. I'd rather stay close by."

"There's a nicer place, not too far away, where we can sit. You don't want to wait for hours standing with the leeches, do you?"

His lips stretched into a wide smile as he pointed to my feet. Those vile little beasts were already coming toward us. I shuddered. "Lead the way," I said hastily, wincing.

Ajin struggled to hold back a laugh that turned into a chuckle.

Our relationship had changed a lot in the last few weeks, and he was getting more and more comfortable with me. Other than Aftertown and Archer, he was the only one who knew my past. To the others, I was just Nurse Evelyn, who could sing and comfort them.

When, after five minutes, Ajin signalled a halt, I looked around. He had been right to bring us here. The place was beautiful, with large mossy rocks on which to sit comfortably. No leeches.

"If the Japs stay too long, we'll go straight to the camp," Ajin said.

"I'm not leaving my daughter behind."

Stunned by my vehement repartee, Ajin stared at me silently. I could easily read in his eyes what he thought of the little bastard. Finally, he relaxed. "We'll wait."

I sighed with relief. Despite her father and the way Barbara had been conceived, she was still my daughter.

Even within five hundred yards of the village, we could hear nothing, yet I was almost certain that the sound of gunfire would reach us if the Japs started firing.

I made small talk with Ajin to pass the time.

"I haven't seen you since Barbara was born."

"We had an operation near Johor."

"Was it successful?"

"Yes and no." He sighed.

I frowned. He hesitated but then continued. "We blew up an ammunition dump. But we had two dead and three wounded, which is a high price to pay."

Wounded? Alarmed, I stood up immediately.

"You could have told me that they needed my services at the camp."

"I was on my way here when the lookouts reported a Japanese patrol. But there's no hurry. It's not too serious. The men have walked this far. They can wait a few more hours."

I sat back down, and we fell into silence again, each of us in our own thoughts. Were Joan and the children, Ruth and Frances, still alive? What about little Barbara? What to do with her? Sometimes having a baby to look after was too much for me. I had been feeling overwhelmed for ten days. But then I thought about Lillian's children. I had given my word. I now had four youngsters to take care of. With Joan. If they lived. If Joan accepted Barbara. What if she didn't?

"I told them your kid was my brother's, you know," Ajin whispered without looking at me.

My mouth dropped open, and I stared at him uncomprehendingly. "Why did you do that?"

"It will be easier for her." He hesitated.

"Barbara," I said.

"Barbara…Once the war is over, it will be easier for both of you if she's half Chinese rather than half Japanese. You could tell the story of Lam, your lover, who died fighting for a just cause. People will respect you for that."

Ajin was right. That story would be much nicer than the ugly truth. Could I lie to everyone, even my daughter? However, I sensed something else in his words. I looked into his eyes and waited. He looked down.

"I...could marry you. The baby...Barbara will need a father."

He stared at me expectantly. My heart pounding, my cheeks red, I shook my head gently.

"I can't do it. I'm sorry." My voice broke. I felt trapped. His proposal was nothing like James's so long ago. No, it was more personal. "You're a good man, Ajin, quite cute. If things were different, I might consider it, but my heart belongs to someone else."

He simply nodded and murmured between his lips, "The doctor."

I stiffened. How did he know about Joan? With a sad smile, he said, "Don't worry. Your secret is safe with me. Lam...Lam was like you, and I loved my big brother."

That explained a lot. But I wanted to understand.

"How?"

"I spent days observing the camps, noting the habits of the guards, studying you all to decide how to make contact."

"The cashew nuts? That was you?"

Obviously proud of himself, he straightened up and puffed out his chest. "Yes, a good idea, right?"

I remembered fondly the moment when Joan had placed them on top of the infamous food. Tears filled my eyes. "My best Christmas dinner ever. Thank you."

Ajin didn't answer. For many minutes I listened to understand what was going on around us. The shrill sound of a large insect not far away almost prevented me from thinking and covered everything else. A Japanese regiment could have approached without us hearing it.

Finally, Ajin stood up. "I'll go check if they've left. Wait here."

He climbed down from the rock he was sitting on, took two steps, hesitated, then came back to me. "If you find yourself alone after the war is over, my proposal will still be valid."

Without waiting for an answer, with his rifle in his hand, he set off toward the village.

What he had implied…I couldn't, I didn't want to think about it. He was reviving my worst nightmare. No, Joan would survive, and we would end up at the Raffles as planned. Even with Barbara, my life would be too empty without her. My heart would stop beating. Clutching my legs, I rocked back and forth, humming the lullaby "Cinderella, Stay in My Arms" that I used to sing to Barbara.

Chapter Twenty-three

Southern Malaysia, 15 August 1945

Out of breath, Muhammed ran into the small field hospital. His smile indicated good news. "The war is over!"

Stunned, I stared at him without reacting. Repeating his words in his language, even though I now understood them well, I thought I had translated them wrong. The war? Over? My strength failed me, and I fell heavily onto the stool.

"Are you sure?"

"Yes, Puan. Tuan Stephen sent me to tell you that the Americans have dropped two big bombs on Japan. Many dead there. They surrendered yesterday."

Muhammed took care to speak slowly so I could understand him. No mistake, the war was over. My heart immediately went out to Joan, the children, and my friends. Were they still alive? When would I see them again? I had to go to Singapore. I had an appointment to keep. I looked around and winced. There were still wounded who needed my attention, and I had to wait for information on how to proceed.

"Thank you for the wonderful news. Go tell the others quickly."

In a flash, Muhammed left to take the good word to the neighbouring village.

My daughter slept peacefully in her bamboo cradle. Nothing disturbed her sleep. Most of the time, she was a quiet baby, except when she threw monumental tantrums. I had asked the midwife who had delivered Barbara for advice, but she'd shrugged. That was the way it was, and I had to deal with it.

I had fully recovered my strength and weight from before the camps, but with an almost six-month-old child, I had to make some sort of arrangements to reach Singapore. My mind racing, I forced myself to focus on the two patients in the field hospital. One was on the mend and would be leaving the next day, but the other needed more care than I could give him. The war was over, and he might die. I went to him. His blue eyes searched my face. Not speaking Malay, he hadn't understood the news. He had been in Malaysia for only a week before he was wounded in battle and brought to me. I gently took his hand.

"Clarence, the war is over. We have won."

He smiled at me and began to sob. He was so young. To cheer him up I sang "Somewhere Over the Rainbow." He had told me that he loved that song from *The Wizard of Oz*. His tears dried up.

"The war is over, and I'm going to die here," he whispered.

His lips trembled. Finishing the song, determined, I answered him. "I won't let you die. I promise you that."

❖

On 5 September 1945, British troops finally landed in Singapore. Clarence, though still weak, sat next to me by the radio in the middle of the village listening to the event. Barbara, on Ajin's lap, was playing with a big red flower and chirping. Stephen and his men were celebrating with a glass of *tuak*.

Since Japan had surrendered three weeks earlier, I had asked the same thing every day, but Stephen's answer had always been the same. The country wasn't yet safe. I understood that moving around when the Japanese army was still in control was risky, but with our troops now in Singapore, I was determined to leave the camp.

During the past ten months, my body had healed, but I suffered mentally from Joan's absence and the memories that returned to haunt me at the most unexpected times. The other day, as I was washing, I had almost felt as if she were with me, her soft voice whispering words of love in my ear. Alone, I had sobbed for my beloved abandoned somewhere on Sumatra.

I had a date at the Raffles, and nothing and no one would stop me from getting there.

"Now that our troops are here, I must go to Singapore. With or without your help," I said to Stephen, the lieutenant.

A little tipsy, he looked at me and sighed as he took another sip of alcohol.

"You're a persistent woman, Evelyn. I'll give you that."

I couldn't stand his condescending tone. Who did he think he was?

"And I'm a good nurse and a good singer. I have business in Singapore to attend to now that the war has been over for three weeks. Maybe you enjoyed playing soldiers, but I've been putting my life on hold for three and a half years waiting for this moment."

He stared at me hard and then winced. He clearly didn't like for a woman to stand up to him. Yet I could see in his eyes that he wouldn't stop me this time. Excitement overcame me.

"We have orders to leave for Johor tomorrow. You can come with us. From there, I'll find you a transport to Singapore," he conceded in a pasty voice.

My heart was pounding, and I almost jumped into the air with happiness. From Johor I would swim to Singapore if necessary. But I refrained from telling him what I thought. I just smiled and controlled my joy and nervousness. Singapore. Tomorrow I might be standing in front of the Raffles.

My sometimes fussy six-month-old daughter was a charming little princess the whole way. She loved everyone's attention. Sergeant Archer, the Scotsman, had died a few days before the end of the war, and apart from Stephen and Ajin, no one knew the truth about her real father. The story Ajin had created had won me sympathy, not only from the soldiers, but also from the people around us. I was a little ashamed to lie, but it was better that way. I didn't want Barbara to be an outcast. I hoped that Joan and my friends would never see her like that.

"If it's all right with you, Lieutenant, I'll go with Evelyn to Singapore," Ajin suddenly offered as we arrived in Johor. "My family lives…used to live in Singapore. I need to know if anyone survived."

Stephen relaxed. He wasn't happy about leaving me, the poor defenceless woman, on my own, but if Ajin went with me…I could have strangled him for that kind of attitude. He had always been the gentleman, with gentlemanly ideas about women, and I had to fight him all the time about everything I did. A woman shouldn't do this, a woman shouldn't say that…But leaving me with Ajin, an educated man, suited his mentality.

Two days later, I was finally standing in front of the Raffles, my baby balanced on my right hip, tied against me with an old cloth. With my dyed hair, blouse, and sarong, I fit in perfectly with the local population. All the British soldiers and civilians ignored me. To them I was as invisible as a maid.

"Are you sure you want to go there? You could stay in my family's house."

"You don't even know if it's still standing. Go find what's left of your family, Ajin. I'll stay here so you know where to find us if you need me."

One of the officers in Johor had told me that a sorting system had been set up at the Raffles for survivors of the internment camps. It was perfect. I would have accommodations and information at my meeting point with Joan. Leaving Ajin behind, I took a deep breath and walked straight to the main door, the one I had used as a customer the few times I had a drink at the bar.

"You can't go in there, madam." A British soldier blocked my entry by standing in front of me.

Stunned, I locked eyes with him and asked, "Why? Why can't I go in there, soldier?"

Hearing my accent, he flinched. "This is not the servants' entrance," he added in a voice that was now uncertain.

Clearly, doubt was slowly creeping into his mind. Between my accent, my attitude, and, I suspected, the colour of my eyes, he hesitated. "You…you are…British?"

"Yes, I am. And I would like to see the person in charge of the survivors of the civilian camps."

He blushed, then swallowed hard, obviously confused by his mistake. Stammering an apology, he hurriedly pointed to the small office not far from the entrance. In the hall, nurses, soldiers, and civilians were passing each other, meeting and talking. The few survivors I could see were so thin. They looked around, seeming a little surprised to be there. Had Joan already arrived? Was I late? Anxiety knotting my insides, on the verge of tears, I knocked on the open office door. A man in his forties, in uniform, looked up from his files and smiled at me, but all I could think of was Joan. My fears were rising, threatening to overwhelm me.

"Miss, I'm Captain Edward Davington. How can I help you?"

The deep voice of the officer in charge snapped me out of my waking nightmare. I stood in the doorway without moving. Tightening my grip around my daughter's back, I stood up. I would not lack courage now that I had reached my goal.

"My name is Evelyn Baker. I was taken prisoner by the Japanese during the fall of Singapore until November 1944, when I escaped from the Palembang camp. I spent several weeks with Petty Officer Albert Johnson in Sumatra before being extracted to Malaysia. There, I cared for the wounded for several months under the command of Lieutenant Stephen Aftertown. I am now looking for the survivors from my camp. This is important."

The captain gazed at me for a long time in clear astonishment. I had spoken very quickly for fear of being interrupted. I assumed that my local clothes and dyed hair didn't help him recognise a British woman. I had also blackened my skin with plant juice. He remained silent as he stared at me. I had no time to lose, now that my goal was almost in reach. I wanted to know. I asked insistently, "Have you heard from my fellow inmates, Captain? I know that after I left, they were sent to Muntok in November 1944."

My harsh voice made him react.

"Please come in and sit down, ma'am. I need to find my lists."

He opened a few drawers before pulling out a folder with a bundle of papers in it. I smiled to myself. Frances would have loved to have all this paper for her diary. I remembered the sheets we had managed to steal for her. After a moment he looked up.

"Evelyn Baker. Yes, you're on the Japanese list from Palembang New Atap camp, but it says 'Deceased.'"

Always benevolent, the captain never took his eyes off me. He clearly wanted to understand. I sighed. I should have known he would want more details. When did I become so naive? To prove a point, I placed a letter from Stephen on his desk, stating my role in his organisation. My discharge paper, he laughingly called it.

Captain Davington took it and read it before handing it back to me and urging me to explain further. I suppressed my impatience.

"I faked my death to escape. My friends buried me the day they were transferred to Muntok."

I told him about the waiting, being buried in my grave, the walk through the jungle, the list of the dead sung to Albert. When he heard all this, he looked for a sheet of paper in another file.

"Yes. It says here that you provided this information and also the facts about the Australian nurses. Major Tebbutt confirmed your report the day before yesterday as soon as he was released from Changi."

I understood that he had to verify my identity, but I was beginning to lose patience.

He must have recognised my mood. Finally making a decision, he explained, clearly a little embarrassed. "The prisoners were moved from Muntok in April, but we don't know where yet. We are trying to get information, but the Japanese won't say anything."

All my hopes died. The survivors I had seen at the Raffles weren't part of my group. I felt like screaming. I held back and, in a broken voice, asked, "What? But why? Why won't they say anything?"

"From what I know, it seems that they are afraid that we will find many of them dead. It's the same with the male civilians. We don't know exactly where they are, but we are actively looking for them. Don't worry. Paratroopers were sent to Sumatra at the end of August."

What? Not to worry? I couldn't believe my ears.

"Is that all you have to say? My friends risked their lives to save my baby and me, and I shouldn't worry! Do you know what it feels like to starve? To see women and children starving to death? Dying from beriberi or malaria because there is no medicine and only a handful of rice a day to eat? So I will worry, and you will see me here every day until I get an answer!" I had tears in my eyes, but I refused to let them fall.

Red with embarrassment, he gathered his papers nervously. "Where are you staying? Here?"

"I suppose so. I just arrived in Singapore today, and I have no money. I have to check with the bank, but I don't know if my account is still active. I was told that I could reside here for a while."

"That's right. Let me find you a bed. We are grouping together the women and children who have arrived from the camps and are still in good health. The hotel has arranged some rooms, and you can eat free at the restaurant."

Gratefully, I nodded as he called a uniformed soldier from another office.

"Please follow Lieutenant Wilson. She'll help you get settled."

"Thank you, Captain," I said with a serious expression before adding firmly, "I'll see you tomorrow."

"Yes. I'll be expecting your visit, ma'am. I will certainly have some questions to ask you and perhaps some news."

As I went with Lieutenant Wilson, I saw his eyes following Barbara, who was still sleeping peacefully. I suspected what he would ask me. He had probably been counting down the months. I didn't mind his questions, even the embarrassing ones, if I got the information I was looking for in return. Ever since I had arrived in Singapore, Joan had been constantly on my mind. She and the children. The authorities had to find them, and soon…before it was too late.

Chapter Twenty-four

Singapore, 9 September 1945

"Hello, Captain," I said as I entered his office.

He was on the phone and held up a finger while he shuffled through his papers. His smile as he hung up made my heart beat faster.

"Major Jacob's paratroopers found them on September 7th. Sorry. I didn't know earlier. One of the Japanese officers finally confessed. The women and men are in two separate camps on the Belalau plantation in central Sumatra. We've already dropped food and medicine with a unit of soldiers and a doctor. I expect to hear from them soon."

"Do you have any names?"

My voice failed me. I was both eager and so afraid to know that I was trembling inside. She had to be alive. The captain consulted the paper he had just picked up.

"Not yet. I know only that several hundred survived. I'll have more information by tomorrow or in the next few days."

How could I make it until tomorrow? I was imagining the worst, and it was almost unbearable.

"I can't give you what I don't have," he added gently, obviously noticing my distress. "In the meantime, can you testify to what you have experienced?"

I shook my head and, without saying a word, left his office and headed for the bar. I needed a pick-me-up, something strong. They had found them, and I had to wait for the list that would make me happy or desperate. I drank two glasses of whiskey before my nerves calmed down a bit. I had never been in the habit of drinking, and the alcohol went straight to my head. Fortunately, I had left Barbara in the care of one of my roommates.

Waiting was so difficult. To soothe the alcohol burn, I asked the waiter for some water. The musical notes that reached my ears made me smile. A man was playing a relaxing melody on the piano. He looked a bit like James, except he was wearing a uniform and didn't play as well. For the first time since I arrived here, I felt an irresistible urge to sing, a part of me wanting to feel alive again to forget this hellish wait.

When he started to perform "Minnie the Moocher," I joined him onstage singing. Surprised, he stared at me for several seconds, missing a few notes, but continued to play. One song chased the other. I could barely hear the opening notes before my memory picked up the words. A large crowd surrounded us, clapping wildly after each song. A wave of intense happiness washed over me. I was wearing clothes donated by charity, but it didn't matter. Inside, for the first time in months, I felt alive. The prisoners had been found. Joan would be among them. I believed it. Anything else was simply unthinkable.

❖

Every day I went to see Captain Davington to check if he had received the list, but he shook his head when he saw me.

At first he asked me questions about the camps, and I answered them as fully as possible. Most of them were about the guards and their actions. He noted my answers but never commented on them, never judged my decision to escape to save my baby. I was grateful for this response. A kind of mutual respect developed between us.

The room I shared with the survivors was perfect. They came from other camps: Singapore, Java... We all had children, and we took turns looking after them. Barbara was the youngest. When they asked about the father, I told them that he was dead and that he was Chinese, so that suspicions would be laid to rest. They were sympathetic, yet none of us detailed our war-time experiences. No one wanted to talk about the horror, only about the future.

The captain also asked me about my family in England. At the mention of my sister, he suggested that I be evacuated to London. I flatly refused.

I didn't tell him that I had already started sending long letters to Dorothy describing the camps, my escape, and Barbara. Writing the events of those earlier years down on blank paper helped me put my story in perspective and seemed to drive my demons away slightly. I had been sleeping better lately, although images of Joan, hungry and calling me, haunted me.

Ajin came to see me and invited me to eat outside the hotel. This diversion gave me some relief from my dark thoughts.

"How are you, Evelyn? Any news?"

"The army found them in Belalau, but the list of survivors hasn't arrived. I don't understand what's taking so long. Making a list is easy, isn't it?"

At his sad expression, I pushed away my anger, which was useless and wouldn't make things go any faster. "What about you? How are you?"

"I'm leaving Singapore tomorrow. There's nothing left for me here. My house is destroyed, my family is dead. I have a distant cousin in Kuala Lumpur. I'll go and see if he's still alive."

My heart bled for him. I put my hand on his.

"You are my friend, Ajin. Never forget that."

He nodded and smiled. No, he wouldn't forget that, any more than I would forget his proposal. Our friendship had been sealed in blood, pain, and tears. It was indestructible.

"Will you stay in Singapore? Even if Joan..."

Under my burning gaze, he didn't continue.

"My life is here. What would I do in England? I finally have access to my bank account, but I need to find a job soon."

"The Blue Tiger is closed. I walked past it the other day. The Japanese didn't spare the area."

"I'll still check to see if Andy and Mr. Chee survived. Who knows? Maybe I can get some of my stuff back."

❖

"I have a list," Captain Davington immediately exclaimed as I walked through his door.

He was all smiles, a triumphant look on his face. I stopped dead in front of his desk and, my heart pounding in terror, waited. He had the list. Was this my salvation or my downfall? What would I do if Joan was dead, and Elsie, and Leo, and Chester or Ruth, Frances? I looked at the piece of paper in his outstretched hand, so scared I couldn't move. My bottom lip was trembling.

The officer was a kind man, very compassionate. In the last few days, he had seen so much misery, and he knew how to deal with it. He helped me to a chair and offered me a glass of water.

"Give me their names. I'll check for you."

I couldn't find my voice. My main instrument was failing me. I drank some more of the cool liquid and, closing my eyes, blew out, "Joan Cliver."

I waited. He was turning page after page, going backward. Why was he taking so long? If he couldn't find her name, it could mean only one thing.

"Yes, she's here. Who else do you want to know about?"

I opened my eyes quickly. What had he said? She was on the list? My heart beat so fast I had to put my hand on my chest to stop it from coming out. The captain was staring at me.

"Are you all right?"

No. I felt like I wasn't, but I went on. "Ruth Carter, Frances McBride."

More waiting, more turning of papers. Joan was alive. The love of my life had survived.

"Yes. They're on the list too. Any other names?"

Joy flooded my heart. Hope...

"Lillian's three children. Elsie, Leo, and Chester...Ravensburg. I don't know how to spell it. She died four months before I escaped, and Joan and I promised to look after her children."

"The daughter, Elsie, is here. But I don't see the two boys. How old were they?"

"Leo is about twelve, I suppose. Chester was younger...eight?"

Captain Davington took another piece of paper.

"The list of men," he explained. "Let's see. Leo Ravensburg. He's here, but I don't see a Chester. I'm sorry, ma'am. Perhaps the list is still incomplete."

From the sadness in his eyes, I knew he was lying. Chester was dead, but Joan was alive. I felt selfish. I asked for more names like Norah and Margaret, though in the end only one was important to me. I was overcome with grief when he couldn't find Margaret. The dynamic woman who had motivated so many of us, especially with our choir, had unfortunately passed away. But Joan was alive.

"Thank you, Captain. Do you know when they'll get here?"

He sighed and rubbed the back of his neck.

"It's complicated. It seems they're far off the beaten track, on an old plantation in the middle of the jungle. We're trying to send trucks there, because they're too weak to walk. But they have food and medicine now. There's even a doctor. Don't worry."

So I had to be patient again. But this time I knew she was alive. A huge weight lifted from my shoulders. The lump I had carried in my chest since leaving the camp began to shrink.

"Is there any way to get a message across?"

"I could try, but I can't promise anything."

"I understand. Could you tell Joan that Evelyn and her baby are here and waiting for her as planned? My friend helped me escape, but she doesn't know if I succeeded. Good news is very important to keep morale up."

I gave him a pleading look. I had to provide Joan with some motivation to survive the next few days. They were alive, but weak. Every ounce of hope counted.

Finally, the captain understood. "I will do my best."

I don't know why, but the refrain of the song "Jingle Bells" sprang to mind.

Chapter Twenty-five

Singapore, 19 September 1945

When I heard of a plane from Lahat carrying surviving Australian nurses and the sickest women, hope flooded me. Finally, after all those days of waiting, things were beginning to happen. I knew these Australian nurses, whose story had spread, as had word of the massacre on Radji Beach, which had made some newspapers' headlines. Was Vivian among the survivors of the camp? I hoped so. She had to be. Her testimony was too important. And Wilma, their leader? She seemed so tough sometimes, yet underneath the shell, like most of them, she had a tender heart.

Leaving Barbara in the care of a woman in my bedroom, I rushed to Captain Davington's office to confirm that the passengers on the plane were from Belalau. The door was locked. Damn it! I felt frantic, out of control, ready to explode. I had to know. I ran out of the hotel and flagged down a rickshaw to get to the hospital as quickly as possible. The young Chinese man who pulled me through the congested streets of Singapore was strong, and we arrived soon. I rushed straight to the admissions office.

"Hello. How can I help you, ma'am?" asked a pleasant-faced young Englishwoman.

"I heard that some prisoners from the Belalau camp arrived today. Where are they?"

My request clearly surprised the woman, and her expression closed immediately. She shook her head in refusal. Before she could open her mouth, I replied. "They are my friends. I was with them in Palembang but managed to escape, thanks to them. I need...to see them."

If I had to plead or beg, I would. However, judging by the secretary's eyes, I understood that she would not tell me anything. She was one of those people without compassion. I was frustrated and began to think that I would have to look for them myself, even if it meant going through all the buildings shouting Joan's name.

Just behind me, a deep voice called out softly, "Follow me, madam."

Scowling at the interference, the secretary opened her mouth but immediately closed it again. Surprised by the change, I turned back to the man who had spoken. The white coat indicated his position as a doctor, his sad look showing he had seen too much in his short life.

"I was just about to pay them a visit. You can come with me if you like."

His gentle, kind eyes almost made me cry.

"Thank you, doctor. These women are my friends."

He went into a wide corridor, and I followed him. "That was my understanding. I'm sorry. I couldn't help overhearing as I passed by."

As we entered a pavilion, he paused. "Some of them are in pretty bad shape. Medically speaking, we can take care of them. As far as their minds are concerned, the slightest friendly face could make a huge difference at this stage."

Having been swamped by dark thoughts myself after leaving the camp, I understood perfectly.

Because of the heat, the doors were wide open. Several women, wearing light tunics over their emaciated bodies, were standing, sitting, or lying around chatting. Relieved to see them again, I breathed more easily. Hearing their voices did me good.

"Evelyn!"

All the chatter halted, and all eyes turned to me. How thin they were! Yet, despite the emaciated faces, I recognised most of them. Those who could walk came to meet me, arms outstretched. Tearfully, I hugged them gently, one by one.

"After we arrived in Muntok, we were told that your funeral was fake," Wilma explained, the first one in my arms. "It takes guts to do what you did."

She kissed me on the cheek, soon to be pulled aside by another of the nurses, then another. I could feel their protruding bones under my hands and was very afraid I would crush them.

"Vivian...Mavis...Jess..." I was crying so hard my vision was blurring.

"Evelyn!"

My name again. An arm waved slowly in a bed almost at the end of the room.

"It's Frances. Go on," Wilma whispered, propelling me in her direction.

I rushed over. Frances was lying on the white sheets in a light nightgown. She looked so small, so weak. I hesitated to even touch her, but she grabbed my hand and forced me to sit on the mattress.

"You're alive. Thank God. Joan will live again. You know..."

Frances suddenly looked radiant. Her blue eyes sparkled with happiness. The frail, weakened woman seemed to have vanished like magic.

"She's not here?" I asked breathlessly.

Frances shook her head gently. "She was well enough to wait, but don't worry. Now that we have food and medicine, everything will be fine. Ruth is alive, as is Elsie. Leo was sent to the men's camp shortly before we were shipped to Belalau, but I heard he's alive. Chester..."

Frances hesitated and then looked down. I gently tightened my grip on her hand. My tears flowed softly.

"I know. I saw the lists."

"And the baby?" she asked, her eyes hopeful. "Did you have your baby?"

"Barbara is fine and waiting to meet her godmother."

The applause exploded around us. I was so focused on Frances that I didn't notice all the women hanging on every word I spoke, some of them even standing right behind me. Many hands touched my shoulders. They were smiling, all talking together. Frances was crying and laughing at the same time. "I'm a godmother?"

With tears still streaming down my cheeks, I nodded. "You and Ruth."

"You have to bring her. We all want to see her," said a woman behind me.

Wilma's voice. I swallowed hard at the lump in my throat before murmuring, "Tomorrow. I'll come with her tomorrow."

Again, a torrent of cheers punctuated my words. The noise intensified as I heard three claps of the hands.

"Come on, ladies. You need to rest."

A nurse in her fifties, with her immaculate headdress and blouse, sent gloomy looks to everyone, pointing at the patients and the empty beds, while the doctor who had accompanied me smiled. He had achieved his goal. All his patients were glowing with a new joy, moving more easily. I stayed with Frances a little longer.

"How are you? How are you feeling?"

"Now that I know you're alive? Much better. We didn't know if you'd made it, and it was driving us crazy, especially Joan, as you can imagine. Once in Muntok, we never had any contact with our benefactors."

"Albert saved me. Do you remember Albert, the petty officer who helped us with the safe boat during the sinking?"

"The one who escaped capture? Was he alive? Tell me about it. What happened to you?"

Little by little I unravelled the whole story, but after a while Frances fell asleep still holding my hand. I got up carefully not to wake her.

Before leaving, I chatted a bit more with some of them, promising again to come back tomorrow with my daughter.

"Keeping their spirits up is more important than ever," said the nurse in charge as I walked past.

She was tall and sturdy, with an air of not giving a damn. A Wilma number two.

"Some of them have lost everything. We can heal their bodies, but healing their souls will take time."

"I know," I replied softly in a voice hoarse with emotion. "Believe me, I know. I was with them until November 1944."

She stared at me for a long time. A discreet smile stretched her lips for a moment before she nodded. "My name is Sarah. If anyone gives you any trouble here, just mention my name. That should scare them."

I chuckled. Yes, I believed her. "I'll keep that in mind. I'll remember that. Thank you."

I was almost out the door when Vivian's voice caught me. "Evelyn! A song before you go!"

"Yes, Evelyn! A song! Please," other women chanted.

A hand gently squeezed my shoulder. Sarah. Looking at all of them, I couldn't ignore the hope on the faces of my fellow sufferers. I cleared my throat and began to sing "My Baby Just Cares for Me." A little bit of rhythm to cheer them up.

Chapter Twenty-six

7 October 1945

As soon as I reached the pavilion, I heard an angry voice. My heart missed a beat. My breath caught, and I had to stop walking. My emotions were all over the place. How many times had I dreamed of hearing that voice again?

I forced my legs to take another step, to cross the threshold. Draped in a sarong against me, Barbara was sleeping peacefully. I had been coming here with her for three weeks, meeting my old friends, talking to the newcomers, but even though I had heard from Joan vicariously, her return date remained undefined. Until this morning.

"I'm not ill. I just need to eat and rest, not be poked and prodded!"

I entered quietly, enjoying the sight of my beloved. She was so skinny, so bony, but she stood on her two feet, erect, with her arms crossed, in front of Sarah and another nurse. I could see her only from behind, but I would have recognised her voice anywhere. She was wearing a dress, which made me smile. She hated them, especially that shapeless sack style.

"I am a doctor. I know what's good for me. And now I have to go to the Raffles. I've got an appointment."

I was speechless. She had just arrived and wanted to keep our rendezvous? With tears in my eyes, so focused on Joan, I hardly noticed someone was heading straight for me. Ruth. She hugged me and silently shed a few tears of joy.

"Is that…?" she asked, pointing to Barbara.

I smiled and nodded.

"Please let me hold her, and you go see Joan. She hasn't wanted to hear anything since we arrived. They threatened to sedate her, thinking she was delirious with this rendezvous thing."

I couldn't let that happen. Outraged, I untied the sarong and handed my daughter to Ruth before walking straight across the yard to my beloved. Red with anger at the resistance she was meeting, Sarah looked ready to manhandle Joan.

"I told you..."

My love was so agitated she didn't notice someone was behind her. With a look of incomprehension, Sarah stared at me, but I shook my head and began to sing "You Belong to My Heart."

Hearing my voice, Joan stopped immediately. She whirled around. Her anger gone, she slowly reached out with her right arm to touch me, but she was inches short. She seemed to be riveted to the ground. I couldn't move either. My eyes on hers, I could only sing my love to her in front of everyone, but I didn't care. I was crying, she was crying. With a wave of my hand, I angrily wiped away my tears.

Making a superhuman effort, she took a step toward me. Her trembling fingers brushed my cheek. My voice caught in my throat. She threw herself against me and sobbed. I hugged her as if tomorrow didn't exist for us. Tears flooded my face, flowed into Joan's short hair. We were in the middle of the yard, and everyone was staring at us. Some who knew us well were smiling or crying too.

I cuddled her head in my hands, caressed her back, letting her sob about all the misery those savages had put her through. In Sarah's eyes I saw no judgment, only understanding. Nothing and no one would ever hurt the love of my life again. They would have to kill me first.

"I'll never do that again, I swear to God," Joan finally muttered.

"What are you talking about?"

"Bury you and leave you in a grave not knowing what would happen." She sniffed.

She was still crying, and I could feel her shaking.

Wiping away my tears, I smiled and whispered, "I hope the next time you have to bury me, it will be because I died of old age in our bed."

The tears rolled down her cheeks again, but this time more slowly. Still in my arms, she swallowed and inhaled deeply to calm herself. "The British major told us last week that you were alive and in Singapore. I…"

"When the major informed us we had to wait for the truck to return, this pig-headed woman wanted to walk to the airstrip," cut in Ruth, sitting on the edge of the nearest bed. "It was as if food had been injected directly into her bloodstream. She could stand again. The major almost had to tie her up to force her to wait."

Joan stared at Ruth. She had opened her mouth to protest when her gaze came to rest on the baby.

"Is this…?"

"My daughter, Barbara or, rather, our daughter."

My arm around Joan's waist, I took a few steps toward Ruth, who was holding Barbara in her lap. "You saved her, both of you. Without you and Frances, she would have been killed."

Joan slowly reached out to touch her, but she stopped just short. "She's beautiful…like her mother."

"She's got quite a temper too," I added, joy flooding my heart at Joan's blissful smile.

Affectionately, I had put my hand on Ruth's shoulder when I heard, "Evelyn!"

I hardly had time to turn round when a bomb flew into my arms.

"Elsie! Oh, my goodness! You've grown so much. Let me look at you."

I pulled her back at arm's length to get a better view. She was a bag of bones, her head shaved, her skin covered with ulcers. Yet her brown eyes were still beautiful despite her emaciated face. And her huge smile…so happy to see me. I pulled her in and held her close for a long time. She reached just below my chin now. I kissed her forehead.

"Chester…" She sobbed.

"I know."

Elsie merely strengthened our embrace. "I was looking for Leo. They don't know where he is, and I can't find him."

She was upset and babbling. I placed another reassuring kiss on her head.

"Don't worry. He's at the Raffles with Frances. He was quite well, and they needed a bed in the men's room, so I took him with me yesterday."

I was reliving my reunion with Leo. He seemed so shy in his awkward adolescent gestures. So small for a twelve-year-old, too small. The doctor had assured me that with a normal diet he would grow up now.

"Frances and Leo were both happy to move to the Raffles. It was a bit of a struggle, but I arranged a room for us all there."

Behind my back, Joan wrapped her arms around us. Ruth joined in, forgetting about Barbara, who was sandwiched in between and shouting her protest.

"That's a great idea, love. Let's all go to the Raffles to celebrate our reunion," Joan suggested.

"They may be able to go, but you're not going anywhere until the doctor says so," a loud voice objected. Sarah, with her arms folded across her chest, stared at Joan. She wasn't kidding. Joan tried to protest. I took her hand.

"She'll do what she has to do, Sarah. We'll wait for her...I'll wait for her."

Indignantly, Joan raised her eyebrows and shook her head, but I smiled gently and whispered in her ear, "Go, my love. The sooner you see the doctor, the sooner we will be together at the Raffles."

"Come with me, madam. Listen to your friend. She's got a lot of sense, and she sings well too. You're a lucky gal. Don't keep her waiting."

With her hand, Sarah showed Joan the way, and she followed her. Before leaving the room, she just turned her head to look at me, seeming still afraid that I would disappear.

"She's so stubborn, that one," Ruth finally said, "but she forced us to hang on even when we couldn't stand the hunger, even when despair threatened to destroy us. Without knowing if you were alive, she buried her pain and pushed us to overcome everything, to maintain the hope that this day would come. We are alive because of her, you know."

Around us, I heard whispers. Frances had already told me everything that had happened after I left. Joan had done everything possible to save them, even with the little she had.

We had just put on quite a show, but no one seemed to care. Most of them knew me from before. Those who had arrived earlier welcomed me with undisguised pleasure. I was their entertainment for the day with Barbara, my songs and stories about life in Singapore. Of those from the Atap camp who knew my past, only a handful rejected my daughter for who she was, who her father was.

"Do you really have a room for us at the Raffles?" asked Ruth while making faces at Barbara, who was laughing out loud.

Like all those who came out of the hospital and found themselves headed for the pearl of Singapore, she looked sceptical.

"Yes. All the survivors from the camps in Sumatra, Java, or Singapore are staying at the Raffles until a solution is found for each of them. Some have already gone home to England or Australia, like all the nursing sisters. Norah and several others have also left. Others remain to find out what happened to their families. The Raffles is the meeting place at the moment."

"But we have no one," said Elsie in a small voice. "Father died before we got on the boat, and Mum...you know. Our grandparents are dead too. What's going to happen to us, to Leo and me?"

"I told you before I escaped, you aren't alone. I'm here, Joan's here. We promised your mother we'd look after you, even after the war. We just need to make it official with the administration. If that's what you want, of course. You're almost an adult now. You can decide for yourself."

Crying, Elsie rushed back into my arms. I had my answer. Eyes glistening, Ruth smiled. She squeezed my hand. I appreciated her strong friendship.

"What are you going to do?" I asked her. "Go back to England?"

"What for? I haven't had anyone there for a long time. Maybe I'll check with my old school to see if they need me. But, you know, I don't want to think about that for a few days. I need to continue to regain my strength. The paratroopers fed us rations and canned food. After the camp diet, I'll always be grateful to them. And I'm not going to complain about putting some flesh back on my old bones in the last month, but now I'm craving some tasty food. The luxury of the Raffles seems perfect to me."

Had they put on weight? I couldn't believe it. What state were they in when the soldiers found them? I thought of Frances and that first evacuated contingent. Frances, who had to stay in hospital for two weeks before being allowed to leave for the Raffles. If the war had lasted only a little longer...I held back the quivering of my lips.

Ruth looked tired, so I picked up Barbara, but she started to scream. I tried to rock her slowly.

"Can I hold her? I could walk her outside if you like, so she won't disturb anyone."

Elsie looked at me with a pleading expression. Considering her general condition, I doubted she could manage a wriggling seven-month-old baby for long, so I opted for a more reasonable solution.

"Sit with her on your bed. As soon as Joan is released, we'll jump on the next truck out to the city centre."

With Barbara crying in her arms, Elsie moved three beds over.

"I think you've got yourself a babysitter," Ruth remarked, and before I could say anything she added, "It will do her good. She's taken Chester's death very hard. She almost let herself die. Joan, Frances, and I tried to support her, but the Japs had just taken Leo to the men, and, as their big sister, she felt she was a failure because she couldn't protect them. Barbara will be a good distraction."

Ruth hesitated, which wasn't like her.

"What?"

"You really want to keep them with you?"

"I'll have to talk to Joan, but yes, I hope so. I made a promise."

"Well, good. Joan will want to, no doubt about it. After we heard the war was over, we dared to discuss the future. She always included you, the baby, and Elsie and Leo, even though we still didn't know if you had survived. Joan is a wonderful woman."

"I know she is."

Her gaze on me, Ruth just nodded silently. We had been through hell. The future couldn't get any worse.

"Let's go," Joan suddenly said as soon as she returned. "I don't want them to change their mind."

She walked toward me, smiling, her beautiful dimple still present despite her hollowed cheeks. Tilting her head slightly to one side, she stopped, her eyebrows furrowed.

"I know that dress…and that hat. You wore them when we…"

A huge smile lit up her face at the memory of our meetings at the botanic gardens. I whirled around. "Mr. Chee put our things in storage after we left in such a hurry, and I was able to access them. It's not the latest fashion, but I was getting a little tired of these charity dresses."

I pointed to the burgundy floral one she was wearing. Joan grinned as Ruth giggled.

"You could have brought me my clothes," she exclaimed indignantly.

"I didn't know when you'd arrive, but they're waiting for you at the Raffles. They'll be too big," I warned her.

Joan shrugged and pointed at her dress in disgust.

"Anything's better than this. Let's go. I don't want to spend another moment here. I need normality."

I burst out laughing. That was my Joan again, and my heart was swelling.

"Give me a minute, and I'll be right there."

I walked over to Sarah, standing by the treatment trolley and watching us out of the corner of one eye.

"I guess you won't be coming back now." Her gaze drifted to Joan. "She's a handful, that one."

I laughed heartily. "She's got a good heart, and she's a good doctor. She used to work here before the Japanese forced us to flee."

"That's what she told me. Let her heal before she goes back to work. She needs food and rest, even if she says otherwise."

With a serious expression, Sarah turned to me. "She'll also need love, lots of it."

"I can assure you she'll get that. Thank you for your trust from the beginning."

Sarah smiled and held out her hand to me.

"Come see us from time to time."

"I will."

Chapter Twenty-seven

The large room we all shared had been turned into a dormitory with eight beds. Frances and Leo, very excited, were waiting for us when we arrived. Sally and Heather, our old math-loving friends from the camps who had moved in at the same time as Leo, were there too. Once again everyone hugged each other, happy to be here. We were all alive and well.

Sally and Heather left first. They were looking for their families and had an appointment with Captain Davington. Ruth and Frances took the three children for a walk around the Raffles, officially to reacquaint themselves with freedom and Singapore, and unofficially to give me time with Joan.

As soon as everyone was out, I locked the door. It was so wonderful to be in my beloved's arms. In a sort of striptease without music, I undressed in front of her. She laughed out loud at my gestures, at the clothes that flew off in disarray. My heart melted at her joy, and I held back tears. My beloved sat quietly, and we were alone. Naked, I suddenly encouraged her to stand up and slowly caress me as I undid her hideous dress.

Joan was in no condition to make love, but we needed to be in each other's arms, skin to skin. Finally, she had her head on my shoulder, and I was cuddling her tenderly. She was so skinny I was afraid I'd hurt her. Until this day, she had always been the stronger in our relationship. But, today, I could feel her physical and mental fragility. Joan was crying softly, and, as hard as it was, I let her. After more than three years of deprivation and humiliation, she needed to find the energy inside herself to come back to us, to me. Aware of her weakness, I pulled her onto the bed. As usual, it was hot, and, despite the ceiling fan, we were sweating, but the mattress was comfortable and clean: no bedbugs or fleas here.

"I'm sorry. I can't stop crying. One minute I'm laughing, and the next I'm crying. But you're here, and the nightmare is over."

I kissed her forehead and let my fingers slide down her cheek as I whispered, "I love you even when you cry, or maybe even more when you cry. We have had and will have again difficult times in our lives. But one thing will always be certain…"

Seeming curious, she raised her head and looked at me, her beautiful green eyes full of hope and confidence. Tears welled up under my eyelids, and I blinked to chase them away. She caught them with her fingertips.

"Don't cry, my love."

Slowly, Joan kissed my lips with infinite gentleness. I shivered.

"What is this thing that will always be certain, love?"

"My love for you," I whispered. "It will be there until death do us part…as late as possible."

I hesitated to continue, to give her my thoughts, but she had to know the truth.

"Barbara helped me survive. When I found myself without you…When I got out of that grave, I…I was torn in two. Leaving you there was the worst thing I've ever had to do. The despair…I've been concentrating on Barbara these past few months to keep from falling apart. I know it's selfish to say that because she's my daughter and I love her, but my feelings for her are nothing compared to the love I have for you. I realised this when I was deep in the jungle without you, not knowing if I would ever see you again. Not a minute has passed without you being present in me. I'll never leave you again."

"Can you promise me that?"

Joan looked at me with such hope in her eyes that I almost broke down. My voice trembled as I answered. "I promise."

She pressed herself against me and sobbed again. It tore my heart out to see her like this, but I could bear the pain as long as necessary, if my beloved was with me. Since my escape, I had been flayed alive by our separation, and now my soul could begin the long work of repair.

"We could stay in Singapore," Joan suggested after a moment's silence. "The authorities will run out of doctors, and I should be able to get my job back at the hospital. I'm sure nice houses are available now, and, with three children, we need something big enough to have a babysitter, an amah, with us."

She talked about the future for several minutes without stopping, of hope, about the possibility of a bright tomorrow. Her spark of life had suddenly returned. The Joan I had met, who had faith in the future, was in my arms. The lump in my throat disappeared completely. My heart swelled with joy.

I stroked her head, feeling the fine hair, which would grow back as mine had. On the ceiling, the fan spun slowly, ticking off the seconds. For the first time since I'd had to say good-bye to her in Singapore three and a half years ago, I felt able to look forward to the future in a positive light.

Suddenly I checked my watch and, seeing the time, jumped out of bed. Looking surprised, Joan raised herself on one elbow.

"I have to go to work, love."

"Work?"

"I've been singing in the dining room every night before dinner for a fortnight. The management gave me a one-month contract. I wanted to buy some more fashionable clothes, and I didn't know what the future…"

No, at the time I didn't know, but now I did.

"A beautiful dress?"

The wonderful smile that had seduced me when we first met was on her lips.

"Do you want to admire me in my new stage costume?" I loved to tease her.

She swallowed. Her gaze became more intense. My heartbeat quickened. Little by little, I was getting my Joan back. The future wouldn't always be rosy. There would be nightmares, for her as well as for me, and we would share tears, but hope as well, and plans, and children.

While I went to the bathroom to wash off the sweat and clean up a bit, Joan lay there. She was still on the bed, arms crossed behind her neck, when I returned. I could feel her gaze intensely following every step, every movement I made…just like before the war. Thinking of her, of our reunion, I'd had this light blue dress made last week. After seeing the pictures of the new Parisian collection in the magazine, I had asked a Chinese tailor I knew to copy one of the dresses. The tight waist made my chest look bigger. As soon as I put on the dress, Joan's mouth fell open. I laughed gently at her.

"Hey. Don't laugh at my reaction. You didn't look in the mirror. You're…I don't have the words to describe how I feel, Evy." Joan fanned herself with her hand. "Is that what's fashionable now?"

"At least in Paris. The tailor finished it yesterday. It's the first time I've worn it…"

I didn't need to add anything. Joan understood the message. This dress was for her. Even if in fifteen minutes I would stand in front of an audience, my outfit would be only for her. I would be only for her.

Joan sat on the edge of the bed without taking her eyes off me. She looked at me slowly, contemplating me from head to toe. A shiver ran through me. She stood up and stopped right in front of me. Her fingers touched my cheek, ran over my skin, gently following my arm until they took hold of my hand and brought it to her lips. The kiss on my palm was a taste of the pleasures to come.

"You are so beautiful you take my breath away."

She held me captive with her gaze. I couldn't move. I was bewitched, and my fairy was this wonderful woman.

"Aren't you supposed to be downstairs for your show?" called Frances from the other side of the closed door.

Under Joan's naughty smile, I came to my senses.

"I'll be right there. Just a second." I held out my hand for Joan to take. "Are you coming?"

"I wouldn't miss it, but first I have to get dressed, don't you think? Where's my stuff? You're not going to make me put that awful dress back on."

I laughed, pointing to the little chest. With obvious pleasure, Joan slipped on her beautiful dark green shirt under an ecru suit that, before the war, had fit her perfectly. She didn't comment on the floaty look and merely tightened her belt.

Frances was waiting impatiently for us at the door. At the sight of my dress, she opened her eyes wide.

"Wow. It's beautiful. I saw the same one in a magazine downstairs."

I winked at her in agreement as I made my way to the lift, my arm around Joan's.

"Did you get one of those fantastic Chinese tailors to copy one?"

I stopped and twirled slowly in front of Frances. "What do you think?"

"I'm jealous. You'll have to give me his address."

I laughed at the look of envy she gave me.

"Aren't you going to be late?" teased Joan, who was still enjoying the view.

A wave of panic surged through me. I was never late. A good artist should always be on time.

"Hurry up. Come on. Ruth and the kids are waiting downstairs in the bar or the dining room. I don't know what they call this place now. It looks like they've moved everything since I was last here," Frances complained as she boarded the service lift.

"Any news of your husband?" I asked as we got off.

Frances had already spoken to her children on the phone, and they were fine. She sighed.

"Not yet. He was taken prisoner when Singapore fell, and his unit was sent to Thailand. That's all I know at the moment…except that the casualties were terrible…"

Joan put her hand on her shoulder and gently led her down the corridor as soon as the doors opened.

"Many are looking for their families. Give them time, Frances."

I walked briskly past them and heard all of Joan's encouragement. She had always been like that since we met, constantly trying to cheer everyone up. My precious Joan. Without her and the nurses, the losses in the camps would have been much worse.

Ruth waved as we entered the dining room. As Joan and Frances sat down, I kissed little Barbara on the head and gently squeezed Elsie and Leo's arm.

They all seemed impressed with my dress, which made me happy. I had chosen well. It highlighted the colour of my eyes. My hair was still too short for my taste, but the hairdresser had been able to give it a Jean Harlow style. My pianist was waiting for me, and I walked quickly toward him under the admiring gaze of the customers. We had decided on a list of songs the day before, but I wanted to change the first one. He smiled when he heard the title. Yes, I was happy, and I wanted everyone to feel it. The first note of the song "We Just Couldn't Say Good-bye" rang out, and the words poured from my lips.

My love was here with me. All those songs that night were for her. When my gaze landed on her, I didn't see a skinny woman who had escaped from the Japanese camps, but the brilliant doctor who had made my heart skip a beat the first time our eyes met.

CHAPTER TWENTY-EIGHT

After dinner, Joan, the children, and I walked on the playground along the Stamford Canal near the Raffles. It was a beautiful evening—a little cooler than most after the mid-afternoon storm. The smell of plants and earth filled the air.

"I'd like to stay here. To build a life with you in Singapore," Joan said suddenly. "What do you think?"

We'd talked about it the day she returned but hadn't mentioned it since. For the past two weeks, she had just been sleeping, eating, and chatting with those who were still there.

Every day we walked together, farther and farther away from the hotel. I watched with pleasure as Joan and the children gained weight and found a new enthusiasm.

"Don't you want to go back to Australia to see your parents?"

"Yes, of course, but not to stay there. We could all go together when our situations have stabilised. I'm thinking of starting to work at the hospital soon and of buying a house. Mr. Chee's flat is far too small for our large family now, and the damage to it won't be fixed for many months."

A house? She had mentioned it the first day, but I'd been so overwhelmed by my emotions that I forgot. Besides, I wasn't the dreamer in our relationship. I could organise things, and I wasn't bad at it, but planning? Even in the camp, she was the one talking about life after the war.

"You know me. I'm just a singer," I joked. "Wherever you want to go, I'll go."

"Elsie, Leo, how would you like to live in Singapore with us?"

The teenagers had been very quiet for the past two weeks. I could see in their eyes that, despite our promises, they were still afraid of being abandoned and sent to an orphanage. I had spoken to Captain Davington about their situation, and he was formalising our guardianship until we could legally adopt them.

Their faces lit up, and they looked at each other, clearly hoping and wondering. As if to give herself courage, Elsie took her brother's hand.

"We would love to...stay with you. There is nothing we want more..."

Smiling, Joan nodded and turned to me. "And you didn't answer. What do you think, my love?"

"Are you kidding? Living here with all of you would be a dream come true. But I need to work too. My contract with the Raffles won't last for years. They've renewed it for another two months, but with the return of Singaporeans and the economy picking up, they'll certainly want an orchestra again. To them, I'm just a cabaret singer."

I was clearheaded and didn't want to be a burden. I looked at Barbara, who was sleeping, held close to me by a sarong. *A family? All together? Here?* I could easily imagine it.

"You could teach singing and music. You should talk to Ruth. She might know of a school that's interested. Speaking of schools, you two will have to go back soon. The holidays are over."

Joan winked at them. Leo grinned as Elsie sighed. Joan was right. Even if they didn't want to be with younger children because of missed classes, they needed education and normalcy in their lives.

"Tomorrow we'll start looking for a house. I've already spoken to a guy," Joan explained, "and from what I understand, there are a lot of nice empty houses whose owners won't be coming back or will want to sell cheaply before they return to England. I checked with the bank, and they finally found my account with the money in it."

As I walked, I put my arm around her waist and held her close. "You are an extraordinary woman, my love. If I could, I'd marry you," I whispered so the children wouldn't hear.

Even though we tried not to be too demonstrative with our feelings, Elsie and Leo knew where they stood, but they didn't seem to care. Some of our love trickled down to them, and they absorbed it gratefully.

"Why can't we use our house?" Leo asked after a few seconds. He smiled and seemed very excited about his idea. Nudging his sister, he said, "Well, Elsie, we could go home. That would be nice, wouldn't it? I'd have my old room back."

Like hitting a wall, Elsie stopped, her mouth open. She was staring at the darkest part of the garden, but I could tell from her expression that she was somewhere else, in a past that had been buried so she could avoid suffering. I went over to her and wrapped my arm around her shoulders, pulling her against me. She was crying.

"Leo's right. I'd forgotten. How could I forget we had a nice house here with Mum and Dad?" She looked at me in despair, tears ravaging her face.

"Sometimes the mind does what it needs to do to protect itself," Joan said gently. "We went through something horrible we'll never forget. In the camps everyone coped in a different way. Surviving and being free was our only goal. Now that we've achieved that goal, we have to get on with our lives, for ourselves and for those no longer with us today."

"Like Mum and Dad," Leo added sadly.

"Or Chester," murmured Elsie.

Wordlessly, Joan placed a kiss on the temples of our two teenagers. Despite the nightmares that plagued our nights, compared to others, we were lucky, and we knew it.

"We'll never forget them," I said.

"Where was your home?" Joan's voice seemed a little too loud in the silence. Of course, a tropical evening is never really silent with all the critters. In Singapore, there was a background noise of engines and shouting as well.

"On Tanglin Hill, near Tanglin Road. It's not too far from the botanic gardens. We used to go there often with Mum. There was a hospital next door. Maybe you could work there, Joan."

Elsie seemed hopeful now that she was recalling the happy times with her parents. After so many days of sitting sadly in the corner and not caring about anything but Barbara, she was finally getting excited about something.

"Did your parents own it? Or did your father's company?"

Leo shrugged. He was too young to remember. Elsie hesitated for a moment. Frowning, she seemed to be trying to remember all the information she'd had to erase in order to survive.

"I think we owned it. Father worked in a bank. He was an assistant manager, but he was hoping for a promotion. I remember my mother telling my father that they should have bought a house closer to the city centre. My father just laughed. He loved riding, and with this house we could keep our horses on the premises."

"Maybe we could go there tomorrow and check it out, but now it's time for bed," I said, taking Elsie's arm with one hand and Joan's in the other.

Barbara continued to sleep, although a little compressed wrapped in the sarong.

Smiling, Leo walked ahead of us toward the Raffles. He was going home tomorrow. Joan's fingers tightened on mine.

"Now that we're together, everything will work out. You'll see."

❖

"My God, this is beautiful."

The taxi dropped us off in front of a huge colonial house and drove away.

I was amazed. The white house had two floors and a large wooden veranda that seemed to surround it. The beautiful park was very well maintained. How could this be? The Ravensburg family had abandoned this house three and a half years ago. From the entrance gate, I could see the lush vegetation perfectly trimmed and the grass well mown.

"I couldn't agree with you more. This house is a gem."

Joan was as surprised as I was at the immaculate state of the place, but the children were so excited I didn't need to ask if this was the right location. Elsie couldn't stand still, and I was glad she wasn't carrying Barbara today. Before I could react, she had already climbed the three steps to the terrace and was heading for the front door when I stopped her.

"Elsie! Wait a minute! This house isn't abandoned. Someone lives here."

A string of foreign words came from the garden.

The speaker emerged, wearing only a sarong, leaving his muscular torso in plain sight. He wasn't old, but his face already showed the marks of time. With his serious gaze he took us in, and I was a little worried because of the machete he held in his right hand.

"Bapak Aris," Leo shouted, running toward him. "You're alive."

Leo was crying as he rushed into the arms of the stunned man, who blinked in clear surprise.

"Master Leo? Miss Elsie?"

The tool slipped from his fingers, and he hugged Leo tightly. I let out a sigh of relief.

"I think this is the right place," Joan whispered with a smile.

"Miss Elsie? Master Leo?" A tiny woman ran up to Elsie and hugged her affectionately.

"Mayli," Elsie said between sobs. "Mayli. Mummy is dead, you know. So is Chester."

Tears immediately rolled down Mayli's cheeks.

At that moment, I knew we had made the right decision. Joan was right. Our lives were in Singapore with our three children.

"I want to see my room!" Leo suddenly exclaimed. Without waiting, he rushed to the front door.

"Leo! Manners!" Joan reminded him in vain as he disappeared into the house.

"Please, Madam Mayli. Would it be possible for Leo to see his old room?" I asked, trying to excuse Leo's bad manners.

As if the years of Japanese occupation hadn't happened, Mayli smiled and replied. "Master Leo's room is ready. Your room too, Miss Elsie."

Still in tears, Elsie ran into the house after her brother.

"How can this be?" I asked Mayli. "It looks like the house is inhabited. There's no damage, nothing."

"Japanese officers used to live here. Before she left, I had promised Madam to look after the property. So my husband and I stayed, and when the soldiers arrived we welcomed them and served them. After the Japanese left, with my husband and sons, we cleaned and prepared the rooms for the children and Mrs. Ravensburg. We knew that Mister Ravensburg had been killed before they left."

"Mrs. Ravensburg, along with her youngest son Chester, died in the camps in Sumatra. We promised her we would look after her children," Joan explained as she entered the hall. "I'm Joan Cliver, and this is Evelyn Baker."

Joan stopped as soon as she crossed the threshold, appearing stunned. The teak-wood floor was perfectly polished and beautiful, but the most amazing thing was the furniture. Nothing was broken, and everything seemed in its place. By what miracle? I had heard horrific stories from other survivors when they returned to their homes. Some were so devastated that it was better to destroy everything and rebuild.

As if reading our minds, Mayli explained. "When Mrs. Ravensburg went abroad, we hid the most valuable furniture in the storage shed and piled up old things in front of it. I asked my boys to put everything back after the soldiers left."

"It's really a beautiful house."

"Are you going to stay here with the children?"

Reassuringly, Joan smiled at her. "Don't worry. If we move in, you and your husband can continue to work for us. It seems that Elsie and Leo adore you."

"I've seen them born and grew up," Mayli explained.

Joan nodded. "We just need to check with a lawyer that we have the right to live here."

Although seeming relieved, Mayli still had concern in her dark eyes. I encouraged her to speak up.

"What is it, Mayli? Is something wrong?"

"Some men came to inquire about the owner of the residence. They said they had a buyer. My husband explained to them that the householder was coming back, but I don't think they believed him. I heard stories…"

Worried, I glanced at Joan. We too had heard warnings about this kind of unscrupulous predator.

Joan rubbed her chin. The teenagers were running from room to room upstairs.

"Is the house ready for us, Mayli? Is there any work to be done before we move?"

"No, ma'am. Everything is prepared. I just need to send my husband to buy some provisions worthy of you."

Mayli hesitated before saying, "We are short of money though, Madam Joan. The Japanese paid us when they thought about it."

"Don't worry. We'll go tomorrow. Fried noodles tonight will be fine. We'd like to avoid rice for a while."

"So now if anyone asks again, you can say the owners are back. How many rooms are available?" I added.

"Five upstairs, Miss Evelyn, but there is an office right there. It is possible to make another room. Come and see."

Mayli was clearly excited. All her immediate worries had just vanished. She pushed open the door, and I was immediately struck by the very masculine look of the furniture.

"It was Mister Ravensburg's," Mayli said.

"This could be your office if you want to open your own medical practice."

"Or the music room, so you can give singing lessons at home," Joan retorted with a smile. "Five rooms will be fine, won't it?"

"If we take Barbara with us, yes."

Joan frowned. I could see the wheels of her brain turning. We needed only four rooms. I smiled.

"I'd like to offer Ruth and Frances a place to stay until they get their bearings. What do you think? The more people we have, the fewer unwanted visitors will bother us."

From the look on her face, I knew that if Mayli hadn't been there, Joan would have hugged me. She just smiled brightly.

"That's a great idea," she said. "I like the way you think. Stay here with Elsie and Barbara. I'll go back to the Raffles with Leo to bring back our few possessions and let them know where we are now. I'll ask Frances and Ruth if they'd like to move in with us, for a while at least. Now it would be nice to get a taxi or something."

With all these plans and the prospect of a full house, Mayli's eyes glowed with apparent happiness.

"The soldiers stole the car, but there are bicycles in the shed."

"Bicycles? Perfect. Leo! Leo, come down!" Joan shouted from the bottom of the stairs before turning to me. "Check out the place and choose our room. We won't be long."

"What about the ownership documents? We don't own this house."

Joan laughed. "I don't think anyone will be bothering us about that. We'll sort it out at the same time as the adoption of the children."

Striding down the stairs, Leo arrived, out of breath. "Do you need me, Joan?"

"Help me get the bikes out of the shed, and come into town with me. I'll explain," Joan said, leading him outside.

A few minutes later they were already leaving the property when Elsie joined me on the patio.

"Where are they going?"

"To the Raffles, to get our things and ask Ruth and Frances to move in with us."

"Today?"

"Why wait? It's your and Leo's house, isn't it?"

Barbara chose this moment to wake up and began to fidget. I winced. At eight months old, she was already quite heavy. As I untied the sarong, Elsie held out her arms. "Let me carry her. She's so cute."

I had noticed in the camp that Elsie had a natural gift with babies. Losing Chester had been a blow, but she loved children and would be a great mother one day.

Holding Barbara, Elsie showed me around the rooms, telling me stories about her past life. Although emotions were still high, she smiled more than she cried. She showed me the portraits of her ancestors hanging on the walls. The day was beautiful, and I was so happy. After all those horrible years, Joan and I finally had a home and a family. A little song began to play in my head. I hummed along to the music, taking a few steps as we walked into a beautiful room. Elsie laid Barbara down on the big Indian rug.

"This was my parents' room," she said.

As I continued my dance steps on the beautiful floor, she looked at me with wide, bemused eyes.

"What are you doing?"

"I'm dancing a Lambeth Walk. Don't you know it?"

Intrigued, Elsie slowly shook her head. I grabbed her hand and sang "The Lambeth Walk" at the top of my lungs. Laughing, Elsie imitated my steps. Yes, this house would be full of laughter, music, and friends. I could easily envision our future here.

Chapter Twenty-nine

Singapore, December 1957

"Ruth, how nice to see you here. I didn't think you'd come before Sunday," I said as I descended the last steps of the terrace to greet my old friend. I gave her a hug and then led her out onto the patio.

Ruth pointed to the tents set up on the lawn and the tables and chairs waiting to be placed by a host of workers bustling about.

"I see preparations are in full swing."

"What can I say? It's not every day that Leo gets engaged. I thought he would bring back a wife he met while studying in England, but no. He stayed true to his childhood sweetheart."

Discreetly, Mayli placed some refreshments on the coffee table. I nodded as Ruth smiled at her before she left. Things had changed since the end of the war. Ruth had lived with us in the house for several years before finally buying a small flat near the school where she worked.

It was barely ten o'clock, but like every day, the temperature had already started to rise. I watched for a moment as the workers finished putting up the last of the tents.

"Is everyone okay?" Ruth asked as she sipped her iced tea. "By the way, I love your new Audrey Hepburn hairdo. Very chic."

I smiled and touched the tips of my short hair. After seeing Hepburn's last film, I hadn't resisted going to the hairdresser's two days later. Joan's reaction had been unforgettable, as had our evening.

"Thank you. I love it, and in this heat, it's so nice. Much more practical than my longer cut. To answer your question, Elsie and her family are doing well. The kids are growing too fast for my taste, and I don't have enough time to enjoy them. If you mean Joan, she's working too hard, as usual. Barbara's getting difficult, like a teenager, but I'm certainly not telling you anything. As for Leo, he loves what he does and swears only by architecture. He has big plans for Singapore. You'll hear him talking about how this city will be the future jewel of Asia."

Ruth laughed. Although we met often, I missed my friend. We had shared so many confidences over the years.

"So nothing's new. But your son is certainly right. After Parliament rejected David Marshall's request for autonomy, I wasn't optimistic about our fate, but it seems that Lim Yew Hock has a better chance. If our colony becomes independent, things will change a lot in the region."

I pouted. "Provided the communists calm down a bit. They're doing their cause a disservice with their armed actions in Malaysia and even here."

"You should ask your boyfriend to calm down his buddies," Ruth joked.

I smiled at the teasing between us. After learning that Ajin had proposed to me, Joan didn't really appreciate the fact that I'd kept in touch with him. Yet she tolerated him and also participated in the heated debates he ignited here on the rare occasions he visited. Ajin had often been arrested as a communist sympathiser, but he had always been released.

"Ajin doesn't really have any power over the extremists in his party. I'm not even sure he believes their ideas himself. In any case, if we get independence, he'll be busy."

Ruth looked at me in amazement. "Since when have you been pro-independence?"

I grabbed my glass and took a sip before answering.

"A long time ago, I suppose, but it's only become clear recently in talking to Leo and Elsie. They were born here, and Singapore is their home. As for me..." I swept the landscape with a wave of my hand. "I never thought of going back to England, even after the war. When we went there in 1950 to accompany Leo to Oxford, I found it sad and cold."

I looked up. During our time there, I had missed the blue sky, the green trees all year round, the colourful birds here, even though I had enjoyed reconnecting with Dorothy. We had talked about her love lost in 1945 somewhere in the Ardennes and about our mother, who died of cancer just after the war. Apart from the newly reopened shops, little else had brightened our stay.

"My life is here."

Ruth raised her glass and toasted.

"So, here's to our independence."

Surprised, I smiled and patted her forearm. "You never told me you were pro-independence as well."

"I'm being discreet. I'm not sure most of my students' parents would like that. They're not like us."

She was right. After the war, many newcomers from Britain had moved to Singapore to take advantage of the colony's economic boom, and the majority didn't understand this desire for autonomy. Ruth remained silent for many minutes. I sighed.

"Why are you really here, Ruth? The engagement ceremony is in two days, and you didn't come to talk politics since tomorrow is the first day of the school holidays and you must be very busy."

I stared at her without blinking. She held my gaze. The flash of sadness in her blue eyes alarmed me. When she took a deep breath, I knew that what was coming next would not please me.

"One of Barbara's teachers told me of a disturbing problem. She heard Barbara chatting with a friend in a corridor."

Waiting for her to continue, I frowned. Ruth hesitated. This was definitely not her style, and I didn't like it at all. "I'm listening."

"Barbara was talking about you."

Not understanding, I pouted and spread my hands, urging her to clarify.

"About you and Joan," she explained.

A shiver of fear ran up my spine. Neither with Ruth nor with Frances had we openly mentioned what was going on between Joan and me. That she should broach the subject now indicated the urgency of the situation.

"And?"

Ruth put her glass on the coffee table, looked around as if to make sure no one was nearby, and leaned forward. "Evy, I'm not fooled and never have been. No one who knew you in the camps or at the liberation is fooled. This love between you and Joan has helped us all bear the unbearable. Every time I see you together, I envy you. It is your strength, but with one misplaced word, it could also be your undoing."

Ruth looked at me, obviously to see if I understood. I nodded.

"What does this have to do with Barbara?" I croaked, afraid to totally understand.

"The teacher told me what was said. According to her, Barbara said that you and Joan were indulging in abominable acts in your room and that you and she couldn't go to London for Christmas because that pervert Joan was keeping you from seeing your real family, and she would tell everyone…"

I closed my eyes. My worst nightmare was coming true because of Barbara. Elsie and Leo had never said anything or even mentioned anything. Would the scandal come from my own daughter? She whom I had saved from certain death? I stood up and wrapped my arms around my middle before leaning against the railing. The pain threatened to crush me inside. If Barbara started spreading stories like that, even if people didn't listen to her and didn't believe a twelve-year-old, some people would find our life together suspicious.

"I thought it best to warn you before things got out of hand," Ruth added, standing in front of me with her palms on my shoulders. "You have the holidays to think about it."

"Did everyone in the camps know? Really?" I asked with tears in my eyes and a slight smile on my face.

Without answering, she held me close. I enjoyed her solid presence for a few seconds before pulling back.

"Thanks for the heads-up, Ruth. I'll talk to Joan about it tonight." I wiped away the last of the tears with my fingertips. "Don't worry. I've seen it all before," I joked.

Ruth smiled. "I know you have. I trust you to do the right thing."

Apart from the ten-year reunion, we rarely mentioned the camps when we were together. Along with Frances, who had moved with her husband to a plantation near Johor, Ruth had remained my closest friend. The painful months of our lives when we met belonged to a time we preferred to forget.

"I have to go. As you said, with the Christmas holidays starting tonight, I have work to do."

Ruth gave me another hug before leaving. I was left alone to gaze at the garden and the labourers who were working in it, calling out and laughing. My brain was struggling to sort things out, to find a solution. Mayli came to collect the glasses but, obviously realising my condition, didn't even try to start a conversation. She too knew, yet nothing in her attitude had ever betrayed anything.

Elsie and Leo knew. I had often seen them smile and exchange a knowing wink as they looked at Joan and me. Why would Barbara betray us? Her requests about the identity of her father had been increasing for some time. Like all teenage girls, she was curious. I had given her Ajin's version of a Chinese father who died in the war. Ajin had confirmed it and talked about Lam the last time he was here. So why? Because we had refused to let her go to London for Christmas with her best friend? Things had gotten out of hand that night. Barbara had made irrelevant accusations. Joan had become the cause of all her misfortunes, from her father's death, to the ban on a dream holiday to London, to my caring more about Joan than her. The rage, the jealousy of a teenager. I could remember her face twisted with fury.

What could I do? I sighed. As long as we were discreet, we could live our love, but if she started to spread rumours, our small, self-righteous local society would reject us without delay. My beloved's reputation would suffer. Our lives were here.

"Granny, Granny!"

Two balls of energy landed on the patio and jumped into my arms as I crouched down. Eton, at four years old, had a little more restraint than his younger sister, Isabel, who would be turning three in two months.

As I nearly fell on my buttocks landing them, behind me, Elsie laughed.

"I'm sorry to be here so early. They couldn't wait. I could hardly contain them until now. Are the horses here?"

I pointed toward the end of the garden. "In the old stable."

Eton was already bouncing in their direction, his sister trying in vain to follow him.

"Mayli?" I called. She arrived immediately. "Could you ask Bapak Aris to go with them?"

Knowing that Elsie and her children were coming, I had suspected her husband wouldn't be far behind. She smiled and set off after the children herself.

"Are you all right, Evy?" asked Elsie as soon as we were alone. She looked at me worriedly.

"Don't mind me. Just a little upset." I forced a smile so she wouldn't concern herself and changed the conversation. "Did you get to see the caterer?"

"Yes. No problem. Everything is ready for Sunday. I can't imagine what the wedding will be like. Leo could have made the engagement a little less gigantic. Did I invite the whole of Singapore when I got engaged?"

I giggled and raised my eyebrows. Elsie looked at me and laughed.

"I admit it wasn't ideal. That the fiancé had to leave in a hurry was not on the agenda, but it was for a good cause."

Peter had had to rush to the hospital after an unplanned, difficult delivery. Being married to a doctor was no picnic, I knew that. What was I going to do with Barbara? I couldn't let her soil the reputation of our entire family.

"Evy?"

I realised that Elsie had spoken to me, but I hadn't listened. She knew me so well. Tears of frustration welled up in my eyes. Without thinking, I blurted out, "Barbara is gossiping about Joan and me. Ruth just told me, and I don't know what to do."

What had I said? I held up my hands to stop her reply. "I'm sorry. It's not your problem. I'll figure it out."

Elsie bit her lower lip. "I should have told you, but since we've never talked about it openly…I didn't dare."

"You didn't dare what?"

"A few months ago, she asked me about her father and then about you and Joan. I didn't like the accusatory language and the way she talked, so I curtly rebuffed her and told her to shut up. I'm sorry. Maybe I should have handled it differently. It's just that the words she used…"

Clearly feeling at fault, Elsie bowed her head. I took her tenderly in my arms. Letting herself be cuddled, she rested her forehead on my shoulder as she did when she was younger.

"You and Joan, in my eyes and Leo's, will never be what she said. You saved us, loved us, encouraged us to live again. Without you, we would have been placed in an orphanage until we came of age."

"It's not your fault. It wouldn't have mattered, Elsie. Barbara was a difficult child, and she's my problem. It's just that I'd gotten used to a smooth and gentle life these days."

"Maybe you should have told her the truth about the camps, her conception. We all spared her. Maybe…"

While I remained silent, she added, "If you need me…"

"I know. Go help Aris with your monsters before he has to play the horse himself like last time. He's not that age anymore, even if he loves cavorting with children."

Watching Elsie walk down the patio steps and away to the back of the garden, I knew what I had to do and headed for the study. This was my den, where I gave singing lessons. As soon as we had the money, we had redecorated it to give it a more modern, feminine touch. I loved the new record player that sat on the secretary's desk. Barbara had been very excited when she saw it, and we had already spent hours listening to music together.

A wave of sadness came over me at the thought of what I was going to do, was forced to do. To break the heavy silence, I turned on the radio and sat down at the desk. A mirthless smile came over my face as I heard Elvis Presley singing "Love Me Tender." God, I loved that song! Each time I thought of Joan.

Joining my voice to his, I grabbed the stationery. The words about love till the end of time sounded so true when I thought of my beloved.

Epilogue

London, 2000

Still in shock, Thea slowly put the letter back into the envelope. It was getting dark. She had spent most of the day reading her grandmother's mail. After the initial revelations, she and Pat had shared the most recent letters to see if they contained anything important. From '46 onward, they provided news of the children and grandchildren, the development of Singapore, and how it was becoming the great city it is today. Only the letter of December 1957 unearthed by Pat was interesting. Short, but informative.

Dear Dorothy,

I need your services. I have to send Barbara to a boarding school in England, and I would feel better if you could keep an eye on her. I will arrive with her in London as soon as possible.

Since she found out about my real relationship with Joan, she has threatened to expose us. Barbara is acting like a jealous teenager. She thinks I betrayed her father and abandoned him for Joan. She wants to know everything about him. If I give in to her desires now, soon she'll demand that Joan leave the house. I can't let that happen.

How can I explain to her that I've lied all this time? I never told her about the camps. As I wrote to you, she does not have a Chinese father, and I never want to remember or mention that fateful day and that horrible soldier again.

*I love my daughter, but Joan is my life, my joy, and my soul mate.
We are happy here. It's a shame you don't have a phone. But I will
talk to you soon.*
    With all my love,
    Evelyn

"Your mother was a bitch when she was young," Pat concluded, placing the mail back in the box. "I went through the most recent letters. Evelyn asked about her daughter in each one. I guess Dorothy must have given Barbara some of the letters, because it seems that if Evelyn wrote to her daughter, she never wrote back. At least nothing is mentioned in the letters between the two sisters."

"While I can understand how unsettling it can be to have two mothers as a teenager, I can't approve of the way my mother obliterates everything about her family, her life in Singapore. I've never even heard her talk about Elsie or Leo." Thea stood up, her anger growing by the minute. "I'm sure Elsie must have looked after her at some point and acted like a big sister. But just to write off her brother and sister because of the love between Joan and her mother? That's homophobia, pure and simple."

Pat stopped her and grabbed Thea's hands.

"You don't need to get worked up over your mother. You always told me she was a lost cause." An idea crossed her mind. "But you could write Evelyn. We have her address."

"Who? My real grandmother? She doesn't know me."

"I saw your name in one of the last letters. Your great-aunt must have kept her informed of everything that was going on in her daughter's life and yours. We'll have to read each of the other letters carefully."

Gently, Thea placed her fingertips on her lover's cheek and kissed her. On this grey, rainy day, Pat's smile washed away the depressing atmosphere.

"I love you, and I'm so happy you agreed to come live here with me. I don't care what my parents think. We have friends and family of our own. And you're right. I'll write Evelyn. Who knows? Maybe we can expand our circle."

Spontaneously, Pat hugged Thea. Savouring this contact after all the shock of discovery, they stayed entwined for many minutes.

"How about coming to Australia with me for our next holiday? We could stop in Singapore for a few days and meet Evelyn and Joan."

Still snuggled in Pat's arms, Thea laughed.

"That's a great proposal. Meeting your family and mine in one trip. You have so many good ideas, my dear. I can't imagine how my mother will react."

❖

"What? What kind of absurd idea is that? Your grandmother was Dorothy. Why do you want to go see this Evelyn? She doesn't matter."

From across the dining-room table, Thea glared at the small woman with dark hair and eyes. How could a simple sentence explaining that she was going to visit her grandmother make her mother so angry? It was a three-person dinner, as there were fewer and fewer of them. She couldn't stand her father's silences any more than she could her mother's reflections and bitterness.

Barbara leapt to her feet, her hands on her hips, her dark eyes shooting flames. With a loud crash, the chair fell to the tiled floor, but no one reacted.

"I forbid you to go to Singapore!"

Thea laughed. Not the best thing to do with her mother, but her reaction was so comical.

"How old do you think I am? Five? I'm thirty, Mum, and I can do what I want. I don't need your permission. I'm going to Singapore to meet my grandmother, whether you like it or not."

Thea refused to look down. For the first time, she was openly defying this mother, who had never been loving. As usual, her father was silent, but she sensed by the glint in his eyes that he was proud of her.

"If you leave, you'll never set foot in this house again," Barbara spat.

Clearly incredulous, her father stared at his wife with round eyes. Would he say anything? Would he object to his wife's dictatorial attitude for once?

"What did she do to you, Mum? Are you upset because she loved Joan and still lives with her? Is that it? I think you were jealous of Joan. Were you jealous of Elsie and Leo too?"

"You don't know what you're talking about. They're sinners. God will punish them."

Thea's blood ran cold. Pure bigotry. She couldn't help but judge her mother. "Evelyn gave you everything. She protected you from certain death by putting her own life in danger. She could have abandoned you, but she didn't do it—"

"That is all lies! She rejected my father, and after he was killed, she did everything she could to prevent me from meeting his family. And for what reason? For a bloody woman!"

Incredulous, Thea shook her head.

"Stop twisting the truth and writing the story you want to hear! I read Evelyn's letters. While she was a prisoner in the civilian camps during the Japanese occupation, an enemy soldier raped her. Joan and her friends helped her escape when she discovered she was pregnant with you. And do you know why? Because the Japanese killed their bastard children as soon as they were born!"

Thea was so upset by her mother's attitude that she forgot all restraint. For more than ten minutes, she spouted off everything she had learned about the camps and the atrocities committed.

"And one more thing. I'm a lesbian too. My girlfriend Pat and I are flying to Singapore next month to meet these two brave women, and after that we're going to Australia to meet Pat's family, who is not homophobic!"

Pale-faced, Barbara opened her mouth, then closed it again. Hoping for support, Thea stared at her father, who looked down. Because he wanted a trouble-free life, he had never opposed his wife and obviously wouldn't start now.

Without another word, under her mother's furious gaze, Thea left the dining room and grabbed her purse and coat. She glanced around for the last time. No more boring mandatory dinners. When she closed the door behind her, no one made a sound.

❖

Singapore

Thea could hardly contain her excitement. In a few seconds, they would be walking through the airport exit door, and someone from her family would be waiting for them. Pat quietly patted her lower back.

"Relax. Evelyn said someone would be here."

"I can't believe we're in Singapore, and I'm meeting my grandmother for the first time. Do you think she'll come in person?"

Pat chuckled. "When I heard your first phone conversation with her, I understood you two had immediately connected. And every call since then seems to have strengthened your bond. Walk through the door, Thea, and you'll get your answer."

A large crowd was waiting. Thea hesitated. So many people were everywhere. She turned her head in all directions. Some had names written on a piece of paper, and others stretched their necks, without a doubt hoping for the imminent arrival of their loved one.

"There!"

Pat grabbed her arm and guided her toward a woman about forty-five, holding a piece of paper saying *Thea & Pat*. Thea was a little disappointed not to see Evelyn.

"Hi. I'm Thea, and this is Pat."

Smiling, the dark-haired, dark-eyed woman held out her hand "I'm Isabel, Evelyn's granddaughter." Making an apologetic face, she immediately corrected herself. "Sorry, habit. I'm Elsie's daughter. I've always considered Evelyn and Joan my grandmothers."

"I understand," Thea replied with a smile.

"Evelyn and Joan wanted to pick you up themselves, but at their age they can't stand for too long. My mother had to argue, almost threatening to tie them to a chair. I'll drive you. You can't imagine how excited they are to meet you."

"They're not the only ones," joked Pat.

"Pat!"

Isabel laughed loudly.

"You'll fit right in with the family, then. No patience from anyone. My mother has already organised a big party for tomorrow at lunchtime. Everyone will be there. We're a curious bunch, and nobody wants to miss meeting Barbara's daughter."

"Who will be there?"

"My mother and father, of course. My ex-husband and his wife, and my two sons. My brother Eton and his offspring, not to mention my Uncle Leo's family, his wife, their two daughters and a son, along with most of their children, I suppose. My mother is in charge, and I don't have all the details. As I was free early this morning, I came to fetch you."

Thea was a little surprised to discover how huge her new family was. As they reached the car park, she asked Isabel, "What do you do for a living?"

"I'm a doctor, like Joan. We have several in the family. Joan passed on the gene." Isabel grinned.

Pat exclaimed enthusiastically, "'I'm a doctor as well, and Thea is a nurse."

"That's what Evelyn said. We have several nurses in the family too, but Evelyn focused on your singing career when she mentioned you, Thea."

Thea blushed. Compared to Evelyn, she felt like an impostor.

"I'm not sure I can call it a career. I just sang one night a week in a cabaret as an amateur. It's more of a hobby than anything else."

"Leo is quite good at the piano, and one of my sons has taken up the guitar. We're all planning to sing tomorrow. It's a tradition. Evelyn taught us all. You can't get away from it," she added with a laugh. "Here we go."

Isabel pointed to a dark grey car and opened the boot.

Early in the morning, the traffic was still flowing. Isabel explained how the restricted area worked, the electronic-fare zone, the metro, and talked about the changes that had taken place over the years. Thea was fascinated by the tropical vegetation, the palm trees and banyan trees along the avenues. Buildings flashed before her eyes—some old, some very recent huge glass towers. But, for her, the most surprising thing was the cleanliness that prevailed everywhere.

"Here we are," Isabel finally said as she turned into a narrow, quiet street surrounded by lush vegetation.

"Evelyn and Joan still live in the same house. We just sold the park, piece by piece, to pay our university bills. With that money, Eton went to Oxford, as did Leo, and I went to Sydney in the 1970s.

Leo built his house on the land over there." Isabel pointed to a house with a more modern look not too far away.

The car moved slowly through a well-kept garden.

"I live in a flat a few blocks away. Vegetation grows fast in the tropics, so it's better to have a small garden."

The house was exactly as described in Evelyn's letter to Dorothy.

"This is beautiful."

"Yes. Not many like it are left in Singapore. My biological grandparents bought it before the war, but according to Leo it was built in 1922," Isabel explained, pulling up alongside the house. "Only eight o'clock in the morning, so we were quick. Breakfast should be ready. I suppose they heard the car."

Isabel pointed to the two white-haired women who stood waiting just outside the front porch. One wore a beautiful blue dress, and the other was in cream-coloured trousers and a light green shirt.

Thea's heart beat faster. Her grandmother and her lover, at last. Without waiting, with a big smile, she got out of the car and walked toward them, Pat at her side. Despite the wrinkles, Thea recognised Evelyn at once from the photos they'd found at Dorothy's house. The blue eyes and the smile were the same.

With one hand against her back, Joan gently pushed Evelyn forward. "Go, dear."

"Grandma," Thea whispered, falling into her open arms.

"You're home at last," Evelyn replied with tears in her eyes. "One of my dearest dreams is finally coming true. My granddaughter is here. This is a wonderful day, one of the best of my life."

Without knowing why, Thea began to sing in a low voice, "Take Me Home, Country Road," immediately joined by Evelyn, her voice still velvety despite the years.

THE END

HISTORICAL NOTES

The ship *Giang Bee* was sunk by the Japanese on the date and in the manner described in this book. Of the four lifeboats, only two could be launched. For more information, see https://www.roll-of-honour.org.uk/evacuation_ships/html/hms_giang_bee_history.htm.

The Radji Beach Massacre sadly took place on 14 February 1942. Twenty-two Australian nurses who had survived the sinking of the *Vyner Brooke*, together with wounded, sailors, and civilians, were coldly executed in small groups by Japanese soldiers. Posing as dead, one of the nurses, Vivian Bullwinkel, managed to survive and was captured only a few days later. She was interned with the civilians in the Palembang camps until the end of the war, when she was finally able to expose the massacre.

The camps of Muntok, Palembang, and Belalau existed. I have tried to respect the chronology and the way of life in the different camps as much as possible. For more information, see http://muntokpeacemuseum.org/?page_id=380.

Norah Chambers and Margaret Dryburgh formed a vocal orchestra that rehearsed in secret until the first performance on 27 December 1943. They continued to sing for months until they were too weak or too few in number. The 1997 film *Paradise Road* told their story. In 1985, a choir paid tribute to them with music arranged by Norah and Margaret. https://www.youtube.com/watch?v=JTlmBQJ-HKA.

Although the Japanese surrendered unconditionally on 15 August 1945, the Belalau prison camps on Sumatra were among the last to be liberated. It was not until 7 September 1945 that British parachutists were able to enter the Belalau camps and organise the air drop of food. On 17 September, the evacuation began under difficult conditions and was not completed until 8 October. http://muntokpeacemuseum.org/?page_id=380. The captives had suffered for three years and eight months, and more than 500 of them had died.

SONGS MENTIONED IN THIS BOOK

Minnie the Moocher—*song by Cab Calloway 1931*

Stormy Weather—*written by Harold Arlen and Ted Koehler 1933*

We're in the Money—*lyrics by Al Dubin and music by Harry Warren from the movie* Gold Diggers *1933*

Isn't It Romantic?—*music was composed by Richard Rodgers, with lyrics by Lorenz Hart 1932*

I Ain't Got No Home—*song by Woody Guthrie 1931*

Let Yourself Go—*song written by Irving Berlin for the film* Follow the Fleet *1936*

How Deep Is the Ocean—*song written by Irving Berlin 1932*

My Funny Valentine *is a show tune from the 1937 Richard Rodgers and Lorenz Hart musical* Babes in Arms

I've Got You Under My Skin—*song written by Cole Porter in 1936*

Smoke Gets in Your Eyes *is a show tune written by American composer Jerome Kern and lyricist Otto Harbach for the 1933 musical* Roberta

Dream a Little Dream of Me—*song with music by Fabian Andre and Wilbur Schwandt and lyrics by Gus Kahn 1931*

Me and My Girl *is a musical with music by Noel Gay and its original book and lyrics by Douglas Furber and L. Arthur Rose 1937*

It's a Long Way to Tipperary *is a British music hall song first performed in 1912 by Jack Judge, and written by Judge and Harry Williams*

You Are My Sunshine—*song copyrighted and published by Jimmie Davis and Charles Mitchell 1940*

There'll Always Be an England—*composed and written by Ross Parker and Hughie Charles 1939*

Rock-a-Bye Baby—*possibly published by John Newbery in 1765*

But Not for Me—*song written by George Gershwin and Ira Gershwin for the musical* Girl Crazy *1930*

Cheek To Cheek—*song written by Irving Berlin in 1935 for the film* Top Hat

Only Forever—*written by James V. Monaco and Johnny Burke for the 1940 film* Rhythm on the River

Somewhere Over the Rainbow—*ballad composed by Harold Arlen with lyrics by Yip Harburg for the 1939 film* The Wizard of Oz

The Muffin Man—*traditional nursery rhyme, children's song 1820*

When I'm Gone—*known by its longer title, "You're Gonna Miss Me When I'm Gone"—is a popular song written by A. P. Carter 1931*

We'll Meet Again—*music and lyrics composed and written by Ross Parker and Hughie Charles 1939*

I've Got Rhythm—*song composed by George Gershwin with lyrics by Ira Gershwin 1930*

Wish Me Luck as You Wave Me Goodbye—*song by Phil Park and Harry Parr-Davies 1939*

Night and Day—*song by Cole Porter that was written for the 1932 musical* Gay Divorce

Cinderella, Stay in My Arms—*song by Michael Carr 1938*

Jingle Bells—*written by James Lord Pierpont 1857*

My Baby Just Cares for Me—*written by Walter Donaldson with lyrics by Gus Kahn for the film version of the musical comedy* Whoopee! *1930*

You Belong to My Heart—*composed by Mexican songwriter Agustín Lara 1941*

We Just Couldn't Say Goodbye—*written by Harry M. Woods 1932*

The Lambeth Walk—*lyrics by Douglas Furber and L. Arthur Rose and music by Noel Gay, from the 1937 musical* Me and My Girl

Love Me Tender—*lyrics are credited to "Vera Matson," though actual lyricist was her husband, Ken Darby, and Elvis Presley himself; this song was adapted from the melody for "Aura Lea," a sentimental Civil War ballad, so its music is credited to English composer George R. Poulton 1956*

Take Me Home, Country Road—*song written by Bill Danoff, Taffy Nivert, and John Denver*

About the Author

French author Kadyan has been living abroad for almost twenty years, especially in Asia and Oceania. With her spouse and her dog, she is now back in France as a full-time writer. Since 2003, she has published seventeen books in French, spanning genres from historical novels to thrillers to science fiction. Her debut novel, *The Secrets of Willowra* (2021), was a finalist for the GCLS General Fiction award. In her free time, she loves to garden and to tinker, using all the cool tools.

Website: http://www.kadyan.fr/

Books Available from Bold Strokes Books

Lucky in Lace by Melissa Brayden. Straitlaced stationery store owner Juliette Jennings's predictable life unravels when a sexy lingerie shop and its alluring owner move in next door. (978-1-63679-434-1)

Made for Her by Carsen Taite. Neal Walsh is a newly made member of the Mancuso crime family, but will her undeniable attraction to Anastasia Petrov, the wife of her boss's sworn enemy, be the ultimate test of her loyalty? (978-1-63679-265-1)

Off the Menu by Alaina Erdell. Reality TV sensation *Restaurant Redo* and its gorgeous host Erin Rasmussen will arrive to film in chef Taylor Mobley's kitchen. As the cameras roll, will they make the jump from enemies to lovers? (978-1-63679-295-8)

Pack of Her Own by Elena Abbott. When things heat up in a small town, steamy secrets are revealed between Alpha werewolf Wren Carne and her human mate, Natalie Donovan. (978-1-63679-370-2)

Return to McCall by Patricia Evans. Lily isn't looking for romance—not until she meets Alex, the gorgeous Cuban dance instructor at La Haven, a newly opened lesbian retreat. (978-1-63679-386-3)

So It Went Like This by C. Spencer. A candid and deeply personal exploration of fate, chosen family, and the vulnerability intrinsic in life's uncertainties. (978-1-63555-971-2)

Stolen Kiss by Spencer Greene. Anna and Louise share a stolen kiss, only to discover that Louise is dating Anna's brother. Surely, one kiss can't change everything...Can it? (978-1-63679-364-1)

The Fall Line by Kelly Wacker. When Jordan Burroughs arrives in the Deep South to paint a local endangered aquatic flower, she doesn't expect to become friends with a mischievous gin-drinking ghost who complicates her budding romance and leads her to an awful discovery and danger. (978-1-63679-205-7)

To Meet Again by Kadyan. When the stark reality of WW II separates cabaret singer Evelyn and Australian doctor Joan in Singapore, they must overcome all odds to find one another again. (978-1-63679-398-6)

Before She Was Mine by Emma L McGeown. When Dani and Lucy are thrust together to sort out their children's playground squabble, sparks fly leaving both of them willing to risk it all for each other. 978-1-63679-315-3)

Chasing Cypress by Ana Hartnett Reichardt. Maggie Hyde wants to find a partner to settle down with and help her run the family farm, but instead she ends up chasing Cypress. Olivia Cypress. 978-1-63679-323-8)

Dark Truths by Sandra Barret. When Jade's ex-girlfriend and vampire maker barges back into her life, can Jade satisfy her ex's demands, keep Beth safe, and keep everyone's secrets...secret? 978-1-63679-369-6)

Desires Unleashed by Renee Roman. Kell Murphy and Taylor Simpson didn't go looking for love, but as they explore their desires unleashed, their hearts lead them on an unexpected journey. 978-1-63679-327-6)

Maybe, Probably by Amanda Radley. Set against the backdrop of a viral pandemic, Gina and Eleanor are about to discover that loving another person is complicated when you're desperately searching for yourself. 978-1-63679-284-2)

The One by C.A. Popovich. Jody Acosta doesn't know what makes her more furious, that the wealthy Bergeron family refuses to be held accountable for her father's wrongful death, or that she can't ignore her knee-weakening attraction to Nicole Bergeron. 978-1-63679-318-4)

The Speed of Slow Changes by Sander Santiago. As Al and Lucas navigate the ups and downs of their polyamorous relationship, only one thing is certain: romance has never been so crowded. 978-1-63679-329-0)

Tides of Love by Kimberly Cooper Griffin. Falling in love is the last thing on either of their minds, but when Mikayla and Gem meet, sparks of possibility begin to shine, revealing a future neither expected. 978-1-63679-319-1)

Catch by Kris Bryant. Convincing the wife of the star quarterback to walk away from her family was never in offensive coordinator Sutton McCoy's game plan. But standing on the sidelines when a second chance at true love comes her way proves all but impossible. (978-1-63679-276-7)

Hearts in the Wind by MJ Williamz. Beth and Evelyn seem destined to remain mortal enemies but are about to discover that in matters of the heart, sometimes you must cast your fortunes to the wind. (978-1-63679-288-0)

Hero Complex by Jesse J. Thoma. Bronte, Athena, and their unlikely friends must work together to defeat Bronte's arch nemesis. The fate of love, humanity, and the world might depend on it. No pressure. (978-1-63679-280-4)

Hotel Fantasy by Piper Jordan. Molly Taylor has a fantasy in mind that only Lexi can fulfill. However, convincing her to participate could prove challenging. (978-1-63679-207-1)

Last New Beginning by Krystina Rivers. Can commercial broker Skye Kohl and contractor Bailey Kaczmarek overcome their pride and work together while the tension between them boils over into a love that could soothe both of their hearts? (978-1-63679-261-3)

Love and Lattes by Karis Walsh. Cat café owner Bonnie and wedding planner Taryn join forces to get rescue cats into forever homes—discovering their own forever along the way. (978-1-63679-290-3)

Repatriate by Jaime Maddox. Ally Hamilton's new job as a home health aide takes an unexpected twist when she discovers a fortune in stolen artwork and must repatriate the masterpieces and avoid the wrath of the violent man who stole them. (978-1-63679-303-0)

The Hues of Me and You by Morgan Lee Miller. Arlette Adair and Brooke Dawson almost fell in love in college. Years later, they unexpectedly run into each other and come face-to-face with their unresolved past. (978-1-63679-229-3)

A Haven for the Wanderer by Jenny Frame. When Griffin Harris comes to Rosebrook village, the love she finds with Bronte de Lacey creates safe haven and she finally finds her place in the world. But will she run again when their love is tested? (978-1-63679-291-0)

A Spark in the Air by Dena Blake. Internet executive Crystal Tucker is sure Wi-Fi could really help small-town residents, even if it means putting an internet café out of business, but her instant attraction to the owner's daughter, Janie Elliott, makes moving ahead with her plans complicated. (978-1-63679-293-4)

Between Takes by CJ Birch. Simone Lavoie is convinced her new job as an intimacy coordinator will give her a fresh perspective. Instead, problems on set and her growing attraction to actress Evelyn Harper only add to her worries. (978-1-63679-309-2)

Camp Lost and Found by Georgia Beers. Nobody knows better than Cassidy and Frankie that life doesn't always give you what you want. But sometimes, if you're lucky, life gives you exactly what you need. (978-1-63679-263-7)

Felix Navidad by 'Nathan Burgoine. After the wedding of a good friend, instead of Felix's Hawaii Christmas treat to himself, ice rain strands him in Ontario with fellow wedding-guest—and handsome ex of said friend—Kevin in a small cabin for the holiday Felix definitely didn't plan on. (978-1-63679-411-2)

Fire, Water, and Rock by Alaina Erdell. As Jess and Clare reveal more about themselves, and their hot summer fling tips over into true love, they must confront their pasts before they can contemplate a future together. (978-1-63679-274-3)

Lines of Love by Brey Willows. When even the Muse of Love doesn't believe in forever, we're all in trouble. (978-1-63555-458-8)

Manny Porter and The Yuletide Murder by D.C. Robeline. Manny only has the holiday season to discover who killed prominent research scientist Phillip Nikolaidis before the judicial system condemns an innocent man to lethal injection. (978-1-63679-313-9)

Only This Summer by Radclyffe. A fling with Lily promises to be exactly what Chase is looking for—short-term, hot as a forest fire, and one Chase can extinguish whenever she wants. After all, it's only one summer. (978-1-63679-390-0)

Picture-Perfect Christmas by Charlotte Greene. Two former rivals compete to capture the essence of their small mountain town at Christmas, all the while fighting old and new feelings. (978-1-63679-311-5)

Playing Love's Refrain by Lesley Davis. Drew Dawes had shied away from the world of music until Wren Banderas gave her a reason to play their love's refrain. (978-1-63679-286-6)

Profile by Jackie D. The scales of justice are weighted against FBI agents Cassidy Wolf and Alex Derby. Loyalty and love may be the only advantage they have. (978-1-63679-282-8)

Almost Perfect by Tagan Shepard. A shared love of queer TV brings Olivia and Riley together, but can they keep their real-life love as picture perfect as their on-screen counterparts? (978-1-63679-322-1)

Corpus Calvin by David Swatling. Cloverkist Inn may be haunted, but a ghost materializes from Jason Dekker's past and Calvin's canine instinct kicks in to protect a young boy from mortal danger. (978-1-62639-428-5)

Craving Cassie by Skye Rowan. Siobhan Carney and Cassie Townsend share an instant attraction, but are they brave enough to give up everything they have ever known to be together? (978-1-63679-062-6)

Drifting by Lyn Hemphill. When Tess jumps into the ocean after Jet, she thinks she's saving her life. Of course, she can't possibly know Jet is actually a mermaid desperate to fix her mistake before she causes her clan's demise. (978-1-63679-242-2)

Enigma by Suzie Clarke. Polly has taken an oath to protect and serve her country, but when the spy she's tasked with hunting becomes the love of her life, will she be the one to betray her country? (978-1-63555-999-6)

Finding Fault by Annie McDonald. Can environmental activist Dr. Evie O'Halloran and government investigator Merritt Shepherd set aside their conflicting ideas about saving the planet and risk their hearts enough to save their love? (978-1-63679-257-6)